Sarah Alderson is a London-born, LA-based writer whose previous books include *Friends Like These* (Mulholland), *In Her Eyes* (Mulholland) and *The Weekend Away* (HarperCollins). Sarah is also a screenwriter; her adaptation of *The Weekend Away* will soon be streaming on Netflix.

You can follow @sarah @sarahaldersonauthor on I

THE
STALKER

SARAH ALDERSON

avon.

HarperCollins*Publishers*
1 London Bridge Street
London SE1 9GF

www.harpercollins.co.uk

HarperCollins*Publishers*
1st Floor, Watermarque Building, Ringsend Road
Dublin 4, Ireland

A Paperback Original 2021

1

First published in Great Britain by HarperCollins*Publishers* 2021

A catalogue copy of this book is available from the British Library.

ISBN: 978-0-00-840004-0

This novel is entirely a work of fiction.
The names, characters and incidents portrayed in it are
the work of the author's imagination. Any resemblance to
actual persons, living or dead, events or localities is
entirely coincidental.

Typeset in Bembo by Palimpsest Book Production Limited,
Falkirk, Stirlingshire

Printed and Bound in the UK using 100% Renewable Electricity at
CPI Group (UK) Ltd

MIX
Paper from
responsible sources
FSC™ C007454

This book is produced from independently certified FSC™ paper to ensure
responsible forest management.

For more information visit: www.harpercollins.co.uk/green

For Vic

PART ONE

Chapter One

Day One

The island is invisible. Dark clouds hang like water-logged blankets over the loch: I can't tell where the horizon ends, and the sky begins. I shiver, wrapping my arms around myself to keep out the chill, damp air. I hoped it would be sunny – it's August after all – but I suppose it is Scotland, and the weather, damp and miserable as it is, seems fitting, as if I've conjured it from inside my head.

I try to remind myself why we're here; it's our honeymoon, albeit delayed by two months and no longer the Greek island paradise we had originally planned, booked and paid for. But, on the bright side, it's going to be just Liam and me. We'll be the only people on the island, staying in an eighteenth-century forge converted into a luxury holiday home. We'll spend a whole week snuggled in front of the log fire, exploring the forests and Celtic ruins, walking the wild and windswept beaches, and trying to put the past behind us — at least that's what I'm telling myself. I'm praying it works out that way.

Liam finishes talking to the boatman and hurries across the pebble beach towards me. He's tall and dark and even from this distance I can make out the arctic blue of his eyes.

My mum thought he looked like Leonardo DiCaprio in his *Titanic* days. And it's true: there is a likeness, a similar sparkle in his eye and a boyish charm. As he walks towards me across the pebble beach, I feel as if someone has called 'action' and I'm an actress starring in a movie. It still feels unreal to me that we're actually married; that I'm Liam's wife. I smile at him and he grins back, making my stomach flip. I suppose it's normal for newlyweds to feel this way, and I sometimes wonder if the butterflies in my stomach will ever go away, because I can't imagine it.

'The man says he'll take us over as soon as the weather eases,' Liam says when he reaches me. The boatman has disappeared somewhere, probably to wait out the weather.

'How long will that be?' I ask, frowning up at the petulant sky.

Liam shrugs. 'Not long. He seemed to think it'll clear up soon. Let's go and grab a beer while we wait.'

'Sounds good.'

Liam steers us away from the water's edge and back up the beach. There's a pub sitting opposite the pier; one of a handful of old, stone buildings that make up the hamlet of Arduaine. Too small to be a village, Arduaine is an outcropping built to withstand the weather. The pub is short and squat, its walls thick as a jail's. Its windows are small beady eyes, recessed deep into heavy sockets.

'The Bucket of Blood?' I say, reading the battered wooden sign nailed over the casement.

Liam opens the door. 'Let's hope they serve a decent IPA,' he laughs, as I duck under his arm and walk inside.

The pub is cosier than its name would have us believe. A fire crackles in the grate and the burnished brass fittings glow as though they've absorbed centuries of polish. It's empty, aside from a middle-aged landlord, with a complexion as weathered as the pub sign outside, and a man in his mid to late twenties who's wearing a camouflage jacket and sitting at the far end of the bar, hunched over and nursing a pint.

'Afternoon,' the landlord says, smiling at us as we lower our hoods and approach. 'What can I get you?'

Liam, always affable and friendly in situations like these, immediately falls into conversation with him about the local ales on tap. I take off my jacket and start to unwind my scarf but stop suddenly, feeling eyes on me, and turn my head. The man at the end of the bar is staring right at me. I smile, trying to be polite, but his gaze remains unflinchingly cold and piercing, so I look away. I wonder what his problem is. Perhaps he doesn't like non-locals in his pub. I wrap my scarf back around my neck, feeling a sudden chill despite the fire roaring in the grate. It feels more like winter, not at all like the dying days of summer.

'Lime and soda?' Liam asks, turning to me.

I nod. 'Yes, thanks.'

'I thought we could wait until we get to the island before we eat,' Liam says.

I nod again. I'm not hungry anyway. The doctor said it can be normal with depression to lose your appetite, and that I should wait for the anti-depressants to kick in. I started taking them a month ago though and haven't yet felt any change, at least to my eating. I'm definitely starting to see some improvement in my mood – a crack of light is appearing in the dark. Who knows? By the end of the week maybe the horrible weight pressing down on me will have been levered off like a giant boulder and I'll start to feel free of it.

It's not that I don't want to be happy; that I don't crave it. But in my memory, happiness is like the chocolate cake my mum used to make for me every birthday since I was a little girl, covered in lashings of chocolate buttercream and decorated with chocolate buttons. I can picture it in my mind's eye – can even recall the feeling of the fork tines against my tongue and the gooey warmth as the first bite hits the roof of my mouth – but for the life of me I can't remember what it tastes like.

As Liam brings our drinks over to a table in the corner, I glance at him, grateful that he suggested we rebook the honeymoon that we'd had to so abruptly cancel. He thought I'd want to go somewhere hot and suggested the hotel on Santorini, but I didn't feel up to going far from home, couldn't imagine myself lying by a pool under a blazing hot sun. And I've always wanted to visit Scotland. My mum and I used to talk about it, both of us having fallen in love with the *Outlander* books, but we never got around to making the trip. Liam's roots are Scottish, and he's really into history, so he seemed happy enough with the idea when I suggested it.

'Cheers,' he says, chinking his glass against mine.

'Cheers,' I answer.

'To us,' he says, leaning across the table and kissing me. 'I love you,' he adds in a whisper, his lips warm against mine.

'I love you too,' I reply, kissing him back. 'Happy honeymoon.'

He brushes a strand of hair behind my ear, his fingers grazing my cheek and sending a shiver down my spine. He grins and I get a flash of memory of the first time I saw him. The very first thing I noticed about him then was the brilliant blue of his eyes and a smile that suggested a certain boyish recklessness and sense of adventure, as well as a level of confidence that I'd only ever aspired to. It's what I first fell for about him.

After taking another swallow of beer Liam jumps to his feet. 'Just going to use the loo,' he says, and strolls towards a door in the far corner of the pub.

I sip my drink and glance around the room. The landlord is sitting on a stool, reading the sports pages of the *Scottish Times*. My gaze drifts to the man sitting at the end of the bar and to my surprise I find him staring back at me with that same piercing look, his eyes hooded and narrowed.

'You heading to Shura?' he asks in a low Scottish burr.

I nod, recognizing the name of the island we're going to. 'Yes.'

'You staying long?' he grunts.

'A week,' I say, wondering why he wants to know.

'You know the place is haunted?'

'What?' I ask, laughing nervously. He's obviously pulling my leg. Yet he isn't smiling; his expression remains sullen.

The landlord looks up from his paper. 'Aye,' he says, glancing at the man before looking at me. 'He's not wrong. Shura's haunted as they come.'

I look between the two men, wondering if they're messing around with me, teasing the newcomer, or if it's some kind of inside joke between them; but the younger man still isn't smiling, and the landlord's expression is completely earnest. He nods again. 'There was a terrible murder there.' He glances at the younger man and then adds, 'I mean, there've been lots of murders there.'

My mouth must have fallen open because he continues in a softer tone: 'The Vikings used to raid all around these parts.'

'Oh,' I manage to say.

'There used to be a monastery out there on Shura. Easy pickings. A lot of monks got killed. Nowhere to run, you see. Or hide.'

'Right . . .' I say, unsure how to react.

'You'll see some ancient burial sites on the island too if you look carefully. Celtic ruins from way, way back.'

I smile politely and nod. Liam will at least like that.

The landlord moves to clear the man's empty beer glass. 'Another?' he asks him.

'Aye,' the man replies with a scowl, before twisting around to face me with a scowl. 'Shura's cursed. You shouldn't be going there.'

I swallow drily, feeling my stomach drop away.

'Come on now, let's not scare the lass,' the landlord admonishes, obviously seeing the anxiety on my face. 'The island's beautiful. You'll have a lovely time,' he reassures me.

The younger man twists back around in his seat to face the bar, shoulders hunched, and the landlord goes back to his newspaper. And I'm left with my imagination, which lurches into overtime. The idea that the place is haunted is unsettling, casting a dark cloud over what's meant to be a romantic getaway. And what does the younger man mean about the island being cursed?

Liam walks out the bathroom just then. Immediately he reads the atmosphere in the room; the undercurrent of tension. 'You OK?' he asks, sitting down and throwing a suspicious look at the other two men.

I nod, still feeling unsettled. 'Fine. They were just telling me about the island.'

'A little bit of history,' the landlord pipes up with a smile.

'Oh, anything interesting?' Liam asks, glancing between them.

'They were saying it's haunted,' I tell him, glancing his way to gauge his reaction.

'Right,' he says, rolling his eyes and smirking. Being a detective means that Liam deals with all sorts of horrible crimes – murders, robberies, assault – so nothing much fazes him, and definitely not the idea of ghosts.

'Ignore them,' he says to me now, taking my hand. 'We're on our honeymoon. And we're going to have a great time.'

'Unless of course the island is haunted,' I joke.

'There's no such thing as ghosts,' he answers, taking a sip of his beer.

I sip my drink and say nothing. I'm not so sure about that.

Chapter Two

The island is visible now. It's shrouded in fog though, wisps of cloud clinging to it.

Liam helps me into the small boat with an outboard motor that will carry us over to it, making sure the straps of my life jacket are done up tight. He knows I'm afraid of water; I have been ever since I almost drowned one time. It's something I still have nightmares about.

Liam sees me eyeing the near-black surface of the water with uneasiness. 'You're all right,' he tells me in the same tone he uses when I jolt awake screaming from a bad dream. 'You won't fall in, I promise. And if you do,' he adds with a wink, 'I'll jump in and save you.'

I force a smile and take a seat at the front of the boat, my right hand gripping the side white-knuckled, despite

Liam's reassurances. He sits opposite me and holds my free hand, his fingers grazing the diamond ring and the simple gold band that was once my grandmother's.

The boatman, wearing a bright yellow rain mac and galoshes, pulls the starting cord and the engine splutters damply to life. We set off, bouncing over the waves, and I fix my gaze on the island in the distance. My hood flies back and the wind whips my hair around my head. I close my eyes as the spray hits my face, relishing the cold scouring my skin. It's awakening, as though it has the power to blast away my sadness.

'Who owns the place?' I hear Liam ask the boatman and I open my eyes to look in their direction.

The boatman shrugs. 'Mystery. No one knows. Was on the market for a few years but no one wanted to touch it on account of its history. Then it was bought a few months back,' he grunts.

'What history?' I ask.

'Oh, just, you know . . . she's got a dark history, Shura.'

'You mean the Viking raids?' I ask.

The boatman glances at me with something of a puzzled expression. 'Aye,' he says, 'that'll be it.'

I frown. It's obvious that there's something more to the island's history, but no one wants to open up and say what it is. And I'm not sure I want to press and find out.

'You're the first ones to visit,' the boatman adds, changing the subject.

'Really?' Liam asks.

The boatman nods. 'Aye. I should know. No other way of getting over there, 'cept by boat. And you're the only ones I've taken.'

'It's our honeymoon,' Liam tells the man. He beams at me as he says it, squeezing my hand, his thumb still rubbing the smooth gold of my wedding ring.

'Congratulations,' the boatman says to us both, but it sounds perfunctory, like he couldn't care less. I notice he's wearing a wedding ring too, dull and scarred and almost welded to his gnarled hand.

'How long have you been married for?' I ask him.

'Forty-three years,' he grunts, but he doesn't look happy about it.

I honestly believe that Liam and I will be one of the one in three couples that stays together 'till death do us part'. Even though we didn't get married in a church because Liam isn't religious, we still said the traditional vows and, when I spoke that part, that was when it really sank in that we were committing to be together forever.

I turn my attention to the island, coming into clearer view now. The forest rises up like a dark, silent army, as if the island is barricading itself to visitors, and the cliffs at the far end almost do make the place seem cursed. I wonder about the history of the place – the Viking invasions that the landlord mentioned and the dark history the boatman just hinted at – and shiver again, despite the extra wool sweater of Liam's that I'm wearing under my jacket. I'm naturally superstitious and I can't shake the sense of foreboding which has settled over me.

As we continue to bounce over the water, edging nearer and nearer to what I can now make out is a slim jetty at the opposite end of the island to the cliffs, the shape of a house starts to materialise, white with dark wood timbers. It's set a little way back from the shore-line. That must be the cottage we're staying in – the old forge.

In that same moment, the sun breaks through the cloud and what seemed to be an inhospitable piece of land rising out of black, unforgiving waters is suddenly transformed as if someone has waved a wand and broken a witch's spell. The beaches shine dazzlingly white and the sunlight glitters off the water, forcing me to squint. The forest is no longer a silent, defending army, but an enchanted wood, begging to be explored. The sun breaks through further cracks in the grey cloud and it makes me think of someone tearing off wrapping paper to reveal the blue gift of the sky beneath. It's like two different islands; one from a nightmare, the other from a fairy tale. Though a lot of fairy tales resemble night-mares when you think about it. I decide to throw off my feelings of anxiety and push the idea of the island being cursed out of my mind. This week is the start of a new chapter.

As the boatman turns off the motor to allow us to drift to the jetty, and the roaring in my ears disappears, I'm struck all at once by the stillness. All I can hear is the water lapping the side of the boat, the wind whispering through the trees and a gull crying overhead.

I turn wide-eyed and still smiling to Liam. 'It's so beautiful.'

He grins back at me and I take his hand, linking my fingers through his, feeling the warmth and strength in them. I know I haven't been easy to live with these last two months, but he's stuck by me regardless, telling me repeatedly that he's not going anywhere. Besides, now we're married, he's got to stick with me through thick and thin, he likes to joke.

'Are you happy?' he asks now, a shade of concern in his eyes.

'Yes,' I say, my eyes drifting back to the island; and it's true for once.

Once we're tied up at the jetty, the boatman points us towards the cottage. It's sitting three hundred feet away, on a piece of higher ground.

'You'll find the key in the lock box by the front door,' he tells us as he sets our bags down. 'I think you've got the code.'

Liam nods and slips him a twenty as a tip. The man pockets the money with a grateful smile. 'I'll be back in a week,' he says as he steps into the boat.

I take out my phone to check the time and notice there's no coverage.

'You willnae get signal out here,' the boatman comments, nodding at my phone.

'There's a satellite phone in the cottage if you need to contact anyone in an emergency. Though I doubt you'll need it,' he adds. He gestures at the loch. 'Just make sure you keep out of the water.'

I grimace; I have absolutely no intention of going anywhere near the water.

'Lots of people drown, god rest their souls,' the boatman goes on. 'Don't realise how deep it is – six hundred foot in places. Deeper than the North Sea. Drops away before you know it. It's the cold that gets 'em. Only takes a few seconds and you're dead.' He snaps his fingers to illustrate his point.

I eye the loch even more nervously, my stomach muscles clenching rigidly, as though someone has just thrown me into the icy depths.

'Don't worry,' Liam reassures the man. 'We won't be going swimming.'

'Aye,' the man says, untying the boat. 'Well, have a nice time. Enjoy yourselves.'

'Thank you,' I call after the man as he pushes off from the jetty.

As the boat drifts away, the boatman tilts his head up to look at the sky, as though reading something in the clouds, which have now almost completely been chased away by the sun. 'Best make the most of the weather,' he says. 'Storm's on its way.'

'The forecast said it would be sunny all week,' Liam responds.

The boatman gives a shrug. 'Weatherman doesnae know anything. Take it from me. There's a storm on its way.'

Liam frowns as he picks up our bags and starts walking down the jetty towards the cottage. I watch the boat disappear into the distance and then hurry after him, feeling a faint stirring of something I can't immediately identify as I take in the view of the island and the cottage up ahead. Excitement. I haven't felt that in so long. I take a deep breath and let it buoy my spirits.

This is going to be the perfect honeymoon, I think to myself as I reach Liam's side.

Chapter Three

Liam locates the key in the lockbox and unlocks the front door. He has to duck to enter the cottage as the doorway is so low, built for shorter men in long-ago times. From the look of it I'm guessing it's at least four hundred years old.

I stop for a moment to admire the lavender and geraniums planted in the flower beds and hanging baskets by the front door.

'Laura, come and have a look!' Liam shouts and I follow him inside.

'Oh wow,' I say, blown away as soon as I enter the living room. There are wooden beams crisscrossing the ceiling and a brand-new cast-iron stove sits in an ancient-looking fireplace. A plush sofa in heathered blue tweed sits on one side of the room, facing a wooden slab of a coffee table and a winged armchair in a damask rose. Warm rugs cover the flagstone floor. Thick, grey velvet curtains hang beside the small windows through which I can see fragments of the loch and sky. 'This place is amazing,' I sigh. And it is; it looks like something out of an interior design magazine.

'Home for the week,' Liam says, clearly also impressed. 'Come on, let's look around.'

We wander through into a kitchen at the rear of the cottage. It's simple but tastefully done, with granite surfaces and state-of-the-art appliances, including a coffee maker, which I know will make Liam exceedingly happy. He loves his coffee in the morning.

True to form, Liam notices it with glee, running his hand over the surface. He then makes for the fridge and opens it. It's full to bursting with groceries: milk, cheese, vegetables, packages wrapped in brown paper, which I assume are the steak and the fish that we ordered in advance. I count two bottles of white wine in the door, as well as six cans of IPA. In the wine rack by the back door I notice another three bottles of red.

'Seems like everything I ordered,' Liam says, shutting the fridge and opening cupboards, to find them stocked with staples and dried food.

We run up the stairs like a couple of giddy teenagers to discover the bedroom. I stop in the doorway and take in the double bed under the eaves, decorated with a warm quilt and several throw pillows, then I cross to the large dormer window.

'Check out the view,' I say as I gaze out over the vast expanse of the loch. It's like we're on a boat at sea.

'I am,' Liam answers.

I turn and find him looking at me from the threshold, grinning in a way that makes my stomach flip over on itself again. I know what he's thinking about, it's clear from his expression, but I need a shower first. We've been on the road since six this morning and I feel gritty and rumpled from the journey.

I make for the en-suite bathroom. There's a clawfoot tub set in front of a window, this one facing the back garden. I peer out to see that it stretches all the way towards the forest, standing proudly several hundred feet away.

Liam comes up behind me and wraps his arms around my waist. He rests his chin on my shoulder. 'Let me run you a bath,' he murmurs into my ear.

I close my eyes and lean back against his broad chest. 'Mmmm, that would be nice.'

Whilst he starts running the taps, I turn and catch a glimpse of myself in the mirror above the sink. I startle, as I often do when I catch sight of myself unexpectedly these days, because it's like a stranger has appeared out of nowhere and is staring at me with a look of shock on their face. I'm so thin. I really need to start eating again. Hopefully all the fresh air will help rouse my appetite.

I head into the bedroom to unpack, folding my clothes neatly into the drawers of the dresser, leaving the top one clear for Liam. I can't help but imagine what it would be like to live here. We keep talking about buying together, although Liam moved in with me a while ago. It made sense, as I have a two-bedroom terrace house and he was living in a flat-share with a colleague. He's been saving up for years to put down a deposit on his own place and now that I have a little inheritance from my mother, we've been talking about pooling our money and buying somewhere bigger.

By the time I head back into the bathroom I find Liam has emptied half a bottle of Molton Brown bubble bath into the bathtub and it's almost overflowing. He grins like a kid and I laugh.

'Go on, get in,' he says.

I undress slowly, aware of Liam watching. I feel self-conscious about my body, always have, but I know how much he enjoys looking at me. And even though I've lost some weight, he's always telling me that I'm gorgeous and paying me compliments. At first, I found it hard to hear and didn't believe him, because no one had ever paid me that much attention before, or treated me the way he did – and even now, eight months later, I still haven't quite got used to it.

I grew up with a father who was always calling my

mother names and yelling abuse at me, too, telling me I was a lazy, fat cow. And before Liam, I dated a couple of guys, one at school and one just last year, both of whom ended up being as awful as my dad, though at the time of course I couldn't see it; I was just flattered that somebody was interested in me. I cringe when I think about it now – how pathetic I was, how needy, and how willing I was to put the needs of undeserving people before my own.

My first boyfriend, Dean, I met at school. I only found out after he dumped me that he'd been cheating on me the whole time. Turns out he hadn't even thought of me as a girlfriend; I was just a bet he'd made with friends, to see if he could make me fall in love with him and take my virginity. I offered it up to him on a plate and the memory still makes me burn with shame. As soon as he succeeded in his goal, he started spreading disgusting lies about me around school, and I ended up dropping out of my final year and finishing my coursework at home because of all the bullying that ensued.

And then there was Paul, who I met at the animal shelter where I used to volunteer. He was older than me and worked for the council's animal control service. He'd bring in dogs, ones that the police had deemed dangerous that needed to be put down. Paul seemed sweet and considerate but after a few dates he ghosted me on New Year's Eve and I never heard from him again.

I'd begun to believe that all men were as bad as my dad, and I'd just about given up hope of ever meeting anyone decent when Liam arrived like Prince Charming and whisked me off my feet.

I shiver as I discard my underwear. The heating isn't on and the cottage is a little cold, so I slip quickly into the bath and beneath the water.

'How is it?' Liam asks, perching on the side as I let the bubbles smother me.

'Bliss,' I tell him.

'I'll go and put the heating on and make a cup of tea. It's chilly isn't it?'

'It is Scotland,' I tell him.

'It's still summer,' he complains.

'At least we've got central heating. Imagine what it must have been like for the Celts and the monks who used to live here.'

He grins. 'True. Glad I'm not a monk. For more reasons than that.' He winks at me.

Once he's gone, I tip my head back against the bathtub and take a deep breath. I let it out in a big exhalation, feeling the tension start to ease from my knotted shoulders. Before I know it, I've started to cry. The melancholy descends on me like a sudden summer storm. The sadness rises up out of nowhere sometimes; a tsunami of grief, and the tears will be pouring silently down my face, soaking my lap, before I even notice I'm crying. Other times it comes in great racking sobs that force me to bury my head in a pillow and scream. And every so often the pain hits me like an axe to the stomach, felling me, making me clutch my sides and gasp for breath, the sob trapped inside of me, unable to escape.

I miss my mum more than I thought it possible to miss a person. The two of us were unusually close, more like sisters, and definitely best friends. After my dad died of a heart attack when I was fifteen it was just the two of us for years. I would quite happily have stayed living at home with Mum forever, but she wanted me to go out and live my life – insisted, in fact, that I did. After graduating, when I found a job, my mum dived into her savings and helped me put down a deposit on a small two-up, two-down terraced house. But even after I moved out, I still spent several evenings a week over at her place. We'd eat dinner and watch *The Great British Bake Off* or *Escape to the Continent*.

It was Mum who encouraged me to pursue veterinary science at the local college, even though I didn't think I was smart enough, and Mum who told me to follow my dreams, even when I didn't feel brave enough. It's why I'm here now – why I told Liam to rebook the honeymoon. I'm trying to move on; trying to be strong. I want to do it to honour her memory. My mum wouldn't want me to be moping and sad and pathetic. She'd want me to pick myself up and get on with my life. Above all, I know she'd want me to be happy.

She loved Liam, too, and I comfort myself with the

fact that she got to be there for the wedding. They say your wedding day is meant to be the best day of your life, but in my case, it was the best day of my mum's life. I'd never seen her so happy; she cried through the entire service, tears splashing onto the paper when she signed her name as witness. I'll never forget the way she looked at me when I came downstairs in my wedding dress, and how she told me I was beautiful before she walked me up the aisle at the registry office. I'll never forget how Liam kissed her cheek and told her *thank you* when she put my hand into his before we said our vows. I'm so grateful that I have these memories, even at the same time that I'm furious I won't get to make any more with her.

Quickly, I wash my hair in the bath, dunking my head beneath the water – careful to keep my face above the surface – then I clamber out, gripping the sides of the bath tightly because my legs feel like they're made of cotton wool. I dry off using a soft white robe that's hanging on the back of the door and then throw on some jeans and woollen socks, as well as a T-shirt and a thick jumper, glad I thought to bring warm clothes, knowing that the weather can be temperamental in the far north of Scotland.

On my way out of the room, I look in the mirror and notice with dismay how badly my roots are showing, my hair not so much blonde as the colour of dirty dishwater. I look alabaster pale, too, and for a moment

I almost crumple in my resolve to be strong, but I take a deep breath and force a smile. *New beginnings*, I remind myself.

By the time I head back downstairs, the tea Liam has made is half-cold, but I sip it anyway and go and sit beside Liam on the sofa. He's leafing through a book and I glance at the title: *A History of the Isle of Shura*. There's a photograph of a grand Gothic castle on the front.

'There's a castle?' I ask, gesturing to the picture.

Liam nods. 'Yeah, it was built on the ruins of the medieval monastery.' He keeps flicking through the pages of the book. 'I didn't know about it either – it wasn't mentioned on the website. We should go and check it out. Maybe we can go inside.'

I look closer at the image. The castle looks like something out of a Brontë novel; lots of arched windows and towers and gargoyles. No wonder people think the island is haunted. If a ghost was looking for a place to haunt, it would definitely feel at home there.

Liam pushes a plate of shortbread fingers my way. I take one but find I can't bring myself to eat it. I feel suddenly nauseous, flushed from the bath, my head spinning, so I set it back down on the plate.

'The castle was in the McKay family for six hundred years,' Liam says, reading out loud. 'They probably had to sell because it was too expensive to keep up – I've read about that happening.'

He turns the page.

'Is that them?' I ask, peering at another photograph, this one of a man, a woman and a boy of about eight or nine standing on the steps of the castle. The massive wooden doors of the castle are open behind them, giving a small glimpse of a wood-panelled interior hall filled with portraits and stuffed animal heads.

Liam reads the description below the photo. '"Andrew and Nancy McKay with their son, Elliot". Yeah, looks like they were the last owners. The book was published seven years ago.'

I study the picture. Andrew, who looks to be in his forties, has a long face with piercing eyes. He's tall and rangy and has a sullen expression on his face as he stares directly into the camera, like he's staring down an enemy.

His wife, Nancy, looks to be in her mid-thirties, beautiful, with a watchful gaze. She's slim and delicate looking, but perhaps that's only emphasised because she's standing beside Andrew.

Elliot looks like his mother: slight, with light-coloured hair, though it's hard to tell the exact colour because it's a black-and-white photo. He's clearly pale though, and I can just about make out freckles dotted across his nose and cheeks. A large Greyhound dog stands beside him and his hand is resting on the dog's back. Similarly, I notice Nancy has her hand on her son's shoulder. Meanwhile, Andrew is touching neither his wife nor his son, nor the dog, but stands apart, hands hanging at his sides, curled into fists.

Liam shuts the history book and picks up a map of the island. It's old and creased and he spreads it out over both our laps. He stabs his finger down where the cottage is marked. 'This is us,' he says. 'We're at the south-east end of the island.'

I glance at the key at the bottom of the map and calculate that the island is approximately two miles long and about a mile-and-a-half wide. The castle is marked right in the centre, with the forest to the east and the cliffs rising to the west.

'The book said there's an ancient barrow some-where,' he says, sounding excited.

I shake my head, confused. 'What's a barrow?'

'It's where the Druids and the Picts used to bury their dead,' he explains eagerly. 'A stone and earth chamber. I just read about it in the book. I thought we could go looking for it.'

I remember what the pub landlord said about the ancient burial sites. 'OK,' I say, trying to summon some enthusiasm. I know Liam is a history buff so I'll have to let him drag me around in search of this barrow. 'Does it give any indication of where it is?' I ask.

He shakes his head. 'No, but we'll find it. I am a detective after all.'

I glance at the map. The forest seems to cover about two thirds of the island, with grazing land marked on the far western end, where the cliffs are. It's a large area to scour for what is essentially a mound of earth.

'Looks like a nice beach over here,' Liam says, pointing out a long stretch of sand marked on the northern side. Now that sounds much more enticing. Hopefully Liam will forget his idea of hunting for old graves and want to go there instead.

'Maybe we can go there for a picnic one day?' I suggest.

He nods in agreement and keeps studying the map. I know he's committing it to memory. He's lucky. He has a photographic memory; he can remember names, faces, things he's read or seen in minute detail. He can even recall whole conversations word for word, ones that we've had months before that I have no recollection of. It makes him a formidable detective and interrogator. Whilst he's engrossed, I pick up another book from the coffee table; this one leather bound. 'GUEST BOOK' is embossed on the cover in gold leaf. I flick through the pages, all of them blank, and then stop, surprised.

'He was wrong,' I say.

Liam looks up from the map.

'The boatman,' I explain, showing Liam the guest book. 'He said we were the first guests.' On the first page someone has written an entry in spidery, blue handwriting. 'But this is dated from last Christmas Eve.'

'That's strange,' Liam says, taking the book from me

and looking at the date. 'Maybe they were the last visitors here, before the island was bought and the cottage was converted.'

Liam reads the entry out loud: '*Stay was cut short unfortunately, but it was wonderful until then. Tried looking for the burial site but couldn't find it. I look forward to visiting in the future. A warning to guests: stay away from the cliffs. A fall could be fatal.*'

Liam closes the book and puts it back on the coffee table. 'Fancy an explore?' he asks, jumping to his feet.

'Are we going looking for the barrow?' I ask with a wry smile.

He shakes his head. 'We'll do that tomorrow when we've got more time. Let's go and check out the castle. That'll be a bit easier to find, I suspect!'

Chapter Four

We leave by the back door and Liam locks it, despite the fact we're alone on the island and it's not as if anyone is going to break in and rob us. 'Force of habit,' he laughs, pocketing the key.

There's a stack of chopped wood piled almost five feet high against the side of the house, covered in a tarp. 'Enough wood to see us through a whole winter,' Liam comments, nodding in its direction. 'And the summer too. Christ, it's nippy. I'll put a fire on when we get back.' He grimaces a little, pulling his coat around him to keep out the chill, then takes my hand as we head into the forest. I'm equally grateful for my scarf and the warm coat I brought with me.

The sunlight barely penetrates among the trees and the occasional beam that slips between the dark branches reminds me of light shining through the windows of a church, as does the hushed stillness. I take deep breaths, filling my lungs with fresh air, revelling in the sense of freedom that's germinated in me, just by being here among nature. It's as if I've left the past behind and I'm taking my first teetering steps on a new path. We follow a winding route through the forest; I'm not sure which direction we're heading in exactly. It's dank and mossy and there's no real trail. Very quickly, I feel lost.

'This way,' Liam says, orienting us without a problem.

After a few more minutes, we break into a clearing and I pull up abruptly, stumbling into Liam. Up ahead is the castle – but it looks nothing like it did in the photograph. It's a ruin: fire has gutted it almost completely, and it lies before us like a blackened, half-eaten carcass.

'Guess that's why they didn't mention it on the website,' Liam laughs.

I stare up at it and suppress a shudder. Though it's only five o'clock in the afternoon and won't be dark for ages, the broken timbers of the roof cast a long shadow and I remember the conversation back in the pub – all that talk of ghosts. Did someone die in the fire perhaps?

'I wonder how it burned down,' I say. 'And if anyone got hurt.' I think of the photograph of Nancy, Andrew and Elliot.

We walk along the edge of the clearing, circumnavigating the castle at a distance. It's four storeys tall, but the roof has collapsed in places and the rafters poke up like painfully splintered ribs. One wing of the castle has been totally destroyed, but the other side is still mainly intact – though many of the windows are smashed and probing tendrils of ivy have snaked their way inside.

The ground floor windows look to be boarded up with plywood, though I can't think why. *Perhaps kids sometimes come over from the mainland*, I muse, *looking for some illicit fun*. Or more likely it's to stop animals from going inside and making it their own. It seems odd that it was never torn down, but perhaps it's too expensive to bother, and maybe there's no point. Eventually nature will claim it; it's already starting to.

The back of the castle is in an even worse state than the front. The walls have broken down entirely in places and it looks like a giant doll's house that's hinged wide open. I can even make out floral wallpaper, stained and faded, in an upstairs room, and a wooden rocking horse, sitting forlornly in what must once have been a nursery on the first floor. I wonder at all the memories a home can hold – whether they imprint on the bricks and mortar.

'Shall we see if we can find that beach?' Liam asks, nudging my elbow.

I nod, wanting to get away from the place and its eerie presence; something about it makes me feel uneasy.

We dive back into the forest, Liam navigating our way with ease between the trees, carving out a new pathway through the bracken and undergrowth. I wonder how long it's been since anyone trod where my feet are landing. It's easy to imagine we're the only people in the world out here, or that we've stepped back in time to another era altogether.

When we reach the beach – another ten-minute walk – I'm out of breath. It's been so long since I got any real exercise, and I'm horribly aware of just how unfit I've become. It's all the staying inside, lying in bed and moping. I used to run three times a week, and even managed a 10K a year ago to raise money for Cancer Research, but now I doubt I could run to the other side of the island if my life depended on it.

The sand stretches almost half a mile and it's the most beautiful place I think I've ever seen. The view across to the other side of the loch is extraordinary: mountains rise shadowy and indistinct in the distance. It reminds me of those *Lord of the Rings* films with all its majesty and otherworldliness. It makes me completely forget the sense of horror that overcame me back at the castle.

We stroll up the beach hand in hand, walking into the wind, which feels like fists pummelling us. 'What are you thinking about?' Liam asks after a moment.

I've been lost in thought, gazing out at the water. My thoughts had wandered to my mum, to tell the truth – my mind often slips back to her – but I don't want to admit that because I know he's worried about my depression and wants me to be happy, so instead I smile and say; 'I was just thinking about the wedding.'

'What about it?' Liam asks.

'Just how perfect it was,' I say, leaning into him.

'Even though it wasn't the big wedding of your dreams?' he asks me, looking unsure.

He's asked me this before, and I've told him a thousand times that the intimate wedding we had was all I wanted, but he still worries that I wanted a big blow-out wedding ceremony and reception and that I feel let down.

'It was just what I wanted,' I tell him again. 'It couldn't have been better.'

He puts his arm around me. 'I agree,' he says, pressing his lips to the top of my head.

My smile must have faltered though, probably because the memories of the wedding are so bittersweet, because Liam notices and frowns. 'What's the matter?' he asks.

'Nothing,' I say, trying to brush away the feeling. 'I'm fine. I'm good.'

I don't want him to feel like I'm ruining the honeymoon by moping. I already ruined the first one; we didn't get to experience any newlywed bliss because my mum died the day after our wedding. We were on the way to the airport when I got a call from her neighbour, telling me she was dead.

'You know your mum wouldn't want you to be sad,' Liam says, intuiting my thoughts. 'She'd want you to be happy.'

It's the same lecture I gave myself in the bath earlier and I nod, swallowing away the hard lump that's risen up my throat. 'I just don't get why she had to die,' I whisper, immediately wishing I hadn't spoken the thought out loud.

My mum had breast cancer. She'd fought it for four years, but she was responding well to the treatment and the doctors were hopeful she'd pull through. It's so unfair. She was meant to grow old. She was meant to be a grandmother. She wasn't meant to die so soon. I still can't get over the injustice of it.

'The best thing you can do is live your life,' Liam says to me now. 'And be happy, for her sake. It's what she'd want.'

'I know,' I say, kissing Liam's cheek. 'Isis would love it here,' I add, changing the subject. 'It's a shame we couldn't bring her.'

'She's fine, don't worry,' Liam says as we continue strolling up the beach. 'The kennel's more like a luxury dog spa. It's costing the earth.'

I laugh, though we did get a discount because I know the owners from my time working at the vet. Isis, our black lab mix, will be well looked after, but I still miss her. She's my companion in the daytime when Liam's out at work; she often lies with me, on top of my feet, when I find myself too tired and too sad to get out of bed. It feels strange to be without her now, as though I'm missing a limb. I keep scanning around for sticks to throw her.

'You know this is our very first holiday together?' Liam says. 'Can you believe it?'

I smile. Liam and I had something of a whirlwind romance; we were married after just six months. After Liam proposed, we decided we didn't want to wait. We were impatient to actually be man and wife and the thought of spending a lot of money and planning for months didn't make sense to either of us. On top of that, my mum being ill made us want to do it sooner rather than later. There was always the thought in my mind that time was precious, and you just never knew which way her health would go. Liam wanted something small and intimate. As he explained it; it was *our* special day, *our* promises and nothing and no one else mattered. And it *was* a beautiful day. The last beautiful day.

It's funny, I muse, how the best day of your life can turn into the worst.

'Where else would you like to go?' Liam asks. 'What's on your bucket list?'

'Paris, Australia, Vietnam, Rome, Costa Rica . . .' I say to Liam, rattling off some of the places on my very long list.

'You've really thought about this,' Liam jokes.

I have, partly because I haven't been to many places. We didn't have much money when I was growing up and summer holidays were spent in caravans on the south coast, usually Broadstairs or Hastings. Once, after my dad died, my mum used some of the money from his life

41

insurance payout to take us to the Canary Islands. We loved it, spent the week lying by the pool reading and playing cards. It was my first time on an aeroplane.

I've also been to Spain once, with two friends I met on my veterinary assistant course. But it was a package tour, one designed for young people who liked to party, and it wasn't really my thing. My friends just wanted to get drunk and go out clubbing and I was too shy and ended up staying in most nights and reading a book.

'What would be your dream holiday if you had to pick one?' Liam presses.

'A safari in Africa,' I say, without hesitation. It's something I've long dreamed of, ever since I was a kid and became obsessed with David Attenborough's nature documentaries. 'But, honestly,' I add quickly, gesturing at the view, 'this is my dream holiday. It's a perfect honeymoon.'

'Better than Greece?' he asks.

'Better than Greece,' I say, and I really mean it. 'Here we've got a whole island all to ourselves. Over there we'd have to share.'

Liam grins.

'Thanks for booking it. I really appreciate it,' I say to him.

'You're welcome,' Liam says, looking pleased. 'Come on, let's get back.'

Chapter Five

I can feel Liam's eyes on me as I kneel down in front of the fridge and pull out ingredients for dinner. I glance over my shoulder and find him watching me with a smile, one that makes me feel flustered and almost causes me to drop the food I'm holding. His expression is a mix of desire and pride. I smile at him. 'What?' I ask, my cheeks burning.

'Nothing,' he grins. 'Can't a man admire his wife?'

I flush even redder. I'm still getting used to him calling me his wife. It feels so strange.

'It's just nice to hear you humming,' he remarks.

I hadn't noticed that I was, and the realisation makes me startle and then smile as I put the garlic, scallops and prosciutto onto the counter.

'What are you making?' Liam asks, coming closer and wrapping his arms around my waist.

'I thought I'd do fettucine with seared scallops and prosciutto,' I tell him, unwrapping the scallops. 'We need to eat these first, before they go off.'

He nods, resting his chin on my shoulder. 'Sounds wonderful. Can I do anything to help?'

I shake my head. 'All under control,' I say as I extricate myself to fill a pan with water.

Liam opens a bottle of red wine and pours himself a glass. He offers me a glass of white, but I turn it down. I'm not meant to mix alcohol with my medication. He sips his wine as he leans against the counter, watching me as I move around the kitchen. He likes watching me cook. He says it's an education, because he can't so much as boil an egg, and he finds it sexy.

I'm not sure how sexy preparing scallops is, but I take the knife he offers me from the drawer and start cleaning the scallops and wrapping them in prosciutto slices. My stomach fights nausea as I do, and I have to grit my teeth against the swell of it rising up my throat. I still don't feel hungry, despite the walk earlier and all the fresh air.

I begin to peel the garlic, trying to remember the steps of the recipe because I can't look it up on my phone. I never used to be a good cook; I've become one in the last few months, which is ironic given that during the same period I've lost my appetite. While I've been battling depression, I haven't felt in the mood to read my normal romance and thriller novels, but I've been able to page through recipe books, and every day I make dinner for Liam for when he gets home from work. At least then I feel like I've achieved something with my day, and I know he appreciates the effort. Liam grew up with a single mother who worked all hours. He was a latchkey kid who lived on TV dinners, and as an adult, working erratic hours and moving around a lot for work, he says he's lived on junk food and Pot Noodles.

My mum would laugh to see how good I've become in the kitchen. I was spoiled as a girl because she would always make home-cooked meals every evening and even when I moved out, she'd still cook for me multiple nights a week. On the other nights I'd head back to my place and warm up a can of soup or a Marks & Spencer ready meal – knowing how to use the microwave was the extent of my culinary expertise. Now I'm capable of delivering three-course meals that would make a Michelin-starred chef envious – at least according to Liam.

I bend down to search for the lemon squeezer in the drawer and Liam comes up behind me again, pulling me back towards him. 'You're so sexy,' he says, burying his face in my hair and kissing my neck.

My legs go weak as they always do when he touches me. I turn around to face him and he pushes me back against the counter and kisses me. Things quickly start to heat up, his hands stroking up my back, my breath becoming ragged, and it's only when I hear the pan sizzling behind me that I leap out of his arms, laughing and catching the pan before the oil can splatter.

'I'll behave,' Liam laughs, moving away to refill his glass.

I put the scallops in the pan and hear the satisfying crackle of the prosciutto as it starts to cook. I need to time things carefully, so the scallops don't overcook, and the pasta is perfectly al dente. There's nothing worse than undercooked pasta and overcooked fish.

Twenty minutes later I set two plates down on the table, adding a squeeze of lemon with a flourish to the scallops. I sit down opposite Liam and watch him take a bite. He chews thoughtfully and then a smile spreads across his face. 'Incredible,' he says. 'You should go on *MasterChef.*'

I smile back, happy he likes it, and take a small bite of my own. I can't taste it though and the slippery, almost fleshy texture of the scallop makes me queasy. I end up pushing the rest of my food around my plate.

'Have you thought about going back to work?' he asks, reaching for the salt.

'I don't know,' I answer, hesitantly. 'I mean, I'd like to at some point.' I quit my job at the vet just after my mum died and I was too depressed to go in. 'I miss my job. Being around animals,' I admit to Liam.

'Maybe you can go back soon,' he suggests. 'I mean, if you think you're up to it? No pressure though, of course.'

I take a deep breath, then let it out. 'I think I might need a few more months,' I say.

'Of course,' he answers. 'Take your time. Are you done?' He gestures to my plate.

I look down and see I've eaten nothing more than that first bite, but I nod. 'Do you want dessert?' I ask, standing up to clear the table.

'Sure,' he says.

I put the plates in the sink and then cross to the fridge, but Liam catches me by the wrist and pulls me into his lap.

'You don't want dessert?' I ask in a teasing tone.

He grins. 'I want you.'

He kisses the spot on my neck that always makes me gasp. I close my eyes as a shiver runs up my spine. His touch is like fire and ice at the same time, almost painful, like the burn you get when you hold snow in your palm for too long. His hands slide up beneath my skirt and he groans.

When we first started dating, I didn't have much experience. I'd only had two previous boyfriends, neither of whom had cared much about giving pleasure, only receiving it, and Liam had to take the lead. I was shy and self-conscious, and I still am to a degree, but much less.

We make love against the kitchen table. Liam tugs at his belt and yanks down his trousers in his haste and I brace myself with one hand against the wall, hearing my own cries of pleasure as though they're far away and belong to someone else. Only Liam's hands gripping my thighs and his voice in my ear bring me back to the moment.

When we finish, Liam pulls up his trousers and I hop down from the table on shaking legs. Liam pulls me to him and kisses me. 'I love you, Laura Carrington,' he murmurs against my lips.

'I love you too,' I answer, looking into the arctic blue of his eyes.

How did I end up with him? What did I do to deserve it? I guess it was fate after all, like Liam likes to say.

Liam takes my face in his hands and kisses me again, gently this time, and then suggests we head upstairs.

In bed I lie beside him, listening. There's no noise of traffic or sirens or car alarms blaring, but the peace and quiet is almost as deafening. It takes a while to adjust to the roar of it in my ears.

I close my eyes and for the first time in months I manage to fall asleep without any problem.

Chapter Six

Day Two

I'm awake before the sun and calculate that I've slept at least eight hours. I'm used to existing on much less – usually four or five hours at most – and normally in the morning when I wake up it's like crawling out of a coma, dragging myself by my fingernails into consciousness. It takes a while on those days for the pieces of my life to rearrange themselves in my head and for me to remember what's happened. I like that magical moment upon waking where, for a whole minute sometimes, I don't remember that my mother is dead. I wish I could live in that space always.

This morning though I feel different; alert, awake and with a sense of anticipation for what the day will bring. I haven't felt like this in months and I hope that it lasts. I rummage through my washbag to find my anti-depressants. Now they're starting to work, I don't want to mess it up. I swallow two pills, as well as my contraceptive, and then, leaving Liam still fast asleep, I make myself a cup of tea. I slip out, mug in hand, to wander down onto the rocky beach in front of the cottage.

The sun is rising and streaking the sky pink. There are only a few clouds and the day promises to be beautiful. I wonder what happened to the storm the boatman mentioned; for all his talk of storms and dark histories, nothing has materialised.

I take several deep breaths of crystal-clear air and gaze out in wonder over the mirror-flat water. It's hard to remember how black and foreboding the loch looked yesterday. Today it looks so enticing that I'm almost tempted to dip my toes in, though remembering how cold it's meant to be I decide not to. I set my tea down and walk for a little while along the water's edge, scanning the beach for rocks, gathering several in my arms before choosing a place above the tide-line and setting them down. I crouch down and build a small cairn, carefully balancing the rocks on top of each other until it rises to about knee-height.

As the sun starts to rise higher, I return to get my tea and then I sit in the sunshine and close my eyes, lifting my face to the breeze, and letting my thoughts drift to the future. It's not something I've been able to do in months. I think about the six days Liam and I have ahead of us on the island and then my mind leaps ahead, beyond the honeymoon, and I start to think about how I'll manage returning to the real world. I told Liam I wasn't sure about returning to work, that I wanted a bit longer, but I wonder if I'll be able to go back sooner after all. I'm definitely starting to feel a shift, and the truth is that I miss working. I miss the banter with colleagues, and I miss being around animals and feeling like I'm making a difference. I want to go back. It's just a case of making it happen.

Footsteps crunch across the pebbles at the top of the beach. I open my eyes and turn around to see Liam walking towards me. I wave and he comes and sits down beside me, putting his arm around my shoulder and kissing me on the temple. 'Morning,' he says.

'Morning,' I reply as he steals my mug and takes a swallow of my now lukewarm tea.

'I woke up and you were gone. I was worried,' he says.

I shake my head at him, amused. 'I didn't want to wake you,' I tell him. 'You didn't need to worry. Where am I going to go?'

He yawns, staring out over the loch. 'Wow, this is beautiful,' he says, taking it in.

'It is,' I agree. The sun is out today and already I'm feeling too warm in my sweater.

'How are you feeling?' Liam asks me.

'Good,' I say, with a nod.

He narrows his eyes at me a little, as though wondering if I'm being honest. I smile reassuringly. 'I slept really well,' I tell him. 'Must be all the fresh air. What about you?'

He nods. 'Same. Out like a light.'

He notices the cairn of rocks and pebbles further down the beach. 'Did you do that?' he asks.

I laugh falteringly. 'Yeah. A little memorial for my mum.' My stomach clenches as I say it and my throat constricts with that acidic tightness I've come to expect when I think of her. 'She'd have liked it here,' I say sadly. I really wish we'd made that trip we always talked about.

Liam frowns at the mention of my mum. Not wanting to put a dampener on the mood, I squeeze his hand. 'Shall we get breakfast?' I say.

Liam nods. 'Yeah. Then I thought we could go for a walk.'

'Let me guess,' I smirk. 'To find the barrow?'

'Why not?' he laughs. He takes my hand and pulls me to my feet, and we head back to the cottage where I rustle up a breakfast of scrambled eggs and toast. I manage to eat a few mouthfuls, which is encouraging, though my stomach has shrunk and I'm very quickly full.

Liam's impatient to get going and make the most of the sunny weather, so I hurry upstairs and pull on a jumper – a blue cashmere that's butter-soft and brings out my eyes.

'I like that colour on you,' Liam says when I come back down.

'Well, you've got good taste,' I joke. He's the one who bought it for me after all.

'I do,' he says, winking at me.

We leave the cottage, Liam locking the door behind us, and stroll along the beach. Eventually it peters out and we're forced to head inland into the woods on the western side of the island that lead toward the cliffs.

'So, what are we looking for exactly?' I ask Liam as we make our way through the woods.

'They're usually raised mounds of earth, and some-times they're topped with stones, a bit like the cairn you built on the beach,' he says eagerly. 'This one is from around the sixth century. It's where the ancient tribes, the Picts and the Celts, used to bury their dead.'

'So, it's a grave?' I ask.

'Yeah' Liam replies.

'Right,' I say, not sure why anyone would want to go looking for an ancient gravesite, but not wanting to mention that to Liam as he's obviously desperate to find it.

'Often, when Christianity first arrived in a place and took hold, the church would build on top of what had been pagan sites of worship,' Liam explains. 'So, I'm thinking that the logical place to look would be around the area where the medieval chapel is. It was marked on the map.'

I follow him as he strides through the woods, on a mission to locate the chapel. He's so keen that I have to hurry to keep up with him.

'Who's buried in the barrow?' I ask.

He shrugs. 'No idea. But probably someone important. The Picts and the Celts didn't always bury their dead; I read somewhere that they left criminals' bodies out in the open to be eaten by animals and the elements. So, people who were interred in the barrows were likely VIPs – kings or priests – but no one knows for sure.'

I muse on that, wondering if women were ever considered important enough to be laid to rest with any ceremony. Probably not.

'Did they bury people with treasure, like the Vikings did with their dead?'

'And the Romans,' Liam adds. 'I think so, yes. There's evidence they carried out human sacrifice too,' Liam says, really getting into the topic. 'The victims were usually people who'd done something bad like betrayed the tribe or committed treason. The tribe would offer them up to the gods. They'd torture them before they killed them, apparently. Stab them multiple times, even disembowel them, and let them bleed to death.'

I glance at him askance, pulling a face. 'That's horrible.'

Liam laughs. 'I forget sometimes that you have a delicate constitution.'

And I forget sometimes that he's become immune to horrible deeds and gruesome acts of violence, thanks to all the crimes he's seen. I suppose if you're around it for so long, get to witness the worst that people are capable of, you probably do develop a thick skin and become inured to it all.

'It was just a different justice system back then,' he comments. 'There were no police or juries or judges. It made sense to them; acted as a deterrent. An eye for an eye and all that. The safety and survival of the tribe depended on it.'

I nod. I know that Liam thinks our current legal system is a joke, and that a lot of criminals get away with murder, often because of technicalities. He doesn't think jail works as a deterrent at all, and he's even told me that he believes in capital punishment for the worst offenders. It's something I find hard to wrap my head around but, then again, I suppose he is closer to it than me: sees the lives these people ruin. And maybe some people are so evil that rehabilitation is impossible, and death is the best option.

'So how do you know all this about the barrows and the Picts and the Celts?' I ask Liam as we walk through the woods, heading for the chapel.

He shrugs. 'History was always my favourite subject at school. The only one I got an A in. This way,' he says, darting between some holly bushes.

I follow him into a small clearing, within which stands a remarkably intact stone chapel – though it's weighted down by ivy, the windows are mostly all smashed and weeds sprout between the stones. It must have been rebuilt many times over the years as it looks more Victorian than it does medieval.

It isn't as creepy as the castle, because it isn't in such a state of decay, but sitting as it is, shadowed by trees, and seemingly derelict with its broken windows and moss darkening the brickwork, it couldn't exactly be called inviting either. It has a forlorn sense about it, something that the tumbledown gravestones, which are scattered around and partly hidden among the under-growth, only help to emphasise.

Liam stares up at the chapel. 'We could have got married here,' he says.

I glance at him wondering if he's joking, but he doesn't appear to be.

'It's a church,' I say, surprised. 'You said you didn't want to get married in a church.'

'I just didn't like the idea of being married by a priest or a vicar. And I don't believe in any of those silly rituals. But I like the setting,' he explains.

I take in the grim and unappealing chapel, not sure what there is to like about it. It's more horror movie than romcom. 'I'm not sure people would have come all this way,' I say.

'Well, it's not like we invited anyone much to the wedding,' he says. 'Apart from your mum.'

I nod. Fair point. Liam's mum is dead and he never knew his father, and because he moves around a lot for work and was new to town he didn't have any local friends, so we decided to keep it small, with my mum as one of the witnesses and the registry office providing the second one.

Liam heads off to explore and search the woods for the barrow and I wander among the fallen gravestones, kicking away brambles and nettles. Most of the grave markers are crooked and the words etched on them have been eroded by time and the weather. I can make out some dates, mainly from the 1700s and the 1800s, and the name McKay is written on most of them, from which I gather it must have been the family graveyard.

Behind the chapel I find two newer gravestones, dark grey granite with white writing carved into them. I step closer to read them. 'In ever loving memory of Nancy McKay. Beloved mother, daughter, sister. RIP.' And on the second stone: 'Elliot Harrison McKay. Beloved son, brother and grandson. Loved and remembered.'

I gasp in surprise. 'They're dead,' I murmur to myself.

I read the dates on the markers. Died November 25th, 2015. Elliot was nine years old; Nancy was thirty-nine. My heart breaks for them. That's awful. I wonder what happened. Maybe they died in the fire? It seems the most likely suggestion. I glance around for a third gravestone marking Andrew McKay, but there isn't one that I can see. Maybe he managed to get out. Though, of course, I'm only guessing. Perhaps they died in some other tragic way.

I notice a dirty vase, tipped over on its side, and the remains of some dried flowers scattered over the ground. Someone obviously used to come and tend these graves, but they haven't been for a while, by the look of things. I pull up some weeds and wipe dirt off the stones.

In the wood I find some little pink flowers growing among the moss, and I pick them and place them on the graves, whispering a little prayer as I do. As I finish, I hear Liam calling my name and I locate him after a minute, standing some way off in the woods. I'm about to tell him about the graves I've discovered, but before I can he grasps me by the arm. 'I think I've found it,' he says, gleefully pointing at the grassy mound in front of him.

'It looks like a hill,' I say. In honesty, it doesn't look like anything much.

'Yeah, but look around here,' Liam says, gesturing for me to follow. The other side of the hill is covered in brambles and Liam has ferreted a path through them to reveal a small arched doorway held up by giant stones. I peer into the darkness of the cave-like entrance but it's too dark to make anything out and there's no way I'm crawling inside for a better look.

'Come on,' says Liam, tugging at my arm.

'Inside?' I ask, horrified at the thought.

He nods and pulls out his phone to light the way.

'Is that a good idea?' I ask as he bends his head and takes a step inside the barrow. 'What if it caves in?'

'It's been around for centuries, it's not going to cave in,' he laughs. 'What's the matter? Are you scared?'

I nod and he grins, amused. 'There's nothing to be scared of,' he reassures me. 'It's only old bones. The dead can't hurt you.'

'Can't they?' I ask, and he looks at me funny. 'I'll wait outside,' I say, backing off, but he takes my hand and pulls me towards the entrance.

'Come on, it'll be fun.'

I sigh and let him lead the way into the barrow. Inside, the air smells loamy and dank, and it's so dark that I can feel the panic start to breed in me like a virus, threatening to shut down my breathing. My thoughts swirl like a blizzard and all I can think about is being buried alive.

Liam grips my hand tightly and drags me deeper along, and I glance over my shoulder at the shaft of daylight behind us, which is shrinking further into the distance with every step. 'I don't want to go any further,' I say, digging in my heels. I've no idea how far back this tunnel goes or where it leads.

'Just a bit more,' Liam urges.

A scurrying noise makes me yelp out loud. 'What was that?' I whisper, clutching his arm.

'Probably a mouse.'

He keeps on for a few more paces and then drops my hand so he can hold up his torch and shine it along the packed-earth wall.

The light suddenly extinguishes, and I scream. 'Liam?' I whisper.

There's total silence to match the total dark. I reach for him but he's not where he was.

'Liam?'

Terror crawls up my spine.

'Boo!' he says, lunging at me and pulling me towards him.

'That's not funny,' I say, annoyed, as he wraps his arms around my waist. 'Let's go,' I say again.

'OK, fine,' Liam says. 'You go, but I'm going to keep exploring.'

I wrench my hand from his and hurry out of the tunnel as fast as I can, emerging into the daylight like a miner who's been trapped below ground. Hugging my arms around my body and trying to rub some warmth back into me, I stand there for a minute waiting for Liam, wondering what on earth he's doing in there.

The trees creak in the wind and I whip around, suddenly feeling as if someone is watching me.

I scan among the trees, my heart racing, wondering if I'm imagining it; my paranoia has been piqued by Liam's prank. A branch snaps and a bird bursts out of the undergrowth, taking flight, and I laugh at myself for being so jumpy. It's all that talk of ghosts and murders.

Wanting to be back in the sunshine, I return to the clearing in front of the chapel and notice that one of the doors is slightly ajar. I push it open with my foot and peek inside. The flagstone floor is cracked, and the wooden pews are dusty and broken in a few places; some have mildewed hymn books still stuffed inside them.

I enter, glancing up at the stained-glass window above the altar which is still intact. I head towards it. It's a triptych: the first panel is Jesus dragging the cross, the second is the crucifixion, and the third and final panel depicts the Resurrection. It's the only part of the chapel that's completely untouched and sunlight streams through the glass, painting the flagstone floor with rainbows. I'm gazing up at it, mesmerised by its beauty – which feels like a contradiction inside this dark shadowy place – when I hear the door swing open behind me.

I spin around to find Liam. 'There you are,' he says to me. 'Why did you run off?'

'I told you I didn't like the dark,' I tell him.

'You didn't have to be scared, you know,' he tells me, brushing a loose bit of hair behind my ear. 'I'd never let anything happen to you.'

I nod. 'What did you find?' I ask. 'Any bodies?'

He shakes his head, looking disappointed. 'I couldn't get very far. It looks like the tunnel's caved in.'

'At least you found it, though,' I tell him.

He shrugs, obviously disappointed.

'I found something too,' I tell him. 'Come and see.'

I lead him out of the chapel and around to the gravestones I discovered. I point at the names and watch the surprise flash across his face. 'They died,' I tell him.

'I can see that,' he replies.

'What do you think happened?' I ask.

'Maybe they died in the fire?'

'That's what I thought too,' I say.

'We should get back.' Liam turns towards the woods. 'It's almost lunchtime. And I'm starving.'

We walk back through the trees towards the cottage, hand in hand, feet crunching over leaves that are already starting to turn orange and drift to the ground ahead of autumn's arrival. I catch a sudden darting shadow in the corner of my eye.

'What was that?' I ask, stopping suddenly, tugging my hand from Liam's and pointing to the bushes up ahead.

'What?' Liam asks, looking in the direction I'm pointing.

'I thought I saw something,' I say.

Liam glances around. 'It was probably just a rabbit.'

I shake my head. 'No, it was bigger than that.'

'A pheasant then. I think there are some on the island. Or maybe a fox.'

We stop and listen for a few moments but all we can hear is the wind stirring the branches of the trees.

'I'm just being silly,' I laugh.

We keep on walking, but the whole time I can't shake the sense that we're being watched. I think about what the men in the pub said about the island being haunted. It definitely feels as if we're being followed by something.

Chapter Seven

After lunch Liam picks up the history book from the coffee table and starts to read it. 'This is interesting,' he says after a time. 'The monks lived on the island from the ninth century through until the 1500s, raising cattle and fishing in the loch to sustain themselves. The abbey was raided several times by Vikings looking to pillage and steal the monastery's wealth.'

I imagine how terrifying that must have been for the monks, with nowhere to flee to. Did they just sit and pray and accept their fate? Or did they try to hide as the Vikings attacked? Did any of them try to fight back?

'Listen to this,' Liam goes on, eagerly. '"The monks were said to have buried the monastery's treasure on the island to hide it. This myth has endured since the fifteenth century."'

I glance at him. I know he's thinking about searching for it, but he doesn't say as much; he just keeps turning the pages of the book.

Later in the afternoon we head back out to the beach in front of the cottage. The sun is still warm, and Liam looks relaxed and happy as he sits beside me on the blanket sipping from a bottle of beer. He spots a flat stone and expertly skims it across the surface of the loch. We watch it bounce a half-dozen times and I cheer. He searches for more flat stones within reach and then tries to teach me, showing me how to angle my wrist and flick with one smooth motion, but I'm not very good and my stone sinks beneath the waves without even bouncing once.

Liam skims another one eight times to show me how it's done. 'I wonder what the world record is,' he says. 'If we had the internet, we'd be able to look it up.' He looks a little put out that he can't discover the world record and I know it's because he'd like the challenge of being able to beat it.

'I'm glad we don't,' I tell him. 'It's nice being cut off from the world.'

'What if something happens though?' he asks, scouring around him for more flat stones to skim.

'Like what?' I ask.

'World War Three could break out, and we wouldn't know about it.'

'We'd probably be better off not knowing,' I laugh.

'It's not as if we could do anything about it. It's like stepping back in time here,' I add. 'And the Celts and the monks didn't have phones or the internet.'

Liam nods. 'Back then they had to rely on signal fires to warn of approaching threats.' He finds a stone and flicks it across the water, frowning when it only bounces three times before sinking. 'Damn,' he mutters.

'I'll look for more stones,' I tell him, getting up and wandering up the beach.

'Make sure they're flat,' he calls after me.

My hunt takes me further along the beach towards the gnarly trees that mark its end. After stooping to pick up a good-sized pebble I stand and catch a glimpse of what looks like a man, standing among the trees. I blink and the person has vanished. I blink a few more times, my certainty that I saw someone fading. There's no one there now, that's for sure, but where could they have disappeared to?

I turn around and head back to Liam, who is standing with his back to me, knees bent slightly, body angled, perfecting his throwing stance. I watch him skim a stone and count the number of times it hits the surface of the water.

'Twelve!' he shouts, pumping his fist and looking around at me for a sign that I've witnessed his triumph.

'I saw!' I say, feigning excitement.

He grins and then picks up another stone to throw. I walk towards him, the small pile of stones I've managed to gather clinking in my pockets. My gaze lands just then on the cairn that I built. Something about it catches my attention and as I get closer, I see that it's because it looks different to how I left it.

I stop and study it. I remember the stone I put on the top was unusual; washed almost white and a perfect flat oval shape. But now another stone sits on top.

I kneel down in front of the cairn and notice the white, oval-shaped stone that I put on top is lying a few feet away. I lean over to pick it up and put it back on the top of the pile, where it was before.

'You OK?'

I startle and look up. Liam is standing over me.

I nod and smile at him, hurrying to stand up. 'Here,' I say, handing over the flat skimming stones I found for him. 'Try these. I think they're flat enough.'

Liam studies the pile I dump into his hands, discarding a couple that don't pass muster. 'Thanks,' he says and turns and hurries back to the shore.

As he walks away, I glance quickly back over my shoulder at the treeline, but of course there's nothing there.

'Watch this!' Liam says.

I turn and hurry after him.

Later that night, I lie beside Liam who has fallen asleep quickly. I can't manage to drift off though. My memory flashes to the man I thought I saw standing among the trees on the beach; there one moment and gone the next. Was I imagining it? Could the anti-depressants be causing me to have paranoid thoughts? Or maybe I'm on edge and the ghost stories those men in the pub told me have aggravated my nerves.

A month or so ago the same thing happened. I was standing at the sink in the kitchen chopping carrots when I had a sudden feeling that I was being spied on. I even started to wonder if perhaps my mother's ghost was hovering around, keeping an eye on me. I didn't tell Liam that time either.

I ease out of bed and tiptoe towards the window. Slowly, I draw back the curtain. Outside there's pitch blackness, broken only by a smattering of stars.

I laugh at myself for believing in ghosts, then pull the curtain across and slip back into bed.

The Stalker

She was just standing at the window looking out. I like watching her when she doesn't know she's being watched.

I watched her on the beach today as she walked along, pausing now and then to pick up stones, her blonde hair whipping about her slender neck as though it was trying to strangle her. I must admit, the thought made me tingle with something halfway between pleasure and pain.

I thought I caught her looking right at me, and I smile as I recall the fear that flashed across her face for an instant. I breathe in deep. I can still smell that fear, lingering in the air.

If she was an animal, she'd be a bird, soft feathered, fragile boned, easily caught and caged. I smile at the idea. She's caged right now. Inside the cottage. On the island. There's no way off. No escape.

Chapter Eight

Day Three

Liam carries the picnic basket that I found in the cupboard under the stairs and I clutch the blanket. We make our way through the forest towards the beach on the northern side of the island where we walked on the first day we arrived. I woke up this morning and in the cold light of day decided I was letting my imagination run far too wild.

'Do you know what today is?' Liam asks.

'Yes,' I say, smiling at him. 'August 26th. Our eight-month anniversary.'

It feels longer because we've been through so much. I've made a special anniversary picnic for us to celebrate: cheese and pickle sandwiches, a chicken salad, and some freshly made shortbread that I cooked up this morning – Liam's favourite. Liam slipped in two bottles of beer as well, though I only intend to have a sip of mine.

At the beach we set the picnic basket down and lay out the blanket, weighing it down with stones on the corners. It's another glorious day, though blustery. 'So much for that boatman's prediction about the weather,' Liam laughs. 'There's a storm coming,' he imitates in a thick Scottish brogue.

'Shall we go for a walk up the beach before we have lunch?' I ask him.

'Sure,' he says, and we stroll along together hand in hand.

'I wonder if I could swim over to that island,' Liam says, pointing to a small craggy island no bigger than a tennis court that sits about a hundred metres out from shore.

'Why would you want to?' I ask.

He shrugs. 'Because.'

How could I forget how competitive Liam is, even when there's no one to compete against? He doesn't like being told he can't do something. He takes it as a challenge to go ahead and do it, almost as though he wants to prove that he's above the law, which I suppose he is in a way.

'Did you forget what the boatman said about how cold the water is?' I remind him. 'And how deep?'

Liam crouches down and puts his fingers in the water. 'Yeah, that's cold,' he admits. 'But I still bet I could do it.'

'I'm sure you could,' I tell him, patting him on the arm. 'But we didn't bring towels, so maybe next time.'

He nods quite seriously, and I wonder if he's joking, because I certainly was, but he doesn't seem to realise that.

We walk halfway along the beach and then Liam stops. 'I'm starving,' he suddenly announces. 'Let's go back and eat.'

'Can we keep going to the end?' I ask. 'I'm enjoying it.'

But Liam is insistent, so we turn back and as soon as we reach the blanket, I find out that he has other things on his mind besides the picnic. He pulls me down onto his lap and fishes a present out of his pocket. It's a small gift-wrapped box.

'Open it,' he says, excitedly.

I do and discover a gold chain with a Celtic cross on it. 'It's beautiful,' I say, touching it.

Liam takes it out of the box, and I lift my ponytail so he can put it around my neck. 'Thanks,' I say. 'Where did you get it?'

He shrugs. 'I got it a while ago. I saw it and I thought of you and, well, it seems fitting, with us being in Scotland.'

I kiss him. 'Thank you.'

Liam's always buying me jewellery – rings, a bracelet, a few necklaces. He has good taste and I feel spoiled beyond measure, as until I met him my jewellery box was mostly full of things from Accessorize.

'Do you like it?' he asks.

'I love it,' I say, turning around to kiss him.

He pulls me closer. I can feel him getting aroused, so I climb off his lap and stretch towards the picnic hamper, but Liam catches me around the waist. 'Where are you going?' he asks, teasingly.

He flips me over onto my back and lowers himself on top of me with a wicked grin.

'What?' I ask, my eyes widening. 'Here?'

He shrugs, his lips just inches from mine. 'It's not like there's anyone here to see.' He kisses me, the grin stretching his mouth wide, and his hands start to rove up inside my sweater. The wind slices against my skin like a razor as Liam eases off my clothes.

Naked, we make love on the blanket as the wind whips sand against us and the seagulls scream above us. Liam seems to like the thrill of it, but I can't help but shiver, my skin coated in goosebumps. I'm distracted; I can't shake the memory of the person I thought I saw on the beach yesterday when I was looking for stones. What if I didn't imagine it? What if they're here right now, watching us? The sense of being spied on grows, averting my attention, making me turn my head and scour the horizon.

I feel self-conscious and I can't relax, and when we've finished, I'm quick to pull on my clothes.

'Was that OK?' Liam asks, stroking my arm as he lies beside me, drowsy and smiling.

'Great,' I say, not wanting to upset him or let him know I've got the unnerving sense we're being watched. I move to open the picnic hamper, taking out the sandwiches and handing both to Liam. 'Not hungry?' he asks.

I shake my head. 'Not really.'

He unwraps his sandwich and takes a bite. 'Hand us a beer?' he says.

I lever off the cap and hand him a bottle and then do the same with my own. Liam knocks his against mine. 'Happy anniversary,' he says. 'Love you.'

'Love you too,' I say, the words whipping away on the wind.

I cast a glance over my shoulder towards the forest, a shiver running up my spine.

Chapter Nine

I dress for dinner, pulling on the slinky black dress that I know Liam likes. 'Very Audrey Hepburn,' he said, the time I wore it on one of our early dates. It was my birthday and he took me for an incredible meal at a Michelin-starred restaurant. That was the first time he told me he loved me, and it was one of the best nights of my life. I remember how I felt that night – like I was floating on air – and genuinely, it was the first time I'd ever felt beautiful.

I smile sadly when I recall my mum telling me how happy she was for me when I called her later that night to tell her how the date had gone.

My mum loved Liam, could see how good he was to me and was happy that I'd found someone who so obviously adored me after my previous two dating disasters. She liked his old-fashioned manners, the fact he was a gentleman; and it didn't hurt that he brought flowers when he met her for the first time. He went up even more in her esteem when he fixed her leaking kitchen tap and mended the garden fence.

'It's nice to have a man around here who's good with his hands,' she'd said to me with a naughty smile, admiring Liam through the kitchen window as he hammered nails into a post.

I notice that the dress hangs loose on me now; looks more like a sheath than the curve-clinger it was a few months ago; but it still works. I touch up my make-up, putting on blusher to mask my paleness, and lipstick too, which I haven't done in a while. It feels strange to wear heels inside the cottage, but it looks weird to be so dressed up and not wear shoes, so I slip them on before heading carefully downstairs, clutching the banister as I go. I'm not used to wearing heels and I feel a little light-headed.

Liam's sitting on the sofa lacing up his boots, but he pauses when he sees me, and his mouth falls open. 'You look beautiful,' he says, eyes widening.

'He adores you,' my mum had told me, noticing the way he was looking at me the first time I brought him home.

I walk over to him and he pulls me into his lap. He's put on a clean blue shirt and his hair still looks wind-swept from our walk earlier.

'I thought maybe we could have a little bonfire on the beach after dinner,' he says. 'I was just going to get it ready.'

'Oh, yes,' I say eagerly. I've always loved a bonfire; the smell of woodsmoke and the crackling flames always remind me of being a kid and burning leaves with my grandad on his allotment. 'I'll make dinner now then,' I add.

Liam heads outside and I go into the kitchen, already knowing exactly how I'm going to cook the salmon and calculating in my head when I should put the crumble that I made earlier into the oven.

By the time I'm sliding the salmon in its foil wrapper under the grill, Liam is back from setting up the bonfire. He washes his hands and opens the wine, pouring a glass for himself which he chinks against my glass of water. 'To us,' he says.

'To us,' I answer.

After dinner we head out to the beach where Liam has built the bonfire. He has dragged out two chairs to sit beside it, and brought out a blanket, which he drapes around my shoulders. I tilt my head back and look up at the sky. 'I don't think I've ever seen so many stars,' I say.

'That's the big dipper,' Liam points out.

'Ursa Major,' I say.

Liam looks at me, surprised that I know the actual Latin name for the constellation.

'My grandad taught me,' I tell him with a small shrug, glancing up at the sky. 'It never sets below the horizon in the northern hemisphere. Slaves used it to navigate north, on their way to freedom.'

'What other stars do you know?' Liam asks. 'What's that one, over there?' He points to a bright star at the edge of Ursa Major.

I shake my head. 'I've forgotten. It's been so long.'

A shooting star suddenly streaks across the blackness overhead and I let out a gasp as it dissolves into the dark. 'A shooting star! Did you see it?'

He shakes his head. 'Did you make a wish?' he asks.

I close my eyes and make one.

'What did you wish for?' he asks.

I'm about to answer but Liam suddenly leaps to his feet.

'What is it?' I ask, turning to look in the same direction as him.

He shakes his head, a frown appearing between his eyes. 'I thought I saw something.'

'What?' I ask, peering past him. The bonfire throws out a halo of light for about twenty feet but beyond that perimeter it's pure darkness: a void. I can't see anything.

He shakes his head and gives a nervous laugh. 'It was probably just an animal.'

He keeps scanning the beach though, frowning, and I do too, wondering what it could have been. After a while he turns to me, forcing a smile. 'Shall we go back inside?' he says.

The bonfire is still going, blazing brightly, but I agree and follow him back to the house, glancing once over my shoulder to scan the beach, wondering what it was that he could have seen. I think back to the shadow of a man I thought I saw yesterday on the beach. I didn't mention it to Liam at the time, and I don't want to mention it now as he might wonder why I didn't say anything yesterday. 'What do you think you saw?' I ask him as he opens the front door and ushers me inside.

'I don't know,' he mumbles, his face dark.

Once inside the cottage, Liam locks all the doors and then goes around checking all the windows. He's acting very spooked and I can feel my own adrenaline starting to pump.

When he's done, he turns to me and smiles, though it seems a little forced, as though he's trying not to worry me. 'I'm sure it was nothing,' he says. 'Probably a fox.'

I offer a reassuring smile in return. Liam takes my hand and pulls me into the living room. I stand beside him as he crouches down and lights a fire in the wood-burning stove. The wood is dry and crackles to life as soon as Liam drops the match. He shuts the door of the stove and stands up. He takes hold of me by my hips, and gives me a look that undoes me, making my whole body quiver in response; then he turns me gently around, so I'm facing away from him.

I suppose he's convinced himself that it really was an animal he saw, and I wish I could do the same; but I just can't stop my mind from wandering, even as Liam slowly unzips my dress, pausing to kiss between my shoulder blades.

A shiver runs up my spine. He unclasps my bra and then slides the dress off, so it pools around my feet, then he turns me back around to face him. My hands fly self-consciously across my body, but I know how much he likes to see me, so I move them to my sides, and he smiles encouragement. He eases off the straps of my bra and I let it fall on top of my dress.

He stands back and his gaze sweeps every inch of me. Goosebumps chase trails across my skin and he draws me nearer, kissing the tender place below my collarbone and then my neck. I tip my head back and draw a tight breath, resting my hands on his shoulders as he kisses down my chest towards my stomach. My fingernails dig into his shoulders.

He pauses to take off his shirt and then he pulls me to my knees and lays me down on the rug. He works out a lot and he's muscled and broad and when he rolls on top of me his weight presses down on me like a rock.

'Do you like that?' he asks.

'Yes,' I whisper in his ear.

'Is that good?' he asks now, kissing the inside of my thigh.

'Mmm,' I say, squeezing my eyes shut.

'Jesus Christ!' Liam yells, leaping to his feet.

I sit up in fright. 'What?'

Liam's on his feet now, staring at the window. 'There was someone there. Looking in the window.' His voice sounds strange, strained, and he looks terrified, as though he's seen a ghost.

'What?' I say in alarm, sitting up and covering my body with my arms. I look at the window, but I can't see anything but sheer blackness. We could be floating in space.

Liam crosses to the window and looks out. 'There was someone there,' he says. 'I swear to god.'

I yank on my dress, disturbed at the idea someone was looking in and saw me naked, and then go and join him at the window.

'It's too dark,' I say, staring out at what looks like an abyss. Nothing is visible; not the loch nor the starlight, only a faint glow from the beach where the bonfire is dying.

A large, dark shadow passes suddenly in front of the flames, and we both jump back from the window in fright.

'There!' he shouts. 'Did you see it?

I nod. 'What was that?' I ask, gripping his arm.

Liam shakes his head. 'I'm going outside to check.'

I grab his arm even harder, pulling him back. 'No,' I say. 'Don't.'

He gives me a sardonic look, one eyebrow raised. 'Laura, I'm a police officer, remember?'

I nod. Of course, I remember, but I don't find it all that reassuring.

'You stay here,' he tells me as he pulls his trousers and shirt back on.

Anxiety buzzes in my sternum. I follow him into the kitchen where he stops to pull on his boots. 'Do you really need to go?' I ask anxiously.

'Yes.' He crosses to the back door. 'Lock it after I go out. I'll knock three times when I come back,' he tells me.

I nod and then he's gone, out the door and swallowed up by the darkness. With a shaking hand I bolt the door behind him and then stand in the kitchen motionless, ears cocked for any noises outside, but I can't hear a thing. The house is as still and silent as a crypt.

He's gone a long time and my anxiety builds with each passing second. Where is he? Has something happened to him? My nerves are electrified and I'm so on edge that when I hear a light thudding sound coming from inside the cottage my heart almost smashes through my ribcage, only relaxing when I realise it's just the fire. A burning log must have fallen against the grate. I walk back into the front room and glance towards the window where Liam saw the face.

I yank the curtain across and then do the same to all

the other windows. I hate the feeling that we're being watched.

Another minute passes and I start biting my nails. What if Liam doesn't come back? But then I hear a rapid knock *knock knock knock* on the back door and run to open it.

Liam enters.

'Was there anyone out there?' I ask.

He shakes his head, turning to lock the back door. 'No, not that I could see.' A deep frown line runs between his eyes, but then he shakes it off and forces a smile. 'It was probably nothing.'

I nod, but I don't believe it. And I'm not sure he does either, because why would he lock the doors if it was nothing? And the shape of the shadow that passed in front of the fire seemed far too big to be an animal. Still, I don't want to push it.

'Shall we go upstairs to bed?' Liam asks, his tone light but forced.

I nod, though I'm not sure I'll be able to get a wink of sleep. Seeing that I'm troubled, Liam puts his hand on my shoulder to reassure me. 'It's all that talk of ghosts,' he says. 'It must have got to us. Don't worry though, I'm here. I'll never let anything happen to you, you know that.'

I give him a grateful smile.

Liam checks once again that the front door is locked, and then we head upstairs. We shut the bedroom door and undress quickly. I pull on a nightdress and Liam gets into bed in his boxers.

We lie in bed together in silence, my head on his chest. I can feel the tension in his body, the muscles rigid, his heart pounding. Finally, when Liam thinks I'm sleeping, he eases his arm from under me and slips out of bed.

I lie awake with my eyes shut, listening to Liam in the bathroom as he moves about, my ears pricked. I can hear an owl hooting in the distance, and something scuttling across the roof; a squirrel or a rat maybe. I'm not afraid of animals though, not even the Pitbulls and the Rottweilers that I used to sometimes have to deal with at work. You could always put a muzzle on them after all. And most animals are predictable and easy to read.

I hear Liam turn on the shower and listen to the water run. My heart is hammering as though I've just run a race. I feel a nervous anticipation that I can't quite put a finger on. The shower cuts out and a few moments later Liam comes back into the bedroom with a towel wrapped around his waist.

He climbs into bed and rolls against my back, putting his arm around me, welding us together. I steady my breathing and listen to the owl hoot. Liam falls asleep almost instantly, but I lie awake for the longest time, unable to sleep. Suddenly, a faint scraping sound, like something scratching glass, makes me freeze. My heart starts to hammer wildly, and I look over at Liam, but he's still sleeping soundly beside me.

I crane to hear and the noise comes again, a screech like nails on a chalkboard, as though someone is trying to cut through glass and get inside the cottage. White-knuckled, I grip the sheet, too afraid to move. Surely it's just a branch tapping the window somewhere downstairs, or the wind rattling the glass. After a moment it stops and my clenched muscles relax.

I still don't sleep though. My heart refuses to settle and every time I try to close my eyes they snap open, staring into the dark void of the room, my mind conjuring monsters. Eventually, exhaustion and the darkness overwhelm me and I slip into a dream-filled sleep.

The Stalker

They were making love in front of the fire. She was naked, her pale skin painted rose gold with the flames, like she was a lacquered ornament. When I saw her, I wanted to take her in my hands, to hold her and marvel at her, and also to smash her to the stone floor. I wanted to annihilate her. And him. For touching her like that.

It made me so angry seeing them together. It made me think of all I'd once had and all I'd lost. It reminded me of how once my heart had been filled with love, but now was broken. It made me think of all the betrayal I'd suffered. And it made me want to fall to my knees and sob at the injustice and the pain of it.

But as I stood there, locked outside in the cold, watching them together inside the cottage, her with head thrown back, her delicate white throat on display, groaning as he pressed into her, I was filled with a searing white-hot rage. I wanted nothing more than to burst in and kill them both.

I backed away from the window before I could be seen, deciding that there was no point in rushing things. I needed to be careful.

I'd take my time with them; let the rage simmer before I brought it to a boil.

Chapter Ten

Day Four

I jerk awake from a nightmare involving a prowling monster hunting me in the dark. A dull grey light fills the room. It's not yet dawn, and when I creep from bed, leaving Liam asleep, and head downstairs I see that Venus, the morning star, is still visible in the light of daybreak. I watch it through the kitchen window as it fades away and finally disappears.

In the cold light of day the nightmares from last night and the fear of an intruder melt away. I play around with the coffee maker – thankfully it's automatic – and try to figure out how to use the steam wand attached to it. By the time I've located the manual in the drawer and made the perfect froth for a cappuccino, Liam is awake and has joined me in the kitchen.

'You're up early,' he says, kissing my cheek.

I hand him a cup of coffee. He notices the heart shape I've tried to draw in the froth with cinnamon and laughs. He takes a sip and nods in appreciation. 'That's a fairly decent coffee. Maybe you could train as a barista. Though,' he adds, 'it would be a waste of your talents.'

I'm about to ask him what he wants for breakfast – I spied all the ingredients for an English breakfast in the fridge and my appetite is stirring and demanding bacon – but he's already heading towards the front door. 'Shall we take it outside, sit on the beach?' he suggests.

His fear seems to have dissipated overnight. He must have resolved in his mind that it wasn't a person he saw after all; definitely an owl. That, or he's pretending in order to make me feel better. Either way, I decide to go along with it.

I nod, pick up my own cup of tea and hurry after him. He undoes the dead bolts on the front door, and we step outside to find that the morning is fresh and mainly clear, with only a few clouds skidding along overhead.

'Still no sign of that stor—,' Liam begins to say, with a slight scoff, but he trails off, his gaze falling to the path in front of us. I follow it and see there's dirt traipsed all over the flagstones. Then I see the geraniums in the flowerbeds are crushed underfoot, as though someone has stomped through them.

'What the hell?' Liam mutters under his breath. He

walks over to take a closer look. There are footprints in the soil right in front of the window – the same window he thought he saw someone staring through last night.

'Oh my god,' I whisper, looking down at them. 'There *was* someone looking in.' It wasn't an animal, and we weren't imagining things. 'Someone else is here,' I whisper in shock. 'On the island.'

Liam bends to take a closer look. 'Looks like a man's eight or nine. Boots not trainers,' he mutters. He stands up and stares at the window. 'He must have stood here last night, looking in at us.'

I swallow, feeling ill at the thought, and starting to shake with fear. I can't stop staring at the footprints – irrefutable proof that we aren't alone on the island.

Liam glances around, following the tracked dirt down the path. 'He ran off via the beach.'

'Look!' I say, pointing at the window, noticing something. Someone has etched random markings into the glass; symbols that don't make sense, like some ancient runes.

'Why would someone do that?' I ask, puzzled.

'Was it there before?'

I shake my head. 'No. I would have noticed when I drew the curtains last night.'

Liam presses his fingernail to the glass. 'It's been done from the outside. With a knife or something sharp.'

I think about the sound I heard last night – of

something scraping against glass — and feel a chill all over my body. 'What should we do?' I ask, looking to him for answers.

'Let's go back inside,' he says.

I glance around. Is whoever did this watching us right now? I feel exposed, as naked as I was last night when someone — this same someone — spied on us through the window.

'We're meant to be on the island by ourselves,' Liam rages, once we're back inside and he's shut and locked the door behind us. 'We're meant to have total privacy, and instead we've got some sicko pervert stalking us, watching us have sex.'

He puts his coffee down on the table and starts to pace the front room.

'Maybe it was some kids from the mainland?' I suggest tentatively, chewing on my thumbnail with worry. 'Or maybe someone's living on the island and they forgot to tell us.'

Liam stops pacing. 'Where? Where would anyone be living? There's no other houses!'

I shake my head and shrug. 'I don't know.' But I think about the castle. Wouldn't that be the obvious place for someone to be living — or squatting?

'And why wouldn't they have warned us? And who the hell sneaks up on a place at night and spies through the window?' Liam mutters, marching back and forth in front of the fire.

'Could it be a groundsman or something like that?' I ask. 'One of the cleaners perhaps?'

'There is no groundsman. And anyway, if there was, why wouldn't they come during the daytime?' he argues. 'They could knock on the door and say hello. Why lurk in the dark, spying on people? They could be arrested for this.'

I perch on the arm of the sofa and think about the person watching us last night. Was the same person following us in the forest earlier in the day? Or was I imagining that?

'It could be a treasure hunter.'

'What?'

Liam nods at the history book. I remember what he said about the monks burying treasure and our silly idea of going to look for it. 'You think someone's here on the island, trying to dig up buried gold?' I ask.

Liam shrugs. 'Why not? Maybe they're trying to frighten us off the island so they can keep up their search.'

He starts pacing again, his fists clenching and unclenching with frustration. Then he stops abruptly and looks at me. 'Didn't the boatman mention a satellite phone? For emergencies?'

I nod.

Liam looks around the room. 'I wonder where it is.'

We search for it, Liam rummaging through the built-in cupboards in the hallway and under the stairs, and me looking in the kitchen. 'Who will you call?' I ask as we search.

'The housekeeper, I suppose. Though I don't know if I've even got her number. We just communicated by email. I could find it though. Worst comes to the worst I can call the pub back on the mainland, someone might know her.'

'I've found it,' I call out suddenly, pulling what looks like a large TV remote out of a drawer by the cooker. I hand it to Liam. 'That's it, isn't it?' I ask.

It looks like a walkie-talkie. Liam takes it and searches for the on switch. He presses it but the phone stays dead in his hand.

'What's the matter?' I say as he keeps playing with the buttons.

'It's not working,' he says, frustrated. 'Damn it.'

'That's weird.' I examine the packaging it came in. 'It looks brand new.'

'The battery must be dead,' Liam says, sighing. 'Does it have a charger?' he asks.

I search through the drawer. 'No, I can't see one.'

'Why would you have a satellite phone with no charger? That's ridiculous!' He's getting agitated.

I keep searching through the other drawers, trying to find one. 'Would it work with an iPhone charger?'

Liam shakes his head. 'No. It looks like it needs a special one.'

He helps me search through the remaining drawers,

but we come up empty-handed. 'Damn,' he says, letting out an angry sigh. 'Maybe, we should see if we can get a mobile phone signal somewhere on the island.'

'The boatman said there wasn't any service out here.'

'There might be if we can get high enough. On the cliffs perhaps.'

I hesitate. 'But what if . . . whoever it is is out there? What if they follow us?'

Liam pulls a face. 'So? I'm not scared of them. In fact, I want to find them so I can have a word with them.'

It's the last thing I want to do, but I have no choice.

'Come on,' Liam says, grabbing his phone from the coffee table. 'Bring yours too, just in case.'

Chapter Eleven

We start walking along the beach, though Liam is practically marching, and I have to hurry to match his pace. The bonfire from last night has left a charred scar on the sand. As we pass it, we glance at the chairs still sitting beside the remains of the fire: reminders of how our evening was ruined.

'What do you think they want?' I ask Liam.

He shakes his head. 'I don't know. Maybe it's not a treasure hunter. It could just be a homeless person. Someone who's living on the island. Trespassing.'

'But how would they survive out here year-round?' I ask. The winters must be brutal – not to mention fresh water and electricity.

'I don't know,' Liam grunts.

When the beach peters out we have to head inland,

through the woods and then up and over a scraggy hill. We can see the cliffs in the distance, and I remember the warning in the book, but when I mention it to Liam, he waves the concern away. By the time we reach them, I have to stop to catch my breath for a moment before I can take in the view. When I do, I can see three hundred and sixty degrees – the whole island spread out before us, as well as the loch stretching in all directions. It makes me feel tiny and insignificant, and also emphasises just how far we are from any help. The loch is really a firth, or a fjord: it leads out to sea, and the mainland feels terribly far away. Looking back over the island, I can make out the forest as well as the roof struts of the burned castle poking up among the trees. The cottage is a small dot more than a mile away, and the jetty appears as thin as a twig stretching out into the dark grey water.

Liam pulls out his phone but the expression on his face tells me he's got no reception. 'What about you?' he asks, nodding at the phone in my hand.

I look down at it and shake my head. 'No,' I say. 'Nothing.'

Liam scowls and then trudges off to a slightly higher point nearer to the edge of the cliffs.

'Don't go too close,' I warn.

He ignores me and holds his phone in the air.

I stand well back, leaning into the buffeting wind and scanning the desolate hillside. It's completely unsheltered, which is probably why it's so barren, apart from one arthritic tree, bent almost double as its roots dig in like claws to keep from being tipped over by the gale force. I feel like at any point the wind might pick me up and sweep me off the precipice too.

'It looks like there's a path over there,' Liam shouts as he heads back over to me. He points to a barely visible track built into the rock face, which looks like it might lead down, though I don't dare step close enough to find out where to.

'It looks dangerous,' I say. 'Come on, let's go home.'

Liam smiles at me, shaking his head as though he's a child indulging an overly protective parent, but he moves away from the edge and we keep going, walking along the perimeter of the island.

The north side of the island runs down away from the cliffs and delves back down into the woods. It's sparser than the forest behind the cottage, which is mainly pine; instead it's filled with ash and rowan and the trees aren't densely packed together but spread out. It's beautiful, peaceful even, like a dell, and completely out of the wind. If only there wasn't this low-level sense of danger thrumming like a discordant note through my body I might actually be able to enjoy it, but I can't stop looking over my shoulder, half-expecting someone to be following us, and I can't escape the sensation of being watched either. And neither, it seems, can Liam. I catch him jerking his head left and right, turning full circles as we walk, as though he expects someone to leap out from behind a tree and attack us.

He walks with his phone in his hand, checking it constantly to see if we've magically walked into an area with signal, but I barely bother looking at mine, knowing the chances are impossible; we're so far from any kind of civilization, and reception was spotty even on the mainland.

We continue on through the woodland, clambering down over boulders in a few places and into steep gullies. We cross a stream and then follow it all the way to the water's edge. On this part of the island, there's no beach; just large rocks jutting into the loch. We head back inland when they become too difficult to climb over and Liam, who has said very little up until this point, leads us into the clearing where the castle sits.

'It makes sense,' Liam says when we come upon it.

'What does?' I reply.

He nods at the castle. 'It's the only place you could shelter on the whole island.'

'You're not thinking of going in there?' I ask him, but I already know the answer.

Liam starts towards the castle. I trot after him and catch his sleeve. 'I don't think it's a good idea.'

'Why not?' Liam retorts, ignoring my hand on his arm.

'Because . . .' I trail off, gazing up at the charred ruin

before us. 'How would we get in anyway?' I ask. 'The downstairs is boarded up.'

'Let's find out,' Liam says, pulling his arm from my grip and striding on.

'I don't think we should,' I mumble to his retreating form. 'It's not safe.'

'I'm not waiting around for this bastard to stop playing games,' Liam calls over his shoulder.

'Maybe whoever it is isn't playing games?' I offer, catching him up. 'What if they're just curious about us? No one's been here for months. They probably just wanted to find out who was staying. We should just leave them alone. And hopefully they'll do the same.'

But it's pointless; Liam's determined to find the person and confront them. I'd do anything to avoid conflict and never used to assume that people had nefarious intentions, but Liam's the opposite. He's like a dog with a bone when he goes after something, and he always assumes the worst in people and situations: another symptom of his police work.

When we reach the castle, I notice just how impenetrable the stone walls are; though weathered and pocked, each slab is at least a foot and a half thick, and there are two towers still left standing among the ruins. I stare up at the pointed arches and buttresses. It reminds me a little of pictures that I've seen of the Notre Dame cathedral in Paris: several leering gargoyles carved into the stonework above the door stick their tongues out at us. It's ugly and imposing, even more so in its decay, and I really want to turn tail and run.

The downstairs windows are all solidly boarded up, with no way of gaining entry unless we had a sledge-hammer or a saw, but Liam walks around the entire circumference of the building, looking to see if any boards have been pried loose, and I follow a few steps behind. When we reach the front doors, we see that they've been covered with two heavy steel panels, the bolts drilled into the stonework on either side. I feel quite relieved that we won't be going inside.

I stand on the scarred stone steps leading up to the entrance, my mind flashing back to the photograph in the book. I'm standing in the exact place where the McKay family stood. I remember the look on Nancy's face, her hand resting on her son Elliot's shoulder, and I shudder as if someone just walked over my grave.

I look around then and notice that Liam has vanished. Panicked, I run around the corner but there's still no sign of him. 'Liam?' I call out, suddenly afraid.

There's no answer. I shout his name again.

'Over here!' I hear him yell back, and then I spot his head emerge from what looks like a hole. As I get closer, I realise he's actually just down some steep stone steps that lead to what was probably once a servants' entrance or maybe even a coal scullery door, judging by the small size of it.

'It's been forced open,' Liam says, pointing at the

boarded-up doorway. 'Look.' He yanks on the plywood covering the entrance and it comes away easily. It was merely there as a prop cover. Liam pulls out his phone and turns the torch on. He shines it into the dark, cave-like interior, then takes a step inside.

I hesitate. 'I don't know if this a good idea,' I say.

'You can wait outside if you like,' Liam answers without even a glance in my direction.

There's no way I'm waiting outside by myself, so I follow him, feeling my way like a deep-sea diver into the murky depths. *There's two of us*, I tell myself, trying to feel brave, *and probably only one of him*. Nothing bad can happen. Can it?

Chapter Twelve

Liam holds the phone up high, though the flashlight does little beyond illuminating a circle of a few feet in front of us. We're in what appears to be a cellar; it's damp and smells of rot or mildew. I cough in the stale air and Liam holds his hand out for me to take as we pick our way across the uneven ground.

I grip it tightly, not wanting to fall or twist my ankle; in places the roof beams have collapsed, and piles of rubble and masonry clog up the space. I worry about the roof caving in completely and trapping us down here. How long would it take before we were found? Too long, that's for sure.

Finally, we reach the far wall and Liam locates a door, but there's a rock wedged in front of it. Did someone place it there? It seems somehow deliberate. He hefts it out the way and pulls the door open; it leads into a stone-walled passage, windowless and airless, which we pick our way along. There are several rooms off the corridor and by the looks of things they were once used as storage or perhaps were even servants' quarters.

There's furniture in some; one looks like a tack room, and another has shelves and several hooks embedded into the ceiling – maybe it was used to hang game. A third has cracked stone sinks and rusting plumbing, and I assume it was once a laundry room. Finally, we find our way into what clearly used to be a kitchen. There's a flagstone floor and an oven so old it looks like an antique. On the shelves of a wooden dresser we see grimy crockery and dishes, and on the old, dusty oak table sits a rolling pin beside an enamel bowl, as though awaiting pastry to roll out. It's as though the clock has struck midnight in a fairytale and everything has been frozen in time. I want to turn back. There's something terrible about the place; haunted or cursed, just like the men in the pub warned. But Liam seems immune to the dark atmosphere; he either doesn't feel it, or he isn't afraid of it like me. Probably the latter.

Off the kitchen we find another stairwell, this one leading up, and Liam starts to climb. Reluctantly I follow behind, almost bumping into him when he pauses halfway up, noting a footprint in the dust.

'He's been here,' Liam whispers. 'I bet this is where he's staying.'

Now I want to turn back even more, and I wonder why we're continuing on.

'I think we should leave,' I hiss to Liam. 'I don't like this. Let's just go.'

He turns and sees the worry on my face. 'Don't worry,' he says, keeping his voice low. 'It'll be fine. I just want to have a word, that's all. Tell him to leave us alone.'

'What if he's dangerous?'

Liam answers by pulling out a switchblade from his pocket. My eyes widen even more in alarm. 'What are you doing with that?' I ask in alarm.

'Protection,' he explains. 'In case we need it.'

I swallow hard. 'This is crazy. We should go back. We shouldn't be here.'

'*He* shouldn't be here,' Liam retorts, tugging his hand from mine. 'He's trespassing.'

He continues up the stairs toward a small wooden door. I watch him push it open and realise that I am faced with a choice; I can follow him, or I can stay here on my own. I don't want to do either, but I figure it's better to stick together and that there's safety in numbers, so I run up the stairs behind him.

We enter a large hallway – what was once probably a grand entrance hall – with a sweeping staircase leading up to a viewing gallery on the first floor above us. Doors lead off the hall, as well as a long corridor running in both directions the length of the house.

Liam puts his phone away. He doesn't need the torch any more: sunlight is streaming in through holes in the broken roof above us. I gaze around. Once upon a time there were probably antlers and portraits of ancestors stuck to the wall, and maybe even swords or coats of arms. I imagine it probably looked like a hunting lodge – but now it's desolate and bare, the stone walls streaked with soot, scorched and blackened from where the flames must have licked it clean. I spot bird nests on the window ledges and droppings all over the pitted flagstone floor. Puddles of water have collected here and there and turned stagnant, giving off a musty odour.

The grand, sweeping staircase that curves around the hallway to the upper level is interrupted in several places, the stones having caved in and formed an avalanche of rubble at the back of the room. There's no way of getting to the upper storeys now, which is something of a relief.

'Come on,' Liam says, walking further into the hall.

Anxiety crawls up my spine and clutches me around the neck like one of those gargoyles outside clinging to the stonework, strangling me and making it hard to breathe.

Liam makes for a room to the right of the stairwell. We enter into what might once have been a drawing room or living room: there's a huge fireplace, filled in now with dirt and stones, and the room is bare of furniture and scarred by soot. Off this room we enter what seems to be a library, judging by the shelves, though all the books have been destroyed. It's dark in here and Liam has to use his phone again to light our way through an open doorway into yet another room. It's hard to tell what this one was used for as there's no furniture and nothing on the walls, just more piles of rubble and a caved-in fireplace, and no signs of life other than streaks of white bird guano and rat droppings.

We find that the doorways going onwards are all blocked up and have to backtrack our way to the hallway. This time, we head in the other direction, heading first into what was once a study to the left of the front doors. For whatever reason, this part of the castle obviously didn't burn at quite the same rate and pieces of furniture remain in place. In front of the window is a regal-looking desk, though the weather has chewed away at the leather top. A broken chair sits in a corner of the room and beside the fireplace there's a metal bucket filled with tools including tongs, a shovel and a poker.

Liam heads through another door, and another, and I follow in his wake, tiptoeing delicately – careful with my step. Some rooms look barely touched at all. We come across a dining table with twelve chairs and it almost looks ready to receive guests, apart from the fact that the dresser is covered in fragments of broken china and glass, as if a giant has crushed his fist down on top of it all. By contrast, in one we find the roof completely caved in and there's so much rubble we can't get across to the far door. We're forced back on ourselves once more, but in the dining room Liam pauses. He points at the wood panelling that covers the walls, which has buckled in places, and crosses towards one panel that has come loose. He pulls it open to reveal a passageway behind.

'Must have been for the servants,' he remarks.

I'm intrigued enough to follow him over to peer inside, but Liam is already headed into the passageway, fumbling his way along, shining his torch. It's a narrow stone corridor with blown-out lightbulbs running down the middle of the ceiling. I can imagine servants scurrying down here, carrying trays of food.

We make our way along the passage, turning several corners. It's labyrinthine and far too dark and who knows if we'll find our way back out again. I start to panic at the thought of being trapped in here, but Liam thankfully doesn't go too far before he finds another doorway. He leans on it and we burst back out into the study. I gasp with relief.

'Let's go,' I whisper, fighting back tears. 'He's not here.'

'He must be here,' Liam answers, through gritted teeth. 'Let's try upstairs.'

'How?' I plead. 'The stairs are broken. There's no way anyone could . . .' But Liam is already striding back into the great hall towards the staircase. 'You can't go up there.' I scurry after him. 'What if you fall? What if . . .?'

I trail off, knowing he won't listen and, indeed, he's already started up them.

He stops at the first gap; a large hole stretches out in front of him and he would need to jump several feet to make it to the other side. But before I can say anything, he makes the leap. My hands fly to my mouth as a piece of masonry crumbles away and joins the pile of rubble at the bottom.

I'm torn between staying where I am at the foot of the stairs and following Liam, but there's no way I'm jumping that distance, so all I can do is watch on tenterhooks. Liam keeps going, gingerly creeping to the edge of the stairs until he reaches the next gap. This one is bigger. I watch him contemplate it. The drop is substantial, some thirty feet to the ground below. He eyes the four feet of empty space that he'd need to clear and then prepares to jump, crouching low and putting his weight on his front foot.

A sudden banging makes him pause just as he's about to go. 'What was that?' he asks, turning to me.

I shake my head in confusion, looking around.

'Where was it coming from?'

I point toward the back of the great hall. 'I think from over there.'

Liam turns and hurries back down the stairs, launching himself over the gap at a pace in his haste to get to me.

'Where?' he asks when he reaches my side.

I gesture towards the pile of debris at the back of the hall. 'Over there, somewhere, I think.'

He frowns and for a moment there's silence. But then we both hear a scuffling sound, followed by a loud thud. It sounds like someone trying to break their way out of a room or knock down a door. Liam puts his finger to his lips to tell me to stay silent – not that I need the reminder – and then he tiptoes towards the noise.

We didn't notice, thanks to the fact it's piled so high, but on the other side of the mound of rubble is a door. It's standing partly ajar. Liam pulls his switch-blade from his pocket and flicks it open. I stick to his back like glue as we clamber as noiselessly as possible over the detritus and plaster and towards the door. The whole time I'm wondering what we're doing. Why aren't we getting the hell out of here? Why are we walking towards danger? But I suppose Liam doesn't see it that way. He's a man after all. Men aren't accustomed to feeling fear in the way most women do, almost all the time, learning from a young age to never walk down a dark street alone and to always look over their shoulder.

I step on a loose stone, causing a mini landslide of dirt, and the banging stops abruptly. We hold our breath, both of us frozen. Liam brings the knife up, holding it like a dagger, and we stare at the door, half-expecting it to fly open and someone to come roaring out in attack mode.

We stay there, unmoving for half a minute, maybe longer, but nothing happens. Finally the banging starts up again, this time sounding even more manic. Perhaps whoever it is knows they're cornered and they're trying to smash their way out of the room.

Out of nowhere, Liam rushes towards the door, throwing it back with his shoulder and bursting into the room with a yell. I glance past him.

There's no one there. It's empty. But then I notice a bird – a crow, black and ugly, slamming itself into the wooden panelling along the bottom half of the wall as it flaps furiously and tries to take flight. The reason for its failure to escape the room through the hole in the roof is immediately obvious: its wing is broken, the feathers sleek on the bird's good side, and scruffy and ruffled on the other.

I let out a gasp and hurry towards it as it hops pitifully. I can see how terrified and exhausted it is. It must have fallen through the roof and been trapped in here. I wonder for how long? The crow caws in terror when I move towards it and skips away, its one good wing flapping desperately. I wrestle off my coat and step slowly forwards, backing the bird into a corner.

'What are you doing?' Liam asks me.

'I'm rescuing it,' I say, without looking in his direction.

I inch towards the wounded creature, murmuring under my breath as I go, trying to soothe it. But the crow is panicked. It caws murder and tries to take flight again, only I'm faster and manage to throw the coat over its head. Before it can fight free, I bundle it into my arms, where the bird struggles momentarily, and then falls still. It's paralysed with terror, and I can feel its little heart thrumming away fast as a hummingbird's wing.

I turn to Liam, smiling in triumph at my rescue.

'Now what?' he asks.

My smile fades. I hadn't thought that far. It's not like there's a vet or a wildlife centre nearby to take it to for treatment. 'We can at least feed it,' I reply, thinking on my feet. 'Give it some water and some food. The poor thing might have been trapped in here for days without any.'

'It's got a broken wing, Laura,' Liam says. 'We'd be better off leaving it or killing it. Putting it out of its misery.'

My mouth falls open. 'What? No! We can't leave it. Or kill it. I can fix it. I'll see if I can splinter the wing.'

Liam raises his eyebrows at me, but he knows I'm a lost cause when it comes to animals. 'Come on then,' he says with a sigh, turning around and heading back out of the room. I follow him, cradling the bird in my arms.

In the great hall he stops and stares at the first floor and the staircase up to it, looking rueful.

'We should get back to the cottage,' I say, hoping that he isn't going to attempt a second climb.

I can see him weighing his choices, but finally he sighs again and faces me. 'Fine,' he accedes. 'Let's go.'

We walk down the servants' stairs into the kitchen. Liam pauses, pulling out his phone to light our way through the dark space and into the cellar.

'I wonder if there's another stairwell,' he says as we walk through the kitchen. 'The servants' stairs maybe. Old places like this always had secret stairs to keep the riffraff out of sight of the posh people.'

He's right. There probably is another stairwell. Perhaps if we kept following the interior hidden passages, we might find it, but I really don't want to explore any further.

'I need to get this crow home,' I argue. 'We haven't even had breakfast yet,' I add, appealing to Liam's prodigious appetite.

He relents, as I'd hoped, and leads the way through the cellar.

'Next time I'll bring a real torch,' he comments as we reach the door.

'Next time?' I ask with dread. 'We're coming back?'

He shakes his head. 'No. *I'm* coming back.'

Chapter Thirteen

The crow has settled in my arms, but I can feel its tiny heartbeat thundering away against my own. I feel its terror inside my own chest too. The darkness I've shrouded it in pacifies it, in a way it never does me, and I keep my grip on it tight, knowing that if I should loosen it and it should struggle free it could hurt itself even more in its desperation to get away. I only want to help, but the bird doesn't know that. If we'd left it there it would have died. At least this way it has a fighting chance.

I ponder the ways you can splint a wing without causing more damage, and where I might put the bird after, to contain it safely while it heals.

Liam smiles at me, shaking his head ruefully as I soothe the bird.

'Tiger used to bring birds home all the time,' I tell him. 'Half dead.' Tiger's my old cat, an orange tabby with an unoriginal name.

'I remember,' Liam laughs. 'Little animal sacrifices.'

He'd bring them to me as gifts, leave them half eaten on the doormat, or even on the bed. I'd try to patch them up, if they weren't already dead. I got my love of animals from my grandad. He would often rescue birds and small creatures like mice that he found on his allotment or on walks through the countryside. One time he saved a baby hedgehog and I helped him nurse it back to health on a cocktail of milk and soaked bread, and then, when it was strong enough, we let it go. I cried, worried that it wouldn't survive on its own without a parent to look out for it, but my grandad reminded me that we'd done all we could; it was now up to the little creature to figure out how to survive in the wild. 'Only the strong survive,' he'd told me. 'That's just nature's way.' I knew he was right, but it still hurt. It didn't feel fair on the vulnerable and the sensitive who didn't choose to be that way. But as he used to point out to me, even the smallest, weakest-seeming insect or animal often has hidden strengths. Take the hedgehog: it's slow and sleepy, but its spikes give it all the protection it needs from predators.

When I was little, I'd line up my soft toys in a pretend hospital, giving them all random ailments and then play-acting the role of doctor. My mum always told me I could be anything I wanted, including a doctor or a vet, but I never had the confidence to pursue my ambitions all the way to the top. Being a veterinary assistant is where my aspirations settled, and I enjoy the work. Or I did. I'm not really sure if I can go back to it though. I left them in the lurch, quitting the way I did, so suddenly and without any warning, and although I think they'd be sympathetic, given all I've had to cope with, I still don't know if they'd want me back. I wasn't exactly the best employee by the end, dealing as I was with my mum being ill and planning a wedding. They will have replaced me by now. There's even a chance they might not give me a good reference if I look elsewhere for a job.

One day at a time, I remind myself, taking a deep breath. *One day at a time.* I'll make it out the other side eventually and start living again. This honeymoon is the fresh start, even though it's turning out to be not quite the romantic getaway that we had planned.

By the time we make it back to the cottage, the sky has turned the colour of a fresh bruise. I cast a look up at it and Liam does too. *That's not a good sign*, I think to myself. Perhaps the boatman was right after all and the storm he warned us about is brewing. Liam must be thinking the same because he frowns unhappily, pursing his lips in a tell-tale sign that he's annoyed.

Liam unlocks the back door as the first fat drops of rain begin to fall, and he ushers me inside. My arms are aching from carrying the bird all this way and I have no doubt that it has done its business inside my coat, but I don't care. All I hope is that it's not for nothing, and that I can somehow fix it, mend its wing so that it can fly once more.

'Where are you going to put it?' Liam asks, nodding towards the bird.

I look around. 'I need a box or a crate of some kind and a towel.'

'I think I saw a box under the stairs,' Liam replies. 'Hang on.'

He goes and retrieves it. It's just big enough.

'Could you fetch me a towel, please?' I say, getting to my knees.

Liam heads to the downstairs bathroom to get a towel and I lower the bird carefully into the box. I'm worried it's gone into shock; that's usually how animals die in these situations. It's huddled, silent, against the side, frozen in fear, and I think it might be too late; but then it turns its beady eye on me and exclaims a furious caw. I exhale with relief. It still has some life in it; it hasn't quite given up the ghost.

I hurry to the cupboard and start searching for something to feed it with. It needs water of course, so I fill a small saucer and place it inside, and then take the oatmeal that I found in the cupboard, soak it in some milk and settle that alongside the water. That should do for now.

Liam comes back with a towel, which I drape over the top of the box. I'm right about the jacket. My new friend has crapped all over the inside of it, and now it reeks. I'll have to try to get the worst out by hand-washing, but I doubt I'll be able to wear it again until I can get it dry cleaned. Given the turn in the weather it's not the best situation to be in, but I'll survive.

'What now?' Liam asks.

'I need to examine it and then figure out how to splint the wing.'

I feel for the first time in ages a sense of purpose; a rekindling of a light that had been almost extinguished inside me. I have a life to save. 'Do we have any tape or gauze?'

'There's a first aid kit under the bathroom sink,' he says.

I run upstairs. In the en suite, I root around in the cupboard under the basin and find a small first aid kit. Inside there's everything I need, and I hurry back down with it.

'I need you to hold the bird,' I say.

Liam looks less than happy at the idea, but I scoop the bird out of the box, and he can't do anything but take it when I proffer it to him.

The bird snaps its vicious-looking beak at me but I fold the towel over its head so it can't see. It struggles in Liam's arms still and I shush it, stroking its feathers, trying to impart that I'm not a predator or a threat, and that it doesn't need to be afraid, but the crow no doubt feels as if it's in mortal danger and can't be soothed. Liam grumbles under his breath.

I examine the wing as gently as I can. I've observed the vet a few times doing this exact same thing and can recall the illustration of a bird's wing that I studied in college, its delicate skeleton structure. They heal fast, I remember that. Bird bones aren't like human bones. For a start they're hollow.

'I think it's a simple fracture,' I say to Liam after a few seconds of gentle probing. 'It's not broken through the skin, which is good.'

I cut off a length of tape and wrap it carefully around the bird, pinning the wing in place and smoothing down the feathers, knowing that the strength of the splinting and the positioning of the tape is key to helping it heal correctly, otherwise it won't ever fly again. It would be kinder to wring its neck if that were to happen, just as Liam suggested back at the castle, but I think the taping is good. It should hold.

Liam curses as the crow tries to nip his finger. He hands it over happily once I'm done and I take it, still bundled in the towel, and place it back in the box. 'There you go,' I say.

I feel a huge sense of pride at a job well done and make a wish that the bird recovers. Somehow, I feel as if the bird's recovery is tied to my own.

After washing my hands, I take my dirty coat from

the side and start scrubbing at it under the tap. Liam is standing at the window glaring out at the overcast sky, as though willing whoever is spying on us to dare show their face.

I'm worried that later he's going to leave me here to go and take a look around the castle by himself. Luckily, it's started to rain so maybe I can convince him to stay inside, and hopefully by the time it stops raining he might have calmed down. Like Liam though I can't stop thinking about it, wondering who it is and why they're on the island.

I carry the crow in its box through into the living room and set it down by the fire, out of the way. The room is dark as a tomb thanks to the fact the curtains are still drawn, and so I move to open them to let in some daylight. As I do, I let out a scream.

Liam comes running, skidding to a stop beside me. I point at the window; the one where the man carved those strange symbols.

Except from this side it's obvious. They're not symbols with some hidden meaning we can't decipher. They're letters. And this way around it's clear what they spell. DEVIL.

Chapter Fourteen

We stare at the word DEVIL etched into the window.

'What the fuck?' Liam curses under his breath. 'Is this some kind of game?'

I've never seen him this rattled before. In fact, I've never seen him afraid, until this moment. Liam marches to the window and yanks the curtain across, erasing the word from view. He turns around and I watch his jaw tensing and untensing, his brow furrowed.

'What do you think it means?' I ask him.

He shakes his head. 'How am I supposed to know?'

I swallow, biting my tongue.

'Devil,' he says. 'It doesn't make sense.' He starts to pace back and forth in front of the window as I stand quietly to one side and watch him. 'It just . . .' He breaks off and stops, yanking the curtain back again to see the word written there, as though he expects it to have vanished. He scratches at his neck, not tearing his gaze from the window.

'Who would write that?' I whisper.

Liam doesn't say anything. Suddenly he makes for the front door.

'Where are you going?' I ask, worried.

'Outside,' he says. 'I want to check those footprints again.'

'Why?'

'Because,' he says, as he opens the door and steps out into the rain.

I follow him, hesitating in the doorway. The rain is coming down in fat drops, the clouds hanging low. I glance up the beach, to where I thought I saw someone standing yesterday. There's no one there now, but the downpour is making it hard to see. I spot the cairn on the beach, still standing exactly as I left it.

Liam is over by the window, crouching down in the flowerbed, examining the footsteps, but the rain seems to have washed them mostly away.

I retreat out of the rain and walk into the living room where I contemplate the word etched into the window again. A cold chill spreads through me, like ice invading my veins. The letters have been carved deeply into the glass, and haphazardly, as if they were done in a hurry, by someone in a rage.

I believe in the devil; I've seen enough to know that

evil exists in the world. In my job – my old job that is – animals were brought in occasionally that had been mistreated and abused, some so badly they had to be put down. So yes, I believe in the devil, but I have doubts sometimes that there is a god. If there is, I don't know how he can let so much suffering occur and do nothing about it.

My faith has definitely been tested this year. My mum always used to tell me to say my prayers whenever I wanted something good to happen, and she always had faith that things would work out for the best; but my father treated her terribly and made her unhappy for most of her adult life, and then she got cancer, and then she died. And I can't understand why any benevolent god would let that happen, and I definitely don't believe in any higher justice. It seems to me that good people, innocent people, and animals often suffer worst in this world, and bad people get away with bad things all the time.

The door bangs shut and I jump, but it's just Liam.

'Did you find anything?' I ask him.

'No,' he scowls, coming to stand by me.

'*Why* would they write that?' I ask again.

'I've already told you,' he says, sounding impatient, 'How would I know?'

'Well, you're a detective, you must have some idea.'

'I'm not a forensic psychologist,' he replies. 'Try not to worry. It's just someone trying to scare us, that's all.'

'But why?' I ask, the icy sensation reaching the tips of my fingers and toes. 'Why would they want to scare us?'

'Because they're crazy?' Liam responds with a shrug. 'Because they think it's funny? I don't know. It doesn't matter why they did it. What matters is not letting it ruin our holiday.'

I press my lips together. It might be a little late for that.

'Do you think they might be out there now, watching us?' I ask, wrapping my arms around myself to keep out the sudden chill.

A frown line appears between Liam's eyes. 'No,' he answers.

'They could be,' I press him. 'We don't know.'

Liam marches forwards and draws the curtain back across the window, then he casts a look over his shoulder as though half-expecting to find someone standing in the room with us. He's spooked. Genuinely spooked. For all his nonchalant talk about not worrying, he really is worried.

He walks into the kitchen and closes the curtains there too, and then he double-checks the back door is locked. 'There,' he says to me. 'No one's spying on us. Shall we have breakfast? I'm starving.'

I know he's trying to put a brave face on it and pretend he's not rattled, so I play along even though I'm not hungry. 'OK.'

We left this morning before we'd had breakfast, and now it's closer to lunch, but I grab the bacon, sausages and eggs from the fridge and put them down on the side. '"Devil",' I muse, lifting the cast-iron pan off its hook and setting it down on the hob. 'It's such a strange thing to write.'

'Probably a religious nutjob,' Liam says. 'Met a few of those in my time. They're usually all bark and no bite.'

I often wonder what kinds of cases Liam has to deal with. He never brings his work home with him and barely ever discusses the crimes he's working on, though I know it's usually robbery and murder. He says it's confidential and that he doesn't want to upset me by giving me any gory details, and to be honest I'm grateful for it; I don't know how he does what he does and stays so sane.

I turn on the hob and add butter to the pan, but nothing happens; the butter doesn't melt, and the pan stays cold. I put my hand over the electric plate and discover that it's still cold. 'I can't get the stove to work,' I say to Liam after a moment spent trying the other rings.

Liam comes over and tries himself, then crosses to the thermostat on the wall and turns it on, but nothing happens with that either. He listens but there's only a click and no answering spark of the electric boiler turning on. He moves the dial back and forth but still nothing happens. He crosses to the light switch next and tries that. 'Shit,' he murmurs under his breath.

We try the light in the hallway and then the one in the living room as well. 'There's no electricity,' he says to me, though I've already figured that much out. 'It's OK,' he adds reassuringly, seeing the look of worry that must be stamped on my face. 'It's probably a tripped switch or something. Let me go and check.'

He throws on his jacket and steps outside again, braving the rain which is now even heavier, and I stare at the saucepan. If we don't have electricity everything in the fridge will go bad.

Within a few minutes Liam's back, his jeans already soaked through. He shuts the door and stands on the mat, dripping rain and shaking his head. 'It's not the fuses. I checked them all. It's the wiring. Someone's cut through the cables.'

'What?' I ask.

Liam repeats himself. 'Someone – that guy – the person stalking us – has cut through the cables.'

'Can you fix it?' I ask.

He shakes his head. 'No. It would need an electrician.'

'Is there a generator?' I ask.

'The power's from a wind turbine on the hill. There's a battery on the side of the house. That's where he's cut the cable.'

I realise I've sunk down into the closest chair and I'm resting my head in my hands. 'Why would they do all this?' I whisper.

Liam shakes his head. Neither of us speaks for a bit.

'Goddamn it,' Liam suddenly shouts. 'This is ridiculous. What the fuck does he want? And what the hell are we going to do without electricity for three more days?'

I don't reply. Silence fills the cottage, both of us no doubt thinking about why someone would write DEVIL on the window or why they would cut our electricity.

'That's it,' Liam says, zipping his jacket back up. 'I'm going out there. I'm going to find him. I want to know what this is all about.'

I stare at him aghast. 'In the rain? Why don't you wait until it clears?'

'No,' Liam says, moving to the door. 'It's only some rain. And who knows when it will stop. I can't bloody believe we thought a honeymoon in Scotland was a good idea.'

'At least have something to eat before you go,' I urge, getting up.

Liam ignores me and opens the door. A barrage of rain slams into his face and a blast of cold wind comes with it and he hesitates. After a brief pause, he steps back into the kitchen and shuts the door. 'Fine,' he says, grudgingly, sinking into a chair at the table. 'But as soon as it stops, I'm going to find him.' He notices the empty pan and the carton of eggs sitting on the side and his shoulders slump even further. 'What the hell are we going to eat?'

I look about, trying to think of something. We can't

have toast or tea, and raw bacon and eggs isn't an option. 'Bread and jam?' I suggest.

Liam looks put out, but it's clear there are no other options, so I hurry and place the cut bread on the table along with the butter and jam. He slaps the bread with butter and lashings of jam while I lean against the side and nibble nervously on a dry crust, glancing occasionally toward the window, half expecting to find someone looking in through the crack in the curtain.

'Jesus Christ, this is not what we signed up for,' Liam hisses, banging his knife down on the table and making me jump. 'We can't stay. We've got to find a way off the island.'

'But how?' I ask. *What are we going to do*, I think to myself, *swim?*

Liam has cracked the curtains open an inch and through the gap we watch the slate sky as we eat. Liam is clearly waiting for the rain to show signs of letting up, but it keeps coming down in torrents. We don't speak; both of us are too on edge. From his furrowed brow and angry glare, I can tell that Liam's anger is growing. When he's finished eating, he drops his dirty plate into the sink with a clatter and walks through into the living room. I follow him as he walks around, checking all the windows are locked tight, as well as the doors. When he's done, he lights a fire in the wood-burning stove, trying to chase away the chill and the gloom that have descended.

'We should have enough wood for the rest of the day,' he tells me, eyeing the pile by the side. He sighs again with annoyance.

I nod, and head into the kitchen, where I wash up, scrubbing the plates to within an inch of their lives. There's no hot water which makes it difficult. I'm frightened; it feels as if fleas are jumping all over my skin. I keep my eyes trained on the window, half-expecting to see someone watching the house, and because it's on my mind I'm convinced that I keep seeing things – shapes materialising through the rain, a person silhouetted against the forest – but the mirages vanish as soon as I blink.

I hang up the wet tea towel and tidy up the kitchen, before joining Liam in the front room. He's poking the fire as if it's a sleeping bear he's trying to prod out of hibernation. I check on the bird in its box; it seems to be doing all right, sitting quietly. I'm guessing it's still in shock, and so I replace the towel and leave it be. I begin pacing to the window and back, too afraid to pull back the curtain and peek out, chewing on the edge of my thumb, wondering what to do next.

I would feel imprisoned, but in a way it's not too different from my life back home. I've been stuck indoors for months there too. I glance at my phone to check the time: it's almost midday. It feels later though – like it should be evening already – not just because of the dim light but because it feels as if we've been awake for hours. *We have*, I remind myself. We were up at the crack of dawn.

I wish that I could text or call someone, but even if we had reception or a landline, I realise that I don't have anyone to contact. A wave of sadness washes over me. I'd normally have rung my mum in a situation like this, and failing that, I used to have a couple of friends I could call on if I ever needed a shoulder: Sonia, who was another assistant at the vet's, and Claire, who I went to primary school with, though she moved to Leeds for university and still lives there, and we haven't seen each other in ages.

Sonia sent flowers for my mum's funeral and Claire sent a sweet card and both called a few times in the months after she died, but I never picked up the phone. I didn't feel able to talk to them. I wonder how I could ever get back in touch now; it feels as if too much time has passed, and they might not understand why I didn't return their calls. I'm not sure I can explain to them either, not when I can't fully explain it to myself. It was just too impossible.

I just feel so ashamed of who I've become: this shadow of my former self; and I'm also a little embarrassed that I never told them about the wedding. I kept it a secret because I didn't want people to feel offended that I hadn't invited them. I'd planned to post something on Facebook after we got back from our Greek honeymoon, but then my mum died, and I didn't feel like blasting social media with pictures of the wedding. I could barely get out of bed, let alone log onto a computer. But perhaps when I get off this island, I'll call Claire and Sonia and find a way to get those friendships back on track. Everything that's happening is making me realise how important it is not to let myself get isolated.

I sit on the sofa and play with my engagement ring, spinning it around and around my finger – it's a big diamond and the band is loose on me now. I force myself to stop. I need to keep busy and distract myself, otherwise it feels like all we are doing is waiting for the next thing to happen, and I can't bear the tension of it. I feel like a soldier in a trench, awaiting the dawn whistle.

'Do you want to play cards?' I ask Liam, who is standing at the window, peering out through a crack in the curtains; though whether he's looking at the water, contemplating how far it would be to swim to the mainland, or searching for our stalker, I don't know. He may even be studying the word DEVIL written on the glass. It's hard to tell. 'We may as well distract ourselves,' I tell him. 'Otherwise we'll go mad.'

He pauses then shrugs. 'I suppose so.'

I saw some cards in the drawer and I go and fetch them. Liam shuffles and deals. We play Whist, a game that my grandad taught me, but I lose every hand to Liam because I'm too preoccupied and I can't keep the suits straight in my head. Though he wins, he seems almost as preoccupied as I am, a permanent frown creasing his forehead.

After an hour Liam gets up and walks again to the curtain. He pulls it back and scowls at the word DEVIL etched there.

Beyond the word, the sky is a thunderous black and the loch is now the colour of unpolished pewter. Liam shakes his head and drags the curtains back across, concealing the letters carved into the glass. 'I can't believe we're stuck here,' he spits, 'completely stranded like this. We should have gone to Greece.'

The Stalker

DEVIL. That was what my mother called me. Her tongue was a lash, and she wielded the word to hurt me. She claimed I was born with the devil inside me and she had to beat him out. She used more than her tongue for that, I'll tell you.

As a boy I believed my mother was right. I thought there must be something wrong with me; if your own mother won't love you what other reason could there be? I had evil inside me and that made me unlovable.

I believed I deserved those punishments; the beating and the starving and the name-calling; that I was worthless. But then I grew up. I got bigger. And I saw one day my mother was afraid of me. That changed everything. Something in me switched. I decided to let that devil inside me loose. I thought to myself, Let me show you what the devil is capable of – maybe then you won't treat me the way you do. Maybe then you'll learn to show me some respect.

And so it was. The devil took over and my mother quickly learned to hold her tongue. The shoe was on the other foot, and it felt good. Her fear grew, and with it my power. I became a new person.

I learned to wear a good disguise in public of course; many disguises; I learned fast that charm and good looks are all it takes to trick people into believing you are who they want you to be.

No one knew the real me except for my mother, who spent every moment when she wasn't working praying on her knees for my soul's salvation.

When I met my wife, I thought she looked like an angel – she was so beautiful and so good – and I wondered if my mother's prayers had come true. I thought that maybe she'd been sent to save my soul. And for a time when I was with her, everything was peaceful and I began to kid myself that the devil had gone away; that maybe my wife's love and my mother's prayers had worked a miracle.

But the devil inside me hadn't gone away. After a time, he began to stir. Out he would come, like a jack-in-the-box, every time my wife crossed me. I started to wonder if she did it on purpose, like a child wanting to press the button despite knowing exactly what's going to come leaping out, because she did it so often, despite knowing the consequences.

She stopped respecting me even though she tried to hide it behind a fake smile. She stopped loving me even though she pretended by offering kisses and smiles and lies coated in sugar. She planned to leave me. And it made me angry. My mother's words rang in my head: you're not loveable; you're worthless; you're a devil; you're damned.

I'm sure she regrets it. She didn't want the boy to die. She begged me not to hurt him. But his death was hardly my fault — it was hers. She made me so angry with her betrayal, and he was collateral damage.

I think about them now. I think about them all the time, in fact. I think about how I chased her out of the house. How she was barefoot and how she ran through the snow, glancing over her shoulder, eyes wide with fear, looking exactly as if the devil was chasing her.

Chapter Fifteen

We while away the hours like condemned prisoners awaiting the hour of execution, on edge and barely speaking. I tend to the bird, disheartened to see that it's weakening. Its heartbeat is rapid and the food and water I gave it remain untouched. If it succumbs to the shock, it won't last the night. I will it to find some strength and fight.

Liam stokes the fire and when it gets too dark inside the cottage I get out the candles and a torch that I found in a drawer in the kitchen, and we listen to the winds start to howl and the rain firing arrows at the windows.

At five o'clock I start dinner but it takes me a while to figure out what to make because my mind is whirring too much to concentrate on the ingredients and without an oven or a stove top, I'm limited in what I can rustle up. I worry about all the food in the fridge going off but there's nothing I can do about it, and in the end I pull out the ham and make a salad, doing a calculation in my head as I rinse the lettuce. If we're here for three more days and we don't manage to get the electricity working, then we're going to have to ration what edible food there is. We only have a loaf of bread, some cheese and ham and salad. There's a jar of pasta sauce and a tin of beans we could eat cold, though I'll save those until we're really hungry. There are also some corn flakes. The milk and the butter shouldn't spoil, given it's not exactly warm inside the cottage. The kitchen is starting to feel like a refrigerator itself.

In the fruit bowl there's a handful of apples, some bananas and grapes, and in the cupboard some trail mix and the rest of the shortbread, though Liam's eaten half already. We could cook the sausages over the fire if push came to shove, I suppose. All in all, though, it isn't much for two of us for three days given how much Liam eats – but at least I don't eat a lot, so we should be able to manage.

I make the salad and slice the bread thin, knowing we may need to make it stretch for three more days, then I lay it all out on the table. I decide not to mention the food rationing situation for now because Liam's already in a bad mood and I don't want to make things worse. We eat again in silence, the atmosphere in the house almost as bad as the weather outside.

Liam drinks several glasses of red wine, and I watch him warily. Normally he's quite controlled and only drinks a glass or two at most; it's another sign that the anxiety is getting to him. He hates not having the upper hand; he's used to being the shot caller, the one in charge.

I make a ham sandwich and eat it.

'Your appetite's coming back,' Liam comments, swallowing the last of his own sandwich.

I look down at my plate, realising with a start that that's the first meal in months that I've actually eaten all of. I shake my head in surprise. 'Must be all the adrenaline,' I say, trying to make a joke of it.

I get up and clear the plates.

'God, I'd kill for a coffee,' Liam grumbles. 'What are we going to do without coffee or tea?'

'How about we play a board game tonight?' I ask, to distract him.

He glances at me with a half-amused expression. 'What, Monopoly?'

I shrug. 'There's the Game of Life as well. And draughts.'

'OK,' he says, not looking particularly enthusiastic. But what else is there to do but go to bed? I don't think he's in the mood for sex, and I'm certainly not, so we'll only lie there staring at the ceiling if we go upstairs now.

I pull out the Game of Life box, which I haven't played since I was a kid. I think the aim is to get married, get promotions, have children, buy a mansion and retire early. It takes me a while to read the instructions as my mind is so preoccupied with other things; I can't stop wondering about the other plans this person has for us and how it all might end. But finally, I lay out the board and hand Liam a plastic car and the dice.

Within a few moves of mostly desultory dice throwing, Liam's got twins. I glance at him as he picks up a pink peg and a blue peg, and places them in his car with a smile. 'A boy and a girl,' he says. He looks up and sees my expression.

'What?' he asks.

'Nothing, just the idea of twins . . .'

'You want children, don't you?' Liam asks, a note of anxiety creeping into his voice.

'Yes,' I say, smiling. 'Just not yet.'

'Why not?' he presses. 'We've talked about this. I thought you wanted children. You said you did.'

'I do!' I say. 'Just not right now. I figure that it's nice to have time as a couple first before you start a family. Once kids come along your whole life changes. And I'm still young enough. I'm only twenty-nine. There's time.'

Liam frowns. 'I just think if we're going to have more than one, we shouldn't wait.'

I had no idea that Liam was so keen on having children, or that he wanted to have one right away.

'How many do you want?' I ask, hoping he isn't about to say eight or nine.

'At least two, maybe three,' he says. 'What about you?'

'I haven't given it much thought,' I admit.

'Well, we were both only children,' Liam says. 'And I don't want that for our child.'

'I loved being an only child,' I say quietly, thinking of how close my mum and I were. True, it would have been easier having a sibling to help deal with things when she got sick and everything fell on my shoulders: going with her to all her appointments and dealing with all the aftercare every time she had chemotherapy. It would have been good too to have someone else to rely on when she died, and I had to organise the funeral while wrung out and torn up with grief.

I still regret how sad and pathetic an affair it turned out; not at all the wake she deserved. I was so upset though, and Liam didn't know what to do, so we cobbled together a gathering in a local pub, and though a lot of people showed up I feel like I was too wrapped up in grief to really give her a good sendoff. Guilt descends on me and I try to push it away. Now's not the time to go there.

'I hated being an only child,' Liam says. 'It was awful. I think if I'd had a sibling it would have been easier,' he tells me. 'Anyway,' he says brightly, brushing off my sympathetic smile. 'We won't be like that. We'll have a boy and a girl.' He pauses, thinking. 'Maybe two girls.'

'I don't think you get to choose the gender,' I laugh.

'How long do you think you'll want to wait?' Liam asks with a small frown.

'Kids are expensive,' I say. 'We should try to save up before we have them. And I'm not working. So maybe in three or four years?'

Liam looks at me in shock. 'Three or four years? That's far too long. If we wait until then you'll be in your mid-thirties and the risks will be much higher. You're in your prime right now.' He pauses and looks at me. 'And it's not as if we haven't been trying,' he says. 'I mean, we don't use protection, so you could be pregnant already.' His face lights up at the idea. 'Imagine, a honeymoon baby.'

I take a deep breath, thinking about the contraceptive pill in my washbag upstairs that the doctor prescribed for me at the same time as my anti-depressants. Liam doesn't know about either pill. I never told him. I realised that I could no longer go on the way I was, moping around the house, bursting into tears every few minutes, feeling completely hopeless. I knew I needed to get a grip; if nothing else then just because I had all the horribly tedious and convoluted admin to deal with surrounding my mother's death. I was the executor of her will and I'd been putting off making calls and sorting things out after I'd broken down in tears on the phone to the bank when I called to let them know she was dead. The doctor prescribed them without any questions, and I've hidden both from Liam inside a box of tampons.

I feel embarrassed about needing them and I don't want Liam to feel like it's his fault that I'm not happy. I was warned not to get pregnant while I was taking them because they can cause birth defects which is why I'm on the pill. That and the fact I don't want children. At least not right now.

It surprises me that the whole time we've been having sex Liam has secretly been hoping I'll get pregnant. I wonder how he'd react if I told him that there's never been any chance of it. I can't tell him. He'd be so upset.

'You're right,' I say to him. 'Let's just see what happens, I suppose. Let fate decide.'

'Really?' he asks, his face lighting up with hope.

I smile back and shrug at the same time. 'I mean, it might take a while. You never know. So, it's probably best we start now, just in case.'

I feel the lie trip off my tongue so easily it scares me. Liam is grinning as though he's won something. My face starts to warm up and I don't want him to see; he's astute when it comes to truth – he is a pro at inter-rogation after all – so I quickly reach for the dice and throw it, then move my plastic car. 'Look! A promotion at work and a pay rise.'

I laugh under my breath. It couldn't be further from the actual truth. I'm aware that by not returning to work, my own career prospects are languishing and all the hard work that I put into getting my degree is becoming pointless. The longer I'm out of employment the harder it will be to get back in – and if I were to get pregnant, I could probably forget ever having a career. I've been over this with myself a million times, and it frustrates me, but I just need to park my worries for the time being.

Liam gets up to stoke the fire, throwing on the last of the logs. He peeks out the window. The rain is still lashing down. He sighs loudly. 'I've got to go out and get more wood. It's not lasted as long as I thought,' he says.

I nod reluctantly, figuring that he's only going to the woodpile and it won't take him long. I watch him put on his jacket and boots and I stand by the back door as he darts out into the rain and around the side of the house. He's back in less than a minute, with a pile of wood in his hands and a fierce expression on his face. He throws the logs down by the back door.

'What is it? What's happened?' I ask.

'The wood's soaked through. Someone's pulled off the tarp that was covering the pile and knocked the stack over, so it's all wet.'

'Are you sure it wasn't the wind?'

Liam shakes his head, his expression darkening. 'It was secured tightly. Someone undid the ropes and pulled it completely off. The wind couldn't have knocked over that stack; it was five feet high. It has to have been deliberate.'

'When could they have done it though?' I ask. 'It

wasn't like that when we got back this morning, I don't think. We would have noticed on our way out, surely?'

Liam casts his eyes about the cottage. The realisation dawns on us. They must have come while we were huddled inside here, hiding from the rain, curtains drawn. The thought makes my stomach clench into knots. There's something truly unsettling about the idea of a stranger prowling around outside like a wolf while we sit in here like sitting ducks.

I look at the fire, dwindling rapidly without fuel.

'Don't worry,' Liam says. 'Hopefully it'll dry out and we can use it later.' But I look down at the pile he dumped on the mat. The wood is soaked through – there's no way it will catch light – and in the damp chill that's encroached on the cottage it isn't going to dry out that quickly.

I sink down onto the sofa. There's a gnawing inside me, like a rat chewing at the end of a fraying rope. Liam prowls the inside of the cottage. He checks and rechecks the locks on the doors and windows as though he's a soldier securing a fortress from an attack.

It's unnerving seeing him like this. I've seen him agitated, but never *afraid*, as he is now. He might be trying to disguise it with anger, but I can see that the pressure is getting to him. I worry he's going to crack.

'It's fine,' he says, more to himself than to me. 'No one's getting inside. And if he does try anything then he'll have me to answer to.'

Adrenaline courses through me; my heart starts to pound as though someone is beating a drum inside my chest and I have to stand up again and keep pacing. The wind howls down the chimney. It sounds as if a thousand ghosts are trying to force their way inside the cottage.

'Why do all this to us?' I ask, wrapping my arms around my body as I pace. 'It must be for a reason.' I look at Liam, who is frowning intently at the empty fireplace. 'You're good at getting in the heads of people,' I say to him, my frustration growing. 'What do you think their motive is? It can't be a treasure hunter. I mean, everything he's doing is so personal. It's vindictive. Don't you think? It's like he's chosen us.'

Liam scowls, chewing the inside of his cheek. He doesn't answer me, but I can tell his brain is whirring.

'Could it be related to one of your cases?' I ask. 'Someone you put away?'

'Not likely,' he says, but he doesn't sound convinced.

I sit down and look around the darkening room with a shiver.

'This isn't a honeymoon, it's a bloody nightmare,' Liam mumbles under his breath. 'It was meant to be a romantic getaway but it's turning into the honeymoon from hell.'

I agree.

Chapter Sixteen

Day Five

The cottage feels like a ship being tossed about on a stormy sea. We've battened down the hatches and are stowed away in the cabin of the bedroom, lying side by side in the bed. Neither of us is asleep though. I find myself clutching the side of the mattress as though at any moment I'm about to be thrown out of it by a large wave colliding into the side of the house. I strain to listen, unsure if it's the rain lashing against the window or someone trying to break in.

Liam's muscles are tense, and he breathes shallowly in the bed beside me. He's wide awake. I know he must be thinking the same thing – worrying that someone is trying to force their way into the cottage – because I noticed he slipped a knife beneath his pillow earlier when he thought I wasn't watching.

I manage to fall asleep at some point, probably because the adrenaline that's been flooding through my system for so long has exhausted me, but I wake before the dawn to the sound of Liam moving about the room. I sit up. 'What's going on?' I ask, pulling the blankets around me to keep out the pre-dawn chill.

Liam's a dull shape in the gloom of the room. 'Nothing. Go back to sleep,' he tells me.

'Where are you going?' I ask, seeing he's opening up the dresser drawers and is starting to throw on clothes.

'Out,' he says.

'Where?'

'To the castle.'

Fear paralyses me. He can't be serious. But of course he is, and it's not like I didn't expect it. I don't want to go anywhere near the castle, I think it's madness, but he can't go alone. I throw off the blankets and jump out of bed. 'I want to come with you.'

He shakes his head. 'No. Laura, I need to go alone.'

'I won't let you,' I argue back. 'Please.' I move to the dresser and start pulling out my clothes too, throwing on a sweater and tugging on jeans. 'You can't leave me here alone. What if that's what they're waiting for? For us to split up? What if you leave and they break into the cottage while I'm here all by myself?'

I can see a furrow deep as a crevice between Liam's brows.

'There's safety in numbers,' I push.

154

Liam concedes with a loud sigh. 'Fine. But hurry up.'

I dart into the bathroom and quickly dress, pulling my hair into a ponytail and throwing cold water on my face. Downstairs I find Liam rummaging through the kitchen cupboards with the help of his phone light. Judging by the dark circles under his eyes, I'm guessing he didn't sleep a wink, but I don't ask because he seems so on edge. He's moving around gathering things, including the torch we took from the drawer and his switchblade knife. I glance at him, but his expression gives little away. He just looks determined, his brow furrowed and his jaw set. A shadow of fear ripples over me. What is he planning on doing to this person if he catches them? Will he try to arrest them? I want to tell him to leave the knife, but I also know that he won't listen.

I check quickly on the bird before we leave, relieved to find it's still alive. It tries to peck my hand and I notice it's eaten most of the food and drunk some water. 'Good girl,' I say to it, deciding it's a female even though I have no idea. 'You'll be fine,' I tell her, re-covering the box with the towel.

'Come on,' Liam says to me, already standing by the back door, impatient to leave.

In the kitchen I slip a bag of trail mix and an apple into my pocket and glance out of the window. The dawn has come, and the sky is still heavy with grey clouds, but streaked with pink. I don't have a jacket to wear as mine is still damp from when I cleaned the bird excrement off it yesterday, but I suppose I'll be OK to go without it. We head out, Liam making sure to lock the back door behind us. He eyes the forest up ahead of us, his eyes darting this way and that, as though he's trying to spot a sniper, hidden among the trees. But it's still dark out; the sky is only just beginning to lighten, and it's impossible to know if anyone is out there, watching us.

Drizzle haloes my hair and when we enter the forest water drips so furiously from the tree branches that it might as well be raining. I regret not bringing my jacket, even if it's damp, as cold slugs of water snake their way between the collar of my jumper and my bare skin. We slog through mud, the wet fronds of ferns and bracken soaking our jeans.

The castle waits for us, lurking in the mist. Today it seems even more ominous and threatening, sitting there under the low-slung sky. Half of me wishes I'd stayed behind in the cottage, but I couldn't let Liam come alone.

Liam puts his finger to his lips to warn me to be quiet before we jog across the clearing towards the side cellar door we entered through last time. He wants the element of surprise on our side, which is why we're here at the crack of dawn. I can hear my breath rasping in my ears and my heart thudding loudly. My stomach flutters with nerves. Liam reaches the cellar door before me, and he pauses; for a heartbeat I wonder if he's having second thoughts. I pray desperately that he is but, as I get closer, I spot what it is that's stopped him in his tracks. Words have been scrawled in red paint across the door: NO TRESPASSING.

My heart explodes against my ribcage and my pulse spikes. I grip Liam's hand, unable to find my voice. I start to pull him away, but Liam doesn't budge. Surely he's not still contemplating going in there? Not with that warning emblazoned on the door. I read it again, blinking a few times as the realisation sinks in: it's not red paint; it's blood. Isn't it? I mean, it can't be paint – where would you find paint out here?

I glance at Liam. His expression is hard to read. I can tell he's afraid, but I think he's also trying to steel himself and hide the fear from me. He's weighing up his options.

'Let's go back,' I plead in a terrified whisper. But Liam's expression darkens. He glares at the words painted on the door.

'No,' he says. 'The bastard's not scaring me.'

My stomach clenches into a knot. 'Liam,' I beg again. 'Please. I don't want to go inside.'

He shakes my hand off his arm. 'You should wait for me here, or in the forest,' he says.

My eyes widen in alarm. He can't be serious. I shake my head furiously. 'No way,' I tell him. 'We can't split up.'

He turns to me, frustrated. 'Laura,' he argues. 'It's not safe for you to go inside.'

'Or you!' I hiss back at him.

'I can handle myself,' Liam tells me.

I know that he can, but I also know that he's stubborn and that he doesn't want to let this person win. *But it isn't a game*, I want to tell him. Not unless two people play. And we don't have to play. We can walk away. But deep down, I know that there's nothing I can say that will stop him.

'Go and wait for me in the forest.'

'No,' I refuse, lunging for his arm again and holding on to him. 'What if something happens to you? What will I do?'

'Nothing's going to happen to me,' he says, touching my cheek and offering me a smile. 'I swear. Stop worrying. Now go and wait for me. I won't be long.'

'What are you going to do to them?' I say, thinking of the knives he's carrying.

'Find out who he is and give him a warning to leave us alone.'

I swallow the lump of fear in my throat and turn to glance back at the forest, caught between the thought of running and hiding somewhere in its dark interior or following Liam into the belly of the beast. Neither option is appealing. But I'd rather be with Liam than wait, alone, not knowing what's happening. 'I'm coming with you,' I say to him.

He purses his lips, frustrated, but then nods. 'OK, but stay back, and stay quiet,' he warns me.

I nod.

We enter the cellar. Liam leads the way through the low-ceilinged space, having to duck because of his height, until we reach the kitchen. I stay glued to his heels, my heart rattling loose in my chest and my breathing quick and fast, fuelled by fear. Every step I half expect the man to come leaping out at us. I wish to god Liam didn't want to confront him.

'There has to be another set of stairs up to the first floor,' he says now in a whisper, looking around. 'We just need to find them. Come on,' he says, gesturing to the stairs we took last time that led up to the great hall. Reluctantly, I follow, and we tiptoe up them, entering the rubble-filled room.

Liam walks swiftly towards the study and I hurry after him, aware of every little noise I'm making. It's almost impossible to stay quiet as our footsteps echo on the stone floors. I worry that the element of surprise will be lost, and we'll walk into a trap.

Once in the study, Liam makes directly for the wood-panelled door and we enter the narrow servants' passage that runs between rooms. My breathing seems riotously loud in the tight space, though it's almost drowned out by the blood that's now roaring in my ears. I recognise it as the start of a panic attack and I fight it, keeping my eyes fixed on Liam's back and trying to screw up my courage. Everything in my body is screaming at me to get the hell away from this place, but, as though I'm under a witch's spell, I cannot turn around. I can only follow Liam blindly on. I'm too scared to leave him and go off by myself, so I choose the lesser of two evils.

We keep following the passage until finally Liam discovers a staircase. 'Here!' he says. 'Found it!'

Liam shines the torch up it and then starts to climb. I follow, my legs like lead, my heart still jackhammering with panic. I draw in huge gasping breaths as I try to fill my shrunken lungs.

We reach the top of the stairs and find ourselves in another passageway, but this one ends at a door. When Liam eases it open, we find ourselves in an upstairs hallway. Liam slips out, putting his finger to his lips again to remind me to stay quiet. My breathing is laboured, and I try to quiet myself down but when I pad out behind him, I let go of the door and it bangs shut behind me. Liam whips around and glares at me, annoyed. I shake my head in apology and mouth 'sorry'.

The hallway is long, with maybe a dozen doors on either side of it. Above us the rafters are open in places, exposing shards of blackening sky. More rain is on its way, by the looks of things. My feet tread in something mushy and I look down to see we're walking on water-logged and rotting carpet, threadbare in places. Beneath, I can see the wooden floorboards are black, and they creak as we walk; an alarm system to thwart our hopes of a surprise attack.

My nerves are frayed, my legs are shaking so hard I can barely stand up, and I feel like I might faint at any moment, but I keep following Liam, sheltering behind his back, terrified that at any moment someone might leap out at us.

Liam opens the first door we reach, and I draw a breath of surprise at the sight of the forest right in front of us. We're in the nursery that we saw from outside. The exterior wall is completely missing. The rocking horse sits forlornly at the edge of what looks like a cliff, staring out over the grounds. We're eye-level with the branches. I glance around; the fire must have burned through the floor above, and the attic, too, but oddly enough, the nursery itself is almost untouched. Besides the rocking horse, there's a chair and a small bed in the corner of the room, complete with the decomposing remains of a mattress.

Liam touches my sleeve and we leave the nursery and keep walking down the hallway, our footsteps silenced by the disintegrating carpet which stinks of fusty mildew. I breathe through my mouth as we keep going, checking every room we pass for signs of occupancy, my fraught nerves ratcheting up with every door handle that Liam tries, until I think I might have to turn tail and run. We find nothing, until we reach the final door.

Liam throws it open and freezes on the threshold. I peer past him and spot a makeshift campsite in the corner of the room; there's a sleeping bag, a stove, pots and pans and other items, but no occupant in sight. Someone is staying here! But who? And why?

Liam steps into the room, crossing quickly to the sleeping bag. He kneels down and places his hand on the bag and then on the pan sitting over the little camp stove. 'It's still warm,' he says.

He must have been here not long ago. We either only just missed him or – I spin around in fright – he's still here, somewhere in the castle.

Panicked, I turn back to Liam. 'We should go, before he comes back.'

Liam ignores me. He's already rummaging through a backpack, upending the contents onto the bed. Dirty socks and underpants tumble out, as well as a couple of T-shirts and a checked shirt. I step forwards, forgetting my panic for a moment. I pick up the shirt and check the label. It's a man's medium size. I notice the boxer shorts too.

Liam opens up a washbag. It holds a cracked mirror, a man's razor, shaving foam, a toothbrush, toothpaste and a small first aid kit. I heave in a breath that doesn't quite fill my lungs, my head spinning. Who is this man and what's he doing here?

Liam searches through the clothes, maybe looking for an ID, and I glance over my shoulder again at the door.

He could come back any moment and we have no idea what he might do if he finds us here.

My attention is drawn to the map of the island that Liam has pulled out of the man's bag and tossed on the bed. Maybe he is a treasure hunter after all. I glance around at the camp. It looks temporary: there's a cardboard box filled with a dozen Pot Noodles and some granola bars. A large gallon bottle of water sits by the fireplace. There's a pile of rubbish in the corner of the room – empty noodle pots and sweet wrappers, a crushed plastic bottle and several crushed cans of beer. It looks like maybe a week's worth of supplies in total.

Liam digs into the inside pocket of the man's backpack and pulls out a pocket radio. Tossing the bag and the radio aside, he pats down the sleeping bag and triumphantly delves inside to pull out a canvas bag that's been stuffed into it. Rummaging through that, he discovers an empty binocular case. Has he been spying on us from afar? When I felt like I was being spied on the other day in the graveyard, was it him?

'Please, can we go now?' I ask as Liam keeps searching through the man's belongings. I'm bouncing from foot to foot and glancing towards the door. What if he comes back and finds us rooting through his things like thieves?

Liam isn't going to be hurried, though. He keeps searching as though he's going to find something to tell us this man's motive for stalking us.

I start to walk back towards the door, but my gaze is snagged by something in the pile of rubbish. Among the wrappers and packets I've noticed a box. I walk over to it.

'Found something,' Liam says.

I turn back around. Liam's flourishing a folded-up piece of newspaper. The paper is yellowed with age, and the ink is smudged from damp. He unfolds it and I come over to see what it is.

'MURDER AT THE CASTLE!' screams the headline. There's a fuzzy black and white photograph of the charred ruins of the castle, alongside another image of Nancy and Elliot. I scan the article, feeling my breathing hitch.

Nancy McKay, 39, and her son, Elliot, 9, were found brutally slain last night at their home on the Isle of Shura. The police found the bodies burned almost beyond recognition after a fire engulfed their ancestral home.

The coroner is yet to release his report, but police are treating the deaths as homicides. A source revealed that the mother and son had both sustained knife injuries.

Andrew McKay, 45, husband of Nancy and father of Elliot, has been declared missing, but whether he also perished in the fire is unclear. It is not yet known if Andrew McKay is a suspect, but it has been reported that he was in significant financial trouble, with the bank threatening to repossess the property. The McKay family have lived on Shura for almost six hundred years and the family are well known in the area.

Andrew McKay's mother, Mary, inherited her late father's seat, and donated much of the estate to Catholic charities when she died. The police are asking for any witnesses, or those who may have knowledge of the crime, to come forward.

I draw in a breath. 'Oh my god,' I say. 'He killed them. Then he set fire to the castle to cover it up.'

Liam nods. 'Looks like it.'

'It's him,' I say, looking around at the campsite. 'He's been hiding here ever since.' Though as I say it, I wonder how he manages, living out here year in and year out. How would he survive the winters? And looking around at his things, it's clear this is a temporary campsite. But maybe he heads back to the mainland for supplies.

I remember then what I'd seen in the pile of rubbish over by the door and I run over to it.

'Liam,' I say in a hoarse voice when I find the item that caught my attention a moment ago.

'What?' he asks, distracted by his own search through the rest of the man's belongings.

'You should come here and see this.'

He comes over and I show him what I'm looking at. It's a box of ammunition. Shotgun shells.

Chapter Seventeen

Liam kicks the ammunition box with the toe of his boot. It's empty. I notice now that there are also a dozen empty shells among the pile of rubbish. Liam hesitates for half a second and then he takes my hand.

'Let's go,' he says, pulling me back into the corridor. I don't need telling twice. We practically run down the hallway and are about to open the door that leads into the servants' stairwell when we hear footsteps coming up it, and skid to a halt.

Liam yanks me sideways into one of the rooms: an old bathroom; and we hide behind the door, pressed up against each other, holding our breath. Liam digs into his pocket and pulls out his switchblade, but I grip his wrist. A knife is no match for a gun.

We hear the squeak of hinges and then the creaking

of floorboards as the footsteps head our way. I feel the hard and frantic scrabble of the panic in my belly clawing up my throat and forcing its way into my mouth. Liam must sense it too, as he clamps his hand over my mouth to stop a scream escaping. The footsteps keep coming closer, a banging noise accompanying them, as though he's knocking his knuckles against the wall as he walks.

The sound of the soft tread stops suddenly, and my scream gathers behind Liam's hand, trying to squeeze past his fingers. My heart feels like it's going to explode out of my chest. It's a miracle the man can't hear it. It's as loud as a jackhammer drilling into concrete, at least to my ears.

I stare up at Liam, whose attention is fixed on the door. He looks like a cornered animal, coiled and ready to spring, his free hand white-knuckled on the knife. We hear another footstep, this one closer. Liam's iron grip on me tightens. I worry he might throw caution to the wind and leap out to confront the man, but then, just as the tension feels like it might snap, the footsteps continue on.

Liam drops his hand from my mouth, and I gasp in oxygen. After a moment he eases the door open a crack and we peek out, just in time to catch a glimpse of the man as he walks down the hall. Is it Andrew McKay? It's hard to tell as we can't see his face. He's dressed all in black, with a long waterproof jacket and a hood pulled up, but my gaze is caught by something else. He's carrying a shotgun in his right hand and dangling a dead rabbit by its ears in his left, rhythmically knocking it against the wall as he walks. He turns and vanishes inside the room where his campsite is set up and it's only then that I remember we left all the man's things scattered and upended on his bed in our haste to get out of there. He'll know we've been here. He may even guess we're still in the castle.

'Move!' Liam says, obviously having the exact same thought. 'Come on!' he shouts at the precise moment we hear an angry yell – a man's voice – swearing blue murder. He must have discovered the mess we made of his things.

Liam pulls me out of the room, and we sprint hand in hand down the hallway. We barrel into the stairway, Liam ahead of me. I trip down a few steps in my panic, but Liam is in front of me, so I fall against his back. My legs are jelly, barely functioning as I career to the bottom of the stairs and into the narrow servants' passage on the ground floor. We plough along in the pitch black. Liam's either lost the torch or doesn't want to waste time trying to find it, so we have to keep our hands out in front of us, ricocheting blindly off the walls, trying to find our way back into the study; but how far is it? And which turn should we take?

What if he's behind us in the passageway? I turn to look over my shoulder but there's nothing but yawning darkness. Liam stops and pulls out his phone and turns the light towards the wall. A clattering noise echoes along the passage behind us and I let out a whimper.

Light floods into the passage suddenly as Liam finds the opening, pushes on the door and it flies open. We stumble out into the study and sprint for the great hall, but as we enter it, making for the stairs that will take us down into the kitchen, I hear a noise and look up. The man is standing on the balcony above us and he's lifting the shotgun to his shoulder, ready to take aim.

I scream and leap into the stairwell behind Liam. We scramble like rats on a sinking ship, desperately heading for the cellar and the way out, but halfway there I catch sight of something that makes me skid to a stop, my legs too frozen by fear to keep moving.

Liam turns around; 'What are you doing?' he yells at me. 'Come on!'

He beckons but I'm completely paralysed. I can't even breathe. He backtracks to me, taking me by the wrist, ready to wrench me along with him, but he stops in his tracks too when he sees what it is that I'm staring at.

'Oh my god,' he hisses under his breath.

We're outside the room with the hooks hanging from the ceiling. It was empty when we passed by it not fifteen minutes ago. But now red strips of fresh meat are hanging from the hooks and blood drips to the stone floor. The stench of torn flesh and faecal matter fills my nostrils and makes me gag. I catch a glimpse of a long, serrated knife, resting on the side.

'Come on!' Liam says again, dragging me out of my trance and pulling me away.

We stumble through the cellar and burst out into the daylight, then we run towards the forest, fully expecting to hear a gunshot blast ring out behind us. He must be watching us now from one of the upper windows. I can feel his gaze lasering me from behind as I run, my lungs burning with the effort.

When we break into the woodland and are hidden by the trees, so we can pause finally for breath, the panic spins like a whirlwind inside me. I lean against a tree trunk, my whole body shaking from adrenaline, the world tipping and sliding beneath my feet. What just happened? I can't quite comprehend it. And what was that in the room hanging from those hooks?

Liam wipes a trembling hand across his sweaty brow and bends at the waist, his hands on his knees, trying to catch his breath.

'What was that?' I whisper, the horror of what we just saw indelibly imprinted on my brain. 'In the room? What was it?'

Liam shakes his head. 'A rabbit.' His voice sounds weak and unconvincing. Was it a rabbit? It didn't look like a rabbit, but I could barely take any of it in, I was so overwhelmed by the blood and gore.

A branch snaps just then a few feet away from us,

the crack of it echoing like a bullet, and we both startle, heads flying up at the sound like prey hearing a predator approaching.

'Let's go,' Liam says, taking my hand, and we tear off again, running as fast as we can, darting between trees, stumbling over hidden roots and thrashing through bracken, until up ahead we see the cottage in its clearing on the edge of the loch.

The Stalker

Run rabbit, run rabbit, run, run, run.

That's the song that played in my head as I watched her run in terror for her life. There was a thrill in her trying to escape. It excited me that she was putting up a fight; that she wasn't making it easy. But also, if I'm honest, a part of me wanted her to escape.

That's always been my problem. I'm a man of two halves. I am constantly torn between conflicting emotions and desires: love and hate, joy and rage, forgiveness and revenge, wanting to be saved and accepting damnation.

It's as if the boy in me who was once eclipsed by the devil still occasionally tries to reassert himself. I start to feel remorse for the crimes I've committed. I want to be forgiven. But then something else happens, I'm triggered, and the devil comes roaring back out.

So I watch her run, knowing she won't get far.

Chapter Eighteen

Liam pulls the key out of his pocket as we race to the back door. He shoves it into the lock, and we fall inside as if the cottage is a burrow that will keep us safe from predators.

I stagger into the front room, panting and shaking. My vision blurs and something comes at me: a dark shape lunging from the corner of the room. I duck and let out a scream, but it's only the crow. I bat her away as Liam comes tearing into the room, switchblade in hand, arm raised in battle.

The bird screeches, flying lopsided with only one wing, and careers into the wall before landing in the corner of the room, cawing in fright.

The panic that has been gathering like a whirlwind inside me finally bursts out in a howling sob. I collapse to the floor in a heap as Liam stands there, knife still clutched in his hand, pumped on adrenaline.

'Fuck,' he exhales. 'Fuck,' he says again, staring around the room.

I see through my tears that the bird has crapped everywhere; there are white streaks on the sofa, the fireplace, the coffee table and the rug.

'How did it get out of the box?' Liam yells.

Another sob rises in my chest. I fight it down. 'I don't know. I'm sorry.' I see that the box has tipped over. She must have wanted to escape her confines: a feeling I can sympathise with.

'Get it the hell out of here,' Liam snaps impatiently.

I struggle to my knees.

'They'll make us pay for the damage,' Liam mutters, waving his hand at the sofas, which are covered in white splotches. 'These sofas are new. It's going to cost a fortune.'

'I'm sorry,' I say, though worrying about the cost of damage seems pointless right now, given we're facing the much bigger issue of a man on the island with a gun.

I move towards the bird, which hops frantically away from me, and I grab the towel from the floor and throw it over its head. I gather it up in my arms, though it fights me, and look around hopelessly. I can't take it outside and leave it. It won't survive with a broken wing. 'I'll put her under the stairs,' I say, reaching for the box.

Liam shakes his head. 'No. Look at the mess it's made. It can't stay.'

'But she'll die if I let her go now,' I argue weakly.

'I can speed that up,' he answers, still fuming.

I flinch in horror at the thought of him wringing the crow's neck and I know he'd do it. He's not a bleeding heart like me. He's pragmatic. And maybe he's right. Maybe I should just let the bird die, let nature take its course. If we hadn't found her in the castle, she would be dead already, no doubt. And there's no certainty that my splint will even do the job. The wing could heal messily; the bird might end up crippled and then it would be kinder to let her die. But still, the thought of Liam killing her is too much. I can't let him.

'Please,' I beg. 'I can't take her outside. What if that man's out there? Let me put her under the stairs. She'll be out of the way there.'

Grudgingly, he agrees. 'Fine. But I swear to god if it causes any more trouble, I'm going to wring its neck myself. I should have done that in the first place.'

I hurry the bird into the box and under the stairs, refilling the food and water saucers, noticing how much my hands are shaking as I do. My heart is still pumping as hard as it was when we were sprinting away from the castle. Liam is barricading the front and back doors with furniture. I try not to think about the man with the gun chasing us back here and I glance at the windows. Are we safe?

After I close the bird under the stairs I turn and find Liam in the kitchen unfurling a map of the island.

'What are you doing?' I ask. 'What is all this?' Then I realise. 'It's his stuff! You took it. Why did you do that? It will only provoke him even more.'

Liam looks at me, his expression so furious I take a step back. 'Are you blaming me?'

I shake my head. 'No, of course not. I'm just saying . . . we don't want to make him angry. He has a gun. And he warned us to stay out.'

The muscle in Liam's jaw pulses.

'I'm scared, that's all,' I tell him.

He softens, seeing the fear on my face. 'I know.' He indicates a map. 'But look, this map is different to the one we have. And there's a boathouse that wasn't on ours,' Liam says, stabbing his finger down on the map. 'We must have missed it when we walked inland along the stream the other day.'

'You think maybe he's got a boat?' I ask.

'How else did he get here?' Liam says. 'I keep wondering about it. It makes sense that he has his own boat.'

'He might have had someone drop him here.'

Liam shakes his head. 'Unlikely, if he's trying to stay off the radar. He's trespassing, remember.'

I nod. He's right. Though the man seems to think we're trespassing, given the warning written in blood on the door.

'If there *is* a boat,' Liam goes on, sounding energised, 'we could steal it and use it to get off the island.'

He looks at me and my eyes widen in terror; we'd have to travel to the other side of the island, past the castle, to get to the boathouse, and the man with the gun is probably out there waiting for us. He may even have followed us back to the cottage. He could be outside right now.

'We're sitting ducks here,' Liam says. 'We can't stay until Friday. Whoever he is, he has a gun. And he's obviously crazy. We're not safe. We need to get off the island, and we need to go now.'

He walks out into the hallway. 'We'll take just one bag; essentials only.'

I follow him. 'What about all this mess?' I ask, gesturing at the destroyed living room.

Liam shrugs. Not ten minutes ago he was yelling about it but now he doesn't seem to care. 'Fuck it,' he says. 'I'm not giving them a penny. They should be paying us compensation. What kind of a bloody holiday is this? They set us up in the middle of nowhere without a phone or any way to get in touch.'

He jogs up the stairs and I follow him, watching as he snatches his backpack from under the bed and starts to toss in a few things. After a second he looks up at me. 'What are you doing?' he asks, staring at me as I stand there, dazed and unmoving. 'Come on, hurry up!'

I snap to and rush into the bathroom, hurrying to

gather up my medication, hairbrush and toothbrush and digging through a box of tampons to find my anti-depressants and the pill, which I stuff into the pocket of my jeans. To me, they are essentials. Liam knocks impatiently on the door, reminding me to be quick, and I leave the bathroom and hand my items to him, to throw into his bag. We head back down the stairs at a run, not even pausing to look around the cottage before we rush for the back door. Liam takes the map he stole from the man's bag, folding it and shoving it into his inside jacket pocket.

Just as Liam opens the door, I remember the bird. *Oh god, I can't just leave it.* But we can hardly take it with us either. I hesitate, not knowing what to do, but then Liam steps out, pulling me with him, and it's too late.

Chapter Nineteen

We move in silence, tramping through the forest. The trees are heavy with rain and creak in the wind, making us jump at every step. Liam's taking us on a circuitous route so we can avoid going near the castle or its grounds, but it's rough terrain and slowgoing, especially as we're trying not to make much noise.

We reach a point in the forest where the trees are thinning and, through gaps, I can spot the flash of water. We pick our way down to a rocky shore, clambering over boulders, and then I see the boathouse up ahead. It's falling apart, the stone walls clad in moss, which camouflages it so well that from a distance it appears as part of the landscape. The clouds have sunk low, engulfing us in soft drizzle, muffling noise and blurring vision.

As we get closer, we see that the boathouse is built

directly over the loch and there's a stone slipway, pitted with age, that juts into the water like an old, greying tongue. We approach the place cautiously, primed for a surprise — for the man to leap out at us with his gun.

I jolt around, turning left to right and scanning the woods, but I can't see anyone.

'Stay behind me,' Liam whispers as we reach the entrance to the boathouse.

I do, sheltering behind his back. He throws the door open; there's no one inside. I breathe a huge sigh of relief. *Thank god*. There is a boat though. It's a wooden rowing boat that's been pulled out of the water and is resting on the slip.

Liam rushes towards it and tosses the bag into the bottom of it. 'Get in,' he says to me, urgently. 'I'll push us out.'

I hesitate.

'It'll be fine,' he reassures me.

But I don't know. I cast a wary look at the boat and, beyond, to the grey, unending sky melting into the loch. The water is choppy, and I remember the boatman's warning about the currents and the cold.

'Come on!' Liam urges.

I glance in the other direction, through the door of the boathouse, to the island. What choice do I have? 'OK,' I say and move towards the vessel.

I climb in and Liam shoves us off into the water. I grip the flimsy sides as Liam jumps in. We rock dangerously and water splashes over the edge, soaking my lap and feet. Liam almost overbalances as he takes his seat, but the boat rights itself and he grabs the oars and pushes us further out into the water.

The wind is high, something we hadn't factored because the boathouse sits on an inlet and is sheltered, but as soon as we're out in the open we're caught in it and the waves get even bigger, slapping hard against the sides. I glance back at the island, now ten metres away, then very quickly twenty metres away. Liam splashes around with the oars, trying to hook them through the oarlocks, but when he finally manages and tries to paddle with them, he can't seem to steer us in the direction he wants to. Instead, we're being dragged along by the tide that the boatman warned us about, slamming into forceful swells that slosh water over the prow of the boat and leave our feet submerged. We're floating through the underworld, it feels, heading away from the mainland and towards the sea.

I shiver as the drizzle turns to heavier rain, coating my face and eyelashes. I can barely see through the cloud and the freezing cold of the water has numbed my hands, which are still clutching the boat tightly. Looking down at the water I think about the unfathomable depths below us and try to overcome my burgeoning panic.

'We should go back!' I shout to Liam, but he shakes his head, fighting to steer a course. He looks over his shoulder to check our progress and just then the boat hits a large wave. It's as if we've been slammed headfirst into a rock. I tumble into the icy loch with a cry of alarm.

Chapter Twenty

The water is so shockingly cold it feels as if I'm being flayed alive. It strips the flesh, rakes at the bone, grips my heart and squeezes it tight. I sink beneath the surface and for seconds I'm too paralysed by shock to fight the terrible downward pull, but finally my survival instinct kicks in and my legs start to move. I kick, breaking the surface and gasping for breath, yet unable to squeeze air into my frozen lungs. The water is cement, encasing my legs and body and tugging me down. I disappear once more, swallowing water, unable to kick my legs or move my arms in order to keep myself afloat. Oh god. I register that I'm drowning.

My mum pops into my head. Since she passed away, I've only ever been able to picture her dead. That one image overrides all the other memories I have of her.

But now, as I find myself sinking into the deep, I see her as she was when she was alive. She's calling my name, urging me to swim, telling me that I need to fight. And I don't want to disappoint her, so I do. I grit my teeth against the cold and ignore the terrible drag of those hungry hands pulling me down. Resisting the lure of just giving up and letting myself sink, I kick with every ounce of strength I have, struggling my way towards the sky.

I break through the water again and this time I'm yanked upwards. Liam has me by the collar of my shirt. He's leaning over the edge of the boat, which is in danger of tipping and throwing him out as well, and he's trying to pull me back in. I cough and splutter, still kicking intensely.

Liam's grip on me tightens. I can hear him yelling my name and the desperation in his voice. Then there's a splash and his grip on me is gone. The boat has flipped, tossing Liam out. He surfaces, gasping, beside me. I dip beneath the waves again, but the fight has been ignited in me now, and I emerge a moment later, thrashing my arms to stay afloat.

Liam is screaming my name as he treads water a few feet away. He grabs for me when I come up beside him.

'Swim,' he splutters.

I can see the boat, floating upside down, drifting away from us, and I realise that we too are drifting further from the island. The choice is either to swim or drown.

I smash my arms into the waves, clumsily. I feel so heavy but force myself to keep going, though I don't seem to be making any progress and I'm growing drowsier with each passing second.

I keep my eyes on the island and even though I'm so exhausted that sinking under the waves starts to feel like a good choice, I force myself to keep going. I don't focus on how far away land is, just on keeping my legs kicking.

Just when I think I can't possibly go any further, and I'm ready to start accepting my fate, my feet scrape the bottom. I can stand. Triumphant, I paddle a little further, before stumbling forward, wading on shaking legs towards the shore, and then all at once Liam is there, catching my arm, dragging me up out of the water and up onto a beach.

We collapse face down beside each other, coughing and shivering violently. My face is pressed into the sand. We must be on the beach on the north-east side of the island, having been dragged along by the tide. I try to lift my head to see but I can't – I'm too weak to move. My lips have started chattering again, so hard my teeth feel like they might shatter. My muscles, too, are juddering as if a current of electricity is being shocked through me.

Liam staggers to his knees and then to his feet, hunched over, trembling. He grips my arm. 'Get up,' he orders, stammering through frozen lips.

I can't.

'Get up!' he grunts again.

I try to open my eyes. His face swims in and out of focus. I can see though that his lips are blue, his skin white. He keeps pulling and I protest at first, but I manage to get to my hands and knees and then force myself to stand, my clothes waterlogged and clinging to my body. Liam takes my arm and we stagger up the beach.

My feet squelch in my shoes and all I want to do is collapse to the ground, curl into a ball, and sleep. I don't know how I'm going to make it back to the cottage – it's so far – but we do, heaving ourselves through the forest, Liam leading the way, hauling me along when I trip.

Finally, the cottage appears in the distance and we stagger across the clearing towards it, neither of us bothering to look out for the man with the gun. All I can think about is getting inside and standing under a hot shower, but as Liam digs for the key in his pocket, his frozen fingers making him fumble and drop it, I remember that there's no electricity, no heating and no hot water. I want to cry.

Liam finally gets the door open and we fall inside. He makes straight for the front room and starts throwing the damp wood he brought in last night into the belly of the wood-burning stove. I collapse down on the floor beside him, tugging the blanket off the back of the chair and trying to wrap it around myself, though my hands are clumsy frozen claws.

Liam's own hands are shaking so hard that the matches keep snapping when he strikes them. He curses under his breath, but keeps going and finally, on the fifth try, he manages to light one. He holds it to a white fire-lighter block, and it catches with a startling whoosh. I stare at the flame like it's a magical element and I have to resist the urge to reach for it and bring it near to me, to cradle it in my frozen hands. Liam shoves it into the stove. The damp wood he's piled inside though merely fizzles and hisses, letting off steam but not igniting. I stare helplessly at the firelighter's flickering flame as it starts to burn itself out.

'Damn,' Liam says, rubbing his hands together to spark feeling back into them. The tips of his fingers are blue. I look down at my own hands: they're wrinkled and white, my fingertips and nails tinged the same blue as Liam's.

Once again Liam drags himself to his feet and disappears into the kitchen. I don't have the energy to follow. I can only lie staring at the wood stove as the weak flame extinguishes. My eyes start to flutter closed. I hear the muffled sound of the back door banging shut and wonder briefly where Liam has gone, but my thoughts are disjointed and fuzzy. I'm starting to drift off.

A loud bang startles me and my eyes fly open. It sounds like an axe smashing into wood. What's happening?

There's another crack, then another, and then a moment later Liam comes through into the living room carrying splintered pieces of varnished wood. It takes me a moment to figure out that he must have smashed up one of the kitchen chairs for fuel.

He kneels in front of the stove and shoves the pieces in, lights another firelighter and shuts the door on it as the wood catches and roars to life.

I crawl an inch closer to the flames, so that my hand is almost touching the cast iron, letting my face bathe in the light and the extraordinary heat. Drowsiness drops over me like a blackout curtain, but there's a frantic tugging at my jeans keeping me from succumbing to the blissful lure of sleep. I grumble something unintelligible, not understanding what's happening, but the tugging doesn't let up.

'Get them off,' I make out Liam saying. 'You need to get out of your clothes. They're wet.'

Feebly, I try to bat him away and pull my legs in tight against my body, trying to curl into a ball, but he's persistent and I'm too weak to protest, so I let him wrench off my shoes and remove my socks. He hauls me into a sitting position and pulls my sweaters off. They come away as if he's peeling off a layer of skin. The cold air stings my bare body and I shake violently, but Liam drapes the blanket around my shoulders.

I curl up on the rug once more and feel Liam wrap

his naked body around mine. He pulls the blanket over both of us and though something is nagging at me, I can't chase the thought, because within seconds I'm falling into the deepest, darkest sleep I've ever known.

Chapter Twenty-One

A bang wakes me. My eyes fly open. It takes me a moment to realise where I am — on the floor in the living room. The fire has died out. It's chilly and the light is muted and purplish. What time is it? How long have we been asleep?

Liam is still out cold. His arm is heavy around my waist and he's breathing deeply. There's another bang, followed by a creak. My heart leaps as though I've been shocked with an electric paddle. I stop breathing, my eyes flying to the kitchen door. Is someone inside the cottage?

But then there's another thud and a blast of cold air and I realise the noise is just the back door, banging in the wind. I force my legs, which are stiff as planks and aching, to move and I roll like an elderly patient out from under Liam's arm and onto my knees. I'm naked and when I stand up, throwing off the blanket, goose bumps cover my skin. I scamper, clutching my arms around myself, to the wooden chest beneath the window and pull out a woollen blanket that I saw in there the other day. Wrapping it around myself I shuffle towards the kitchen.

I find the back door open and flapping in a gusty wind. Did we leave it like that? In our exhaustion, did we forget to close it? I remember now: that's the thought that I was trying to chase before I fell asleep. We should have barricaded the doors before we did anything. Liam must have forgotten after he went out to get the axe. We're lucky the man didn't come looking for us.

I shut the door now, pushing a chair beneath the handle, but not before briefly gazing on the forest. The rain has lifted and though there are still clouds, the sun, which is low, is breaking through and painting them purple. It must be seven or eight in the evening, I'm guessing, by the light and the position of the sun, which would mean we've been asleep for hours. I want to check the time but then I remember that my phone was in the pocket of my jeans when I fell in the loch, and, if it's even still in my pocket, then it won't be working. And the electricity is out so the clock on the stove isn't working either.

I stagger to the sink and gulp down two glasses of water. I'm dehydrated, my head throbbing, and I stare out the window, lost in thought for several minutes. The boatman isn't picking us up until Friday. Two more days until help arrives. I think about the man in the castle, my mind conjuring the image of him standing on the landing, gun to his shoulder. Who is he? What could he want? Worse, how will he react once he discovers his boat is missing?

I turn to head back into the front room and notice that the pile of paper and the map that Liam stole from the man's belongings are still on the kitchen table. I glance at the article again and then I realise that there's another folded square of newspaper lying beneath it. I pick it up and unfold it.

ANDREW MCKAY FOUND

Quickly, I scan the article, hands shaking. It's dated December 9th, two weeks after Nancy and Elliot died.

The body of Andrew McKay was found washed ashore yesterday, two weeks after he disappeared following the murders of his wife and son. The coroner's initial report indicates that McKay drowned. Speculation persists around the murders and Andrew McKay is the only suspect. Police believe he killed his wife, Nancy, and son, Elliot before taking his own life. The brutal murders shocked the close-knit community around Shura.

'It's not him,' I whisper to myself, feeling at once relieved and then in the next instant confused.

Who the hell is the man in the castle then? I wonder to myself.

When I head back into the front room, I see Liam is still dead to the world on the floor in front of the log burner. I don't wake him. Instead, I head upstairs to find dry clothes, hurrying over to the dresser and pulling out fresh underwear, a large jumper and a pair of leggings, then a warm pair of hiking socks which make me groan with bliss when I put them on. I dig out a woollen hat next and pull that on over my dry but still tangled hair. What I would give for a hot shower – but that's a luxury we no longer have.

I pause for only a second to look in the mirror in the bathroom, and as I suspected, it's not a pretty sight. I'm a ghost: skin like a corpse drained of blood, lips pale, hair in ratty strings; but I also see, in my eyes, a flash of something that wasn't there earlier – a spark of life. I remember the fight I put up when I was under the water; how my mum appeared to me and I heard her voice, urging me on. Something ignited in me in that moment and I can see it in my reflection, burning in my eyes – a fierce determination and a will to live that my depression had sucked from me, but that has now returned in full force.

When I head back downstairs, I see that the front room is empty. 'Liam?' I call.

I stoop and gather the wet clothes we stripped off earlier, which are strewn where we left them, noticing as I do the bird crap all over the furniture. The clothes are still sodden. I have to stop myself from shuddering at the memory of the water closing over my head, dragging me down into its depths. I remember that my pill and my anti-depressants were in the pocket and quickly shove my hand inside to find them. They're not there. They must have fallen out when I was under the water. Damn. But I can't worry about it now.

'Liam?' I call again.

There's no answer. I head towards the kitchen, and that's when I notice a drop of red on the carpet by my feet. It looks like blood. I bend down to take a closer look. It's still fresh. And there are several more drops. I follow them, heart pounding. 'Liam?' I say again, this time louder.

In the kitchen I find him sitting in a chair, blanket draped over him like a cape. One foot is resting on the other knee and he's bent over and peering at the sole of his foot.

'What's the matter?' I ask. 'I was calling you.'

'Sorry,' he mumbles. 'I was concentrating. I've got something in my foot. I'm trying to get it out.'

'What?' I ask, coming closer.

'I think it's glass,' he says, wincing in pain.

I frown. 'How did that happen?'

He shakes his head. 'I don't know. I stood in it, just now.'

'Stood in glass?' I reply, confused. 'Where?'

'In the living room,' he answers, grimacing tightly.

I drop the wet clothes on the table and peer at his foot. Dusk has fallen and it's not the best light, but I can still see two big shards of glass sticking out of his sole, and a couple of smaller splinters too, beading with blood.

'Shall I get some tweezers?' I ask.

'Yeah,' he grunts, biting his lip.

I run upstairs and fetch a pair from my washbag, returning quickly to the kitchen. 'Do you want me to do it?' I say.

He nods. First, I fetch the candles from the drawer and light a couple, setting them on the table. Then I take the torch and kneel down and examine his foot. 'Where did the glass come from?' I wonder out loud as I grip one of the bigger splinters and twist and yank at the same time.

Liam lets out a yell and I hold his ankle tight to keep him still. I get a grip on the second piece of glass and start to pull that out, but Liam jerks. The splinter is crushed by the tweezers and half of it remains buried in his flesh.

'Christ,' he shouts. 'Did you get it?'

I examine his foot. 'No, there's still some in there.'

He glowers at me. 'Shit.'

'I could try again,' I offer but he grabs the tweezers off me. 'God, no, let me do it.'

I hand the tweezers and the torch over and then take a candle and walk into the front room, treading lightly and slowly towards the fireplace to make sure I don't tread in any glass myself. I spot the shards immediately, glinting in the light. They're scattered on the rug by the corner of the sofa. I kneel down and examine them. They looks like they come from an ornament of some kind. I pick up a shard and look closer. It's part of a wing.

'What is it?'

I look up and see Liam has hopped into the room and is leaning against the arm of the chair. I show him. 'It looks like an angel.'

Liam stares at the fragment in my palm and I watch him turn pale. He takes it from me and examines it. 'How did it get here?' he asks.

'I don't know,' I say, shaking my head and shrugging. 'I found it right here.' I point at the rug.

Liam frowns hard at the place I'm gesturing to, at the splinters of broken glass still scattered there, and I can see him racking his brains, wondering how it ended up on the floor.

'The door was wide open when I woke up,' I say quietly.

He looks up, startled. 'I shut it. I know I did. I locked it when I came back in.'

'Maybe he has a key.'

We take that in, a hum of terror thrumming through my body.

'But I put a chair in front of the door,' Liam says. He turns his head to the front door, realisation dawning. 'He came in the front,' he says. 'I forgot to bolt it. He must have come in that way and left by the back door. I can't believe I did that.' He curses himself under his breath and hobbles over to the front door, drawing across the bolt.

'It's not Andrew McKay though,' I say, running to fetch the article. 'They found his body. He killed himself.' I show him the newspaper.

Liam snatches it from my hand and reads it.

We fall silent, both of us looking around the chilly front room, staring at the now-dead fire and the rug where we lay sleeping. 'Well, whoever the hell he is, he was here,' Liam says in a hushed voice. 'He must have come in while we were passed out. He stood here.' He points at where he's standing. 'He watched us.'

The Stalker

I stood over them for the longest time. I wanted to kill them both. It was hard not to. I had to fight hard to wrestle the anger and rage and subdue it. I wanted to make them suffer first. I wanted to hurt him in ways that he could never imagine, and I wanted to make her watch. Then she might know some of the pain I've experienced watching her with him.

So I decided to wait.

I glanced at the gift I'd brought for her. An angel made of glass.

'This is for you,' I whispered, setting it down.

Chapter Twenty-Two

I glance down at the splinters of glass on the carpet. 'Why put an angel ornament there?' I ask. 'I don't understand!'

'I told you. He's messing with us.'

'But why?' I shout. 'Who could it be? What do they want with us? Why are they stalking us like this?'

Liam shakes his head and collapses down into the armchair, wincing as he brings his foot into his lap. He presses a tea towel gingerly to it. 'I need to get this glass out,' he says. 'Or I won't be able to walk.'

'I could use a razor blade,' I say, trying to shrug off my terror and focus on the problem in hand, 'and try again.'

Liam glances at me, grim-faced, and then nods,

reluctantly. 'There's a spare blade in the bathroom, with my shaving stuff,' he tells me.

I go upstairs and fetch it, as well as some alcohol wipes from the first aid kid and some clothes for Liam so he can get dressed. The whole time I'm fighting a wave of fear of the man on the island and wondering why in god's name he's here.

When I come back downstairs, my arms full, I see Liam's still sitting in the armchair staring at the fragment of angel wing. He startles when I walk towards him and quickly pulls on the T-shirt and jumper I hand him. I help him hop into some boxers and a pair of jogging bottoms.

'I'm sure this must have something to do with one of your cases,' I say, aware that I'm repeating myself.

He looks at me, puzzled. 'What?'

'Is there anyone who might want revenge on you? Someone who's angry at you? Maybe someone you locked up?'

He shakes his head but avoids my eye. It makes me wonder if Liam has thought of something; if he does know who it is, but he's just not telling me. It's the angel. I think it's triggered something in him, but he's withholding the knowledge from me.

'How are *you* doing?' he asks me, trying to change the subject. 'Are you OK?'

'Fine,' I reply

'You're shaking,' he says.

'I'm cold,' I tell him. I don't think I'll ever feel warm again. I'm frozen through to my marrow. But it's not just the cold making me shiver. I'm petrified. I nod and crouch down in front of him and sterilise the razor blade with the wipe. When I'm done, I look up. 'Ready?' I ask.

He grits his teeth and nods. I slice the blade into his foot; he lets out a roar of pain and I have to grasp his ankle with my spare hand to stop him from yanking it back. My time at the vet has trained me well enough to focus on what I'm doing while wrestling an anxious animal or one in pain so I tune him out, keep a firm grip, and manage to dig out the smaller splinters, placing them carefully in a tissue, but the bigger piece that broke off is stubborn and won't be pried out with any amount of digging.

Liam is turning whiter and whiter as I probe with the tip of the razor's edge. His hands clutch the arms of the chair and sweat beads on his brow. I scrape away skin and pause to mop up the blood. 'It's in too deep,' I tell him with a sigh, finally giving up. 'I can't get it. You need to go to hospital to get that out. It's impossible without a local anaesthetic and a magnifying glass.'

'Do you see a hospital anywhere?' he snaps.

I settle back on my haunches, still holding the razor blade, and don't reply.

'Shit,' Liam grumbles.

He puts his foot on the floor and tries to stand but collapses, hissing through his teeth at the pain. He squeezes his eyes shut and his brow furrows.

I gather up the alcohol wipe and the splinters of glass and dispose of them in the kitchen bin. *What are we going to do now?* I wonder. I hear Liam shuffling into the kitchen behind me and turn to find him hopping towards the table. He looks wrung out, pale and exhausted, his face pinched tight with pain.

'Are you hungry?' I ask him, thinking of my own rumbling tummy.

He nods. 'Yeah.'

I move to the fridge to see what I can rustle up. 'What the hell?' I say as I open it.

'What?' Liam asks.

I throw the door open wide so he can see. The fridge is completely empty. 'There's no food. It's all gone.'

'He's taken it,' Liam says in disbelief. He hops to the cupboards and opens them all. They're all bare as well – all the biscuits and pasta and groceries that were here this morning have vanished. Liam bangs the cupboard doors shut.

'I don't understand. Why take all our food?' I ask.

'I've told you! He wants to fuck with us,' Liam spits. 'We've got no food and no electricity and no gas. And we're here for two more days.' He puts his head in his hands. 'He's playing with us. Drawing it out before . . .' He tails off.

I stare at him wide-eyed. 'Before what?' I ask, my voice catching. 'How do you know what he wants?'

Liam hops toward the sink. He leans on it and looks out of the window at the fast-falling night. He does know something about who this person is. I know he does.

Liam grimaces. 'We could have escaped by now if . . .'

'I'm sorry,' I say, interrupting him, staring at the floor, my shoulders hunched. I know it's my fault that the boat capsized. We could have been on the mainland by now. Although it's more than likely we would have been swept out to sea, and possibly even have drowned. Who's to say?

I glance up and see that Liam's shaking his head, as though fighting frustration, but then he hops over to me and pulls me into his arms. 'I thought I'd lost you for a moment. When you went under like that. I thought you were going to drown.' He hugs me tight, pressing my head into his chest and stroking my hair. 'I don't know what I'd do if anything happened to you,' he whispers into my ear, his voice cracking.

I close my eyes. 'What if he comes back?' I ask. 'What if he discovers his boat is missing? He might have already.'

Liam lets me go. 'We could try lighting a fire on the cliffs,' he says. 'Use it to signal the mainland.'

'How would anyone see it? We're so far away.'

'At night they might,' he argues. 'Or in the day, they might be able to see the smoke.'

'There's no fuel,' I counter. 'Everything's soaked through. What would we burn?'

He's losing patience with me. 'There are things in the castle that are dry. And there's furniture here we could use, too. I could chop up the other chairs. And the table. We could light it on the cliffs.' He's got the idea now, it's taken hold, and I can see he's not going to let it go.

'But what if the man sees it too?' I ask, worried. 'What if he sees the fire and comes looking for us? He's got a gun.' I press my knuckles to my lips pushing back the panic.

Liam scowls. 'I'll take our chances.'

I don't know if *I* want to though. I shake my head at him. 'I think we should find a place to hide,' I suggest. 'Somewhere on the island where he can't find us. We could lie low until the boatman comes on Friday.'

'Where are we going to hide?' Liam asks, looking at me like I'm mad.

'The chapel?' I suggest. 'If the man can't find us, he might think we've found some way to get off the island. He might not even know yet that we stole his boat. So he might think we did get away.'

Liam chews it over. 'You think we should hole up in the chapel and wait it out?' he asks. 'Without anything to eat? Without water?'

I shrug. 'We might be able to find some food. Forage for things,' I say. 'I saw some blackberries.' I shrug. 'It might be safer than staying here. And definitely safer than lighting a giant bonfire.'

'I'm not scared of this bastard,' Liam mutters. 'If he didn't have a gun . . .' he trails off.

I can tell he absolutely hates the fact that he doesn't have the upper hand in a situation where he would normally. He's angry, but he's actually more afraid, and I don't know how that makes me feel because normally he's so in charge; so in control and so confident. But the fact is, this guy has a gun and Liam doesn't.

'Let's do it,' Liam says to me, making a decision.

Chapter Twenty-Three

I dart upstairs and start to gather up clothes and my washbag. I layer on sweaters, wishing my jacket wasn't covered in bird filth, but I take it anyway as it's going to be cold in the chapel.

The jacket reminds me of the bird. I haven't checked on her. Guiltily, I race back downstairs and throw open the door to the cupboard under the stairs.

The box is still there, covered with a towel, which I peel back. The bird opens one beady eye and stares at me. Then she hops over and tries to peck my hand, letting out an annoyed caw, as though angry at having been abandoned for so long, but simultaneously relieved to have been remembered. I smile, seeing how much stronger she looks than earlier today.

Liam gives me a look when I carry the box out into

the kitchen and set it on the table, and mutters something under his breath which I choose to ignore. He's gathered up the blankets from the living room and is packing them into a plastic bin liner to take with us.

We fill a plastic bottle with water and Liam retrieves the wine bottles from the recycling bin and rinses them before filling them up too, plugging them with the used corks. It's not enough water, we both know that; not for two days. 'We'll have to sneak back here,' he says, 'and refill them.'

It's not a great idea, but we don't have much choice. I fill a glass from the tap, down it and then drink another whole glass, hydrating myself as much as I can in anticipation of being rationed. My body is still aching from the swim and my stomach is growling painfully. My appetite has chosen the worst possible moment to make a comeback.

I know Liam must be really starving as he's got a much bigger appetite and hasn't eaten a thing since this morning.

'Why the food?' I ask, shaking my head. 'I still don't understand.'

Liam has no answer.

We leave the cottage and hurry out into an already dark and starless night. Liam takes the axe he used to chop up the kitchen chairs. We have the torch, some firelighters and the matches too, but we don't want to use the torch in case we're seen, so we make our way in the dark along the beach and into the woods, helped only by the palest strands of moonlight. Because of the glass in Liam's foot we make slow progress. He has to hobble, leaning on me, and I keep hearing him hiss through his teeth whenever he accidentally puts pressure on the injured part. He's sweating profusely by the time we make it to the chapel and his lips are white from tightly clamping them shut to stop from whimpering.

Liam pushes on the chapel door and it creaks open. The windows are high up, so once we're inside we risk turning on the torch, though Liam shields the light with his palm to soften it, afraid it will signal the man like a beacon and alert him to our whereabouts.

The chapel is chilly, but at least it's out of the wind. I glance around at the broken pews and the cobwebs clinging to the corners and set the bird in its box down behind the stone font.

A loud scraping sound makes me jump and spin around. But it's only Liam, shoving one of the pews in front of the door as a barrier. It's not a particularly sturdy barricade, but better than nothing I suppose. I go to help him and afterwards we look around the chapel's interior, shining the torch into the dank corners, deciding where best to make our camp.

The torch beam bounces off the altar ahead of us and I notice something sitting on it. 'What was that?' I ask Liam.

'What?' he asks.

'Over there,' I say, pointing. 'Shine the light.'

He moves the torch's beam so it lights up the far end of the chapel. There's definitely something on the altar. We walk down the aisle towards it, unable to make out what it is. As we get closer, though, I see it's a photograph, propped up against a musty hymnal. It's of a girl, or a young woman; maybe mid-twenties, possibly younger; with blue eyes and blonde hair. The photo has been torn in half erasing whoever was standing beside her in the photo, but his arm remains around her shoulders. They're standing on what looks like a mountain with a view of the ocean behind, and the woman is grinning at the camera.

I go to pick it up, but Liam reaches out and snatches my arm, stopping me. I look at him and see his eyes are fixed on the photograph and his expression is one of total terror, as though it's not a photograph but a poisonous snake.

'Who is it?' I ask him. 'Do you know her?'

Liam doesn't answer. He just keeps staring at the photograph, open-mouthed and turning paler by the second.

'Who is it?' I press, feeling panic starting to rise in my chest.

'Mia Watkins,' Liam finally says, his voice barely a whisper.

I glance at the photograph again and then back at Liam. 'Who's Mia Watkins?

Liam pulls his focus from the photograph on the altar and turns to me. 'She was murdered,' he says. 'Her and her boyfriend.'

The breath leaves my body in a sharp exhalation. 'Who killed them?' I ask.

Liam shrugs, shaking his head. 'No one was ever arrested.'

'Was it your case?'

'No,' he says. 'It was in Cumbria. Cumbria police had jurisdiction. They called in Scotland Yard, which is why the file crossed my desk. I remember it because the crime scene photographs were . . .' He breaks off, shuddering at the memory before glancing my way and obviously deciding not to share the details. 'They found a glass angel at the crime scene,' he adds.

Goosebumps cover my skin. I'm rooted to the spot. 'What do you mean, a glass angel?' I ask, although I already know.

Liam turns to me, grim-faced. 'Like the one in the living room that I stood on earlier.'

I slump down into the nearest pew and put my head in my hands, dark spots dancing before my eyes. I try to draw in a breath, but my lungs feel too tight.

'I didn't think about it until now,' Liam goes on. 'It rang a bell, but I didn't put two and two together until' – he gestures at the photograph – 'I saw that picture.'

I glance at him, feeling the cold hand of terror grip hold of my insides and start squeezing.

'It was never confirmed that the suspect left it behind,' Liam says. 'But there was one found on the kitchen table at the crime scene. As if he'd positioned it there to watch.'

'To watch what?' I ask, almost too terrified to hear him answer.

'What he did to them,' Liam murmurs.

I swallow what feels like a twig that's lodged in my throat, my heart smashing loudly in my ears. 'What *did* he do to them?' I hear myself ask. I don't really know if I want to know the answer, but I need to.

Liam frowns, looking pained, as though he doesn't want to tell me.

'Tell me!' I hiss at him.

He takes a breath and then lets it out in a loud exhalation. 'He killed them. We think he tortured the guy first – his name was Will – and that he made Mia watch. Then he dumped their bodies in a ditch.' He says it without any emotion, but I'm sure, judging from the expression on his face, that he's holding back the gruesome details.

'And the police never found out who did it?' I ask.

'No,' Liam admits. 'Whoever it was got away with it.'

'How?'

'He was smart. There was no evidence left at the scene of the crime. Not a trace of anyone. It was a mystery.'

'Why would someone do that?'

Liam shakes his head. 'Who knows? I had a theory that he was in love with Mia. He thought she belonged to him and when he saw her with another man, he got angry. She betrayed him, so he punished her.'

Liam turns away and picks up the photograph. He must be wondering what the hell it's doing here on top of the altar. I wonder at the placing of it there – in a chapel. It's like a memorial. 'What's it doing here?' I ask Liam.

Liam doesn't look at me. I gaze, half-dazed around the chapel. 'It's him, isn't it?' I ask before looking back at Liam. 'He's here on the island with us.'

Liam meets my gaze then comes over and puts his arm around me, pulling me against his chest. 'Don't worry,' he tells me. 'I'll keep you safe. I swear I won't let anything happen to you.'

I extricate myself from his arms and start to walk up and down the aisle, frantic, trying to think it all through. 'Why us though?' I ask, rounding on him. 'Why would he lure *us* here? You didn't work the case. It's got nothing to do with you, has it?'

Liam's thinking hard. Obviously he's been wrestling with this very same thing. 'I don't know,' he finally offers. 'It doesn't make sense to me. I can't figure it out.'

I stare at him, willing him to join some dots.

'Did he stalk her before he killed her?' I ask.

Liam shrugs. 'We don't know. I mean he definitely watched her, yes. He obviously planned things out in detail. That's why he was able not to leave any DNA behind. I'm only guessing from the file I read about the crime scene, but the violence against the boyfriend – the number of times he was stabbed – suggests he was furious about something. Presumably he was angry because he thought the boyfriend had stolen Mia from him.'

I stare at Liam. I know he likes to get inside people's heads, but it's as if he's trying to excuse murder. 'He's a sick bastard. A psychopath,' I tell him.

Liam says nothing. His brow remains furrowed.

'I'm a replacement for Mia,' I say looking up at Liam, my pulse thrumming like a bird's.

Liam glances at me with a frown, as though I'm spouting nonsense.

'Look at us,' I say, stabbing the photo with my index finger. 'We look really similar.'

Liam wrinkles his nose. 'Not that similar.'

'We're both blonde, blue-eyed, roughly the same age.'

Liam looks more closely at the photograph and then at me.

'I think he killed Mia and then transferred whatever he was feeling about her onto me,' I say. My voice shakes when I speak.

Liam pulls a face, a half-smirk. 'That's ridiculous,' he says, dismissively.

'Is it?' I ask him, hands on hips. 'We're being stalked,' I tell him. 'Just like Mia and Will.'

Chapter Twenty-Four

Day Six

We stretch out on the choir pews behind the altar. Liam brings out the blankets and I lie down, my head pillowed on my hands, wrapped up in one of them. I'm guessing it must be past midnight.

Liam stays sitting upright beside me, rigid, gripping his knife in his hand. He hasn't said much more about my theory that the killer is on the island and that he's stalking us, but I know he's thinking about it.

'With any luck he'll think we've left,' Liam mutters now, and I can hear how hard he's trying to convince himself. I'm trying too, but I keep remembering the silhouette of the man standing above me on the landing, gun resting on his shoulder, the room filled with strips of meat and the NO TRESPASSERS sign written in blood.

Liam switches off the torch and I lie still, my hip aching from the hard bench, wondering how I'll ever fall asleep, with the cold and the wind howling, and with the knowledge of what is outside, hunting us.

I do sleep though. I must still be so exhausted from the swim, and from all that adrenaline coursing through my body, that I pass out.

When I wake up, watery sunlight is filtering through the stained-glass window above me, painting rainbows of colour onto the stone floor. I'm stiff as a board, aching all over, and there's a gnawing hunger in my belly. I glance at Liam, still sitting in the pew beside mine. He is staring up at the third panel in the stained-glass window: the Resurrection. With a blanket wrapped around his shoulders he looks like a supplicant monk from medieval times.

'Did you sleep?' I ask him, scrambling to a sitting position and stretching out my aching limbs.

He shakes his head. 'I wanted to stand guard, in case.'

He's been awake all night. He looks exhausted, frayed around the edges; his eyes are sunken and days of beard growth are darkening his cheeks.

'You were talking in your sleep,' he says, glancing my way.

'I was?' I say, surprised. 'I didn't have a nightmare, I don't think.'

'You were mumbling "Help",' Liam clarifies.

'I must have been dreaming about falling in the loch,'

I say, rubbing my face to try and wake up. Or maybe I was dreaming about being stuck on the island.

I reach for a wine bottle of water and take a sip. Feeling Liam's eyes on me I turn. He's staring at me with a strange look on his face.

'What is it?' I ask him.

He pulls something out of his pocket and holds it up to show me. It's my contraceptive and my anti-depressants. My heart sinks and a flutter of nerves hits me. I look back at his face. He looks devastated and hurt and for a moment I struggle to think of what to say.

'What are these?' he asks.

He already knows though. I can tell. 'I . . . I'm on the pill,' I admit to him with a shrug.

His jaw clenches and his shoulders slump. For a moment I think he's going to burst into tears.

'I'm sorry,' I tell him. 'I'm on anti-depressants and I didn't want to tell you. And I can't get pregnant if I'm on anti-depressants as it could be harmful to the baby.'

A frown line forms between Liam's eyes. 'When did you go to the doctor?' he asks.

I take a step towards him.

'Why didn't you tell me?' he asks. 'Discuss it with me?'

I can see he's hurt that I've kept a secret from him.

'I was embarrassed,' I tell him. I sit beside him and take his hand. 'I'm sorry.'

He doesn't respond.

'I won't be on the anti-depressants forever,' I re-assure him.

'Do I not make you happy?' he asks. 'Is that it?'

I shake my head vigorously and squeeze his hand. 'No, of course you do. So happy! I love you. It's not about you. It's because of my mum. But I'm getting better. I'm feeling better. I don't think I'll need to be on them for long. And then we can try for a baby.' I kiss his cheek. 'And let's just focus right now on getting off this island. We can talk about all this later.'

Liam nods.

'I love you,' he says. 'I just want you to be happy. Us to be happy. That's all.'

'I know,' I reassure him.

'You're not keeping any other secrets, are you?' he asks.

I shake my head. 'No, of course not.'

I feel a wash of shame and guilt come over me as he studies my face as though wondering if I'm lying to him. I've broken his trust and I know it'll take some work to regain it.

'I need to go outside,' I tell Liam.

He frowns at me and shakes his head. 'No. We've got to stay here, inside,' he says. 'It's not safe out there.' The whites of his eyes are gleaming, and he looks almost like a man possessed.

'I need the bathroom,' I say apologetically, glancing around at the chapel. It's not like I can go in here.

He scowls. 'OK,' he finally allows. 'But let's be quick.'

He gets up and heads over to the door. I notice that his limp seems more pronounced this morning, his face tightening sharply with pain, and that he's wincing whenever he puts the slightest pressure on the ball of his foot. The glass must have pushed deeper in; I wonder if it may even be infected. I should have brought the first aid kit with me, but we were in such a hurry to leave the cottage I didn't have a chance to think about it.

We move the pew out of the way of the door and then creep outside into the morning. It must be around nine o'clock, I guess, judging by the height of the sun. I hurry to a nearby bush and go to the loo and then Liam does the same

I forage quickly for food for the crow, crouching and digging among the graves with my bare hands, looking for grubs or insects.

'What are you doing?' Liam asks angrily.

'I'm getting some worms for the bird,' I tell him.

'Forget the bloody bird,' Liam hisses at me.

'It won't take a second,' I tell him, tearing at the earth, feeling the cold damp soil beneath my nails.

Liam grips my elbow and tries to pull me away, but I've just discovered a worm and I refuse to budge until I've tugged it out of its hole and caged it in my palm.

Liam drags me back inside, tutting with impatience

and muttering about the damn bird, and I bite my lip and glower at his back. It might be stupid to him, but it's important to me.

I deliver the worm up to the bird and she swallows my offering whole. I stroke her back and the bird ruffles her feathers in response. 'You need a name,' I tell her. 'How about Hathor?' I say, remembering the Egyptian god. It goes with my dog's name, Isis. 'Hathor was the goddess of women,' I tell the bird. She caws her approval. 'Hathor it is then,' I smile.

I fill her empty saucer with rainwater that has handily fallen through a hole in the roof and collected in the font, noticing that my engagement ring is caked in dirt. I brush the worst off, wishing I could scrub my hands or take a shower. I'm still so cold.

The memory of that bubble bath I took on the day we arrived makes me almost cry. I content myself with imagining the first bath I'll take when we get off the island. I close my eyes and let myself really picture it: the warm, soapy water, piled high with bubbles, my body entirely submerged. I might even pour myself a really large glass of wine to drink while I'm in the bath, medication be damned. The last few days have made me readjust my thinking on everything. I've had to remain in the present, not dwelling on the past. I've been forced to be active and to concentrate on survival, and that's pushed all the sadness and grief to one side.

I can make it through this. I will get off this island.

I have to; I've got so much to live for, so much I want to do with my life. I make a promise to myself here and now, that once I'm home I'll get back to work and I'll get back in touch with my friends, too. I'll even make new ones. I'll live up to all the potential my mum believed in, and which, until now, I always somewhat doubted. I'm never going to doubt my worth ever again, or waste another second of my life living in fear.

At the sound of a branch snapping outside, Liam and I both freeze. There's a flapping of wings as a flock of birds takes flight, then another cracking branch. 'What was that?' I whisper, looking at Liam in fright.

Liam turns his head to listen too. We hear it again. Movement. Footsteps perhaps. Someone is outside, walking through the graveyard. Liam tiptoes unsteadily towards the entrance. I pull on his arm to stop him and he turns to look at me.

'What are you doing?' I mouth in alarm.

He points at the door. I shake my head vehemently. He can't go outside. We need to stay in here. We need to hide. We have no idea what this stranger might do to us if we confront him. I look down at the switchblade in Liam's hand and feel a flutter of fear, but before I can argue with him, he pivots and keeps on towards the door.

My heart starts to race as I watch him squeeze past the pew. It would be much safer to stay hidden, but Liam's not that sort of man. He's not going to let this guy get away with what he's done, even if it means taking a risk. What good is a knife against a gun though? And Liam can barely walk. He definitely can't move with any stealth, or run. It won't be a fair fight.

'What about me?' I say, catching up to Liam at the door and taking hold of him once again by the arm. 'If something happens to you, then what will he do to me?'

He pauses, obviously not wanting to confront the thought.

'You promised you wouldn't let anything happen to me,' I whisper, tears stinging my eyes.

He looks anguished for a moment, but then he pulls his arm from my grip, kisses me on the cheek, and vanishes through the door.

Chapter Twenty-Five

I follow him, scanning the view in front of the chapel. The graveyard is empty, and I can't see any movement. There's no sign of the man. Liam's walked to the corner of the chapel's front side and is peering around it. I tiptoe up behind him. Just then another brace of birds erupts into the sky at the rear of the chapel.

'Stay here,' Liam says to me in a whisper, before taking off towards the movement as fast as he can manage on his bad foot.

I ignore him and keep after him, crouching low and trying not to step on any leaves or twigs. We reach a large stone cross covered in moss, its words faded by time, and we duck behind it. Liam glowers at me for tailing him but then peeks out from behind the cross.

'I see him!' he whispers excitedly.

I glance past him and see the man walking at a pace away from the chapel grounds, making in the direction of the barrow and the woods. I can't see his face as he's striding away from us, but his hood is down, revealing wisps of dark hair. He must be about six foot or so and is and of average build.

'He doesn't have his gun on him,' Liam whispers to me.

I look at the man's hands, swinging by his sides. Liam's right; the man's unarmed. He isn't carrying anything in his hands, at least. We watch him stride into the woods and then disappear from sight. Liam makes to go after him, but I snatch his sleeve and yank him back. 'Where are you going?' I ask.

'He doesn't have his gun!' Liam repeats. 'I could take him.'

I raise my eyebrows and widen my eyes in alarm. 'Don't be stupid. It's too dangerous.'

Liam scowls at me, his mouth pursing tight. He glances after the man, weighing it up.

'We don't know if he might have another weapon,' I whisper, almost frantic now. 'And besides, you can barely walk!'

Liam's shoulders slump. 'You're right,' he concedes. His eyes shift as he contemplates his next move. He glances at me, an idea forming, his expression brightening. 'Let's go to the castle while he's gone and find the gun. He must have left it there.'

I hesitate, not liking the idea one bit. 'What if he comes back and finds us there?'

'We'll have the gun,' Liam answers with a shrug. 'Come on.' He's already moving off in the direction of the castle, at a halting pace thanks to his limp.

I glance back once more over my shoulder, worried.

'He's heading for the cliffs,' Liam reassures me, gesturing for me to follow. 'He's probably looking for us. The last place he'll look is the castle.'

If he was looking for us, though, wouldn't he have brought the gun with him? And surely he would have looked inside the chapel – the most obvious place for anyone to hide. Maybe he's discovered his boat is missing and he's already been to the cottage and found us gone. There's a chance that he really thinks we've left. In which case, we should keep hiding. If we steal his gun, then he'll know for sure we're still here.

I rush to catch Liam up and then I pull him to a stop behind a tree. 'I don't think we should take the gun,' I say.

'Why not?' he asks.

'Because then he'll know we didn't escape, that we're still on the island. Right now, there's a chance he knows about the boat and thinks we're gone.'

'I don't care,' Liam says defiantly. 'We'll have the gun. I'd like to see him try stalking us then.' I see then that this is about Liam wanting to get revenge. It's not about keeping us safe at all. He doesn't want the gun to defend us, he wants to use it to confront the man.

Before I can argue with him though he's off again. I sigh and chase after him, knowing that I won't be able to convince him to give up the idea.

Despite his injury he keeps up a pace, never once complaining even though it's obvious he's in pain and can't put weight on his injured foot. We arrive at the clearing in front of the castle out of breath and sweating and rush towards the cellar entrance with its frightening message warning us not to trespass. I try not to focus on it, even though the letters have now dried to a dull brown colour, confirming my earlier suspicion that it was written in blood.

Liam pulls out the torch and lights the way on the now familiar route through the cellar. Once in the downstairs servants' area we both turn our heads to stare into the room where the meat was hanging the other day, only to see that even more strips have joined the others and blood has pooled and congealed on the stone floor. I can see now, with the luxury of slightly less panic, that the meat is rabbit. There are several skins stretched taut on the table. He must be catching them with traps and skinning them, maybe eating them too.

For the first time, I also notice the rusting hunting equipment hanging on the wall. Before I only noted the savage-looking hooks and the strips of bloody flesh, but now I spot the rusting jaws of an ancient-looking gin trap, the kind of thing that looks like it could catch a buffalo, it's so big. What on earth was that used for? Maybe once upon a time there were wild boar on the island. There are also smaller wire snares and a range of contraptions with serrated teeth, probably used to catch foxes or ferrets. Blood roars in my ears. What are we doing here?

We keep going, and I'm sickeningly aware that at any moment our pursuer could return to the castle. He might only be minutes behind us. There's no time to dawdle. We make our way up the servants' staircase and along the hallway towards the bedroom where he's set up his campsite. Liam is panting hard and sweating by the time we reach it, and he has to lean on me.

The room looks much the same as before, except all his belongings have been repacked into his bag and the pile of trash in the corner of the room has grown. Immediately my gaze lands on the stash of pot noodles and the little camping stove. Liam's does too. 'See if there's any food we can take,' he tells me.

I rush over and start rummaging through the supplies. There's a box of granola bars and a few packets of instant noodles, but we'd need the stove to cook the noodles and I'm not sure we should take it. I'm not sure we should take anything, but I shove the breakfast bars into my pocket, half of me wishing I could open one and stuff it in my mouth but knowing there's no time even for that.

Liam is frantically hunting through the man's things. 'Where's the gun?' he mutters angrily.

I glance around and spot it on the other side of the room, sitting on the broken mantelpiece. 'There,' I say, pointing. I can't quite believe the man has left the gun here unmanned. I suppose it's confirmation that he thinks we've left the island.

Liam strides over and snatches it up. 'Grab those shells,' he says to me as he checks if the gun is loaded.

I look at the box he's pointing to and stoop down to pick it up. It's lying among a pile of empty shotgun shells beside the bed. I hesitate for a moment; I still don't think it's a good idea. We should leave the gun, but I don't argue – it's too late for that. I pocket a handful of the red cartridges and stand up.

'OK,' says Liam. 'Let's get out of here.'

I don't need any urging. We've already been here far too long; he could be back any moment. Gripping the gun in one hand and leaning on me, Liam leads us back out of the castle. The whole way back down the stairs my heart races, pounding in my ears, and I'm terrified we'll run into him. Every corner we turn I expect him to be there, but we're lucky. We manage to make it all the way to the cellar and then we're outside and making for the treeline.

Chapter Twenty-Six

Once in the woods we stop for breath. Liam is pale and sweating profusely: it's pouring down his face, and his T-shirt is sticking to him at the collar. He leans against a tree, breathing shallowly, resting his weight on his good foot.

'Does it hurt a lot?' I ask.

He grimaces in answer and waves me off, then takes a deep breath and we head off again. I let him lean on me for some of the way, which slows our pace.

Back at the chapel Liam collapses down on one of the pews, exhausted and panting rapidly, then I move the other pew into place on my own, barricading the door. When I'm done, I sit down and tear into one of the granola bars that I stole from the stash at the castle, handing another to Liam. My stomach growls and I recognize the stirrings of a long-lost appetite, like a beast coming out of hibernation after winter and needing to replenish everything it's lost. Liam however sets the granola bar aside without so much as a bite. 'Aren't you hungry?' I ask him.

He shakes his head. He looks like death warmed up, as my mum would say. I place a hand to his forehead. He's hot. 'You've got a fever,' I tell him.

'Where are those shotgun shells?' he asks, ignoring me and pulling the gun into his lap.

I dig the cartridges out of my jacket pocket and watch him load the shotgun with two of them.

He turns to face the door to the chapel, his face a mask of stone, aiming the gun as though ready to pull the trigger on anyone who steps foot inside.

'Promise you won't kill him?' I plead.

Liam raises an eyebrow in my direction but doesn't take his eye off the door. He lifts his arm and wipes the moisture from his brow.

We spend the next several hours in silence. Liam doesn't once take his eyes off the door in all that time, though I start to see his eyelids drooping when the midday sun begins to warm the interior of the chapel. 'Why don't I take over?' I say to him after his eyelids flutter closed for the third time. 'You need to sleep.'

Liam blinks furiously as though trying to chase the exhaustion away but finally he agrees. 'Wake me up in an hour,' he tells me, moving to stretch out along the bench. 'And don't take your eyes off the door,' he warns.

I nod. 'Do you want to give me the gun?' I ask.

He shakes his head and pulls a face. 'No,' he says. 'You don't know how to use it. You might shoot yourself in the foot. If you hear anything wake me up, OK?'

I nod, and with that he limps off towards the pews at the back of the chapel where the blankets are. I watch him lie down gingerly and bundle a blanket beneath his head. He keeps the gun on the ground right beside him. I glance at the axe, which Liam left by the font, and then, after a beat, I go and pick it up, hefting it in my hands, wondering if I'd ever actually be able to use it as a weapon. I can't imagine myself swinging it at anyone. Still, I carry it over to the pew where Liam was sitting before and perch on the end, staring at the door, waiting, and trying to figure out how I ended up being this man's target.

Am I right about the connection between Mia and me? Is it our similarity that drew him to me? Do I remind him of her? Am I his next angel? Is he a religious fanatic, or does he just enjoy the power that comes from selecting someone to be his next victim? Does he like the control that comes from knowing someone's life is in his hands? What does he want from me? Does he really believe I can save him or offer him some kind of salvation? I want to tell him that there's no salvation or redemption for someone like him. He's not a man but a monster. I remember the word carved in the window. Devil. He is a devil. He knows it. And maybe that's why he thinks an angel can save him. But a devil can't be saved.

I wish I understood why he's chosen me. Did I do something to attract it? I think about what Liam told me earlier, about Mia and Will and how he murdered them, but not before torturing Will. That he's capable of something so horrific and evil fills me with paralysing dread. I stare up at the stained-glass window and think of the monks who probably hid in a chapel built on this very site, terrified for their lives as Vikings rampaged and pillaged. Did they pray as they were preyed upon? Tears slide down my cheeks and I quickly wipe them away.

I picture the man returning to his hideout in the castle and discovering his gun missing. What will he do? Will he immediately come looking for it? Or will he be cautious? I would, knowing we were armed now. But who knows? It might just infuriate him further. He might bide his time and wait until dark. Or he might be outside right now, stalking us.

Perhaps he knows we're in here and he's watching from a perch somewhere, waiting until we leave before he attacks? I stare at the door, expecting it to fly open and trying to imagine what I'll do. My fingers grip the axe handle and I swallow, trying to ignore the way my gut is twisting with anxiety.

I curse at not knowing the time. I don't know if minutes are passing or whole hours. Perhaps it's just seconds.

I get up, leaving the axe on the pew, and tend to the bird, wanting to distract myself from the dread of waiting for what's coming next. Her broken wing seems to be setting well now. She's trying to flap it. It seems I was right in my suspicion that it was just a simple fracture, and all it needed was a few days of splinting to put it right. 'Not yet, Hathor,' I tell her. I'll give it another day just in case.

Hathor is content to sit on my lap and for me to stroke her feathers. I feed her some granola bar and she bumps her head into my palm as though thanking me. I keep stroking her, finding it soothing.

After twenty minutes I check on Liam, tiptoeing closer, and discover he's passed out. His skin looks flushed and his breathing is heavy and laboured. I hover over him wondering what to do, glancing warily at the gun lying on the ground. I wish we hadn't taken it but it's too late now.

In the end I let him sleep for several hours, finally waking him up when dusk is falling. He opens his eyes, groggy and disorientated, and then slowly sits up. He blinks at the purplish light and then looks at me quizzically. 'What time is it?' he asks.

I shrug. 'I don't know.'

He checks his watch, but the face is smashed, and I wonder when it broke. Probably when we fell in the loch. 'Damn,' he says. 'Why didn't you wake me?'

'You needed sleep,' I tell him. 'How are you feeling?' I touch his forehead again. His fever is worse.

He rubs his eyes, squinting as though he has a headache and I hurry to offer him water.

'Here, drink. You look dehydrated.'

He takes the bottle and swallows half.

I offer him a granola bar too, but he shakes his head. He rubs his tired eyes some more, the dark shadows beneath them standing out like bruises, then he stands up, leaning his weight on his good foot. He takes a step and his knee buckles.

'Damn it,' he mutters angrily.

'I think your foot might be infected,' I say to him. 'Let me check.'

Liam reluctantly allows me to undo his shoe and peel off his sock. He lets out a cry as I lift his foot into my lap to examine it. I'm right. It is infected, the skin bright red and swollen around the site of the splinter. I don't know how it's gotten so infected so fast; he must have got dirt in it. I don't have any bandages or antiseptic with me so there's not much I can do. 'I can go back to the cottage and get the first aid kit?' I suggest.

He shakes his head. 'You're not going out there. Not by yourself. It's far too dangerous.'

I look at his foot. 'It's only going to get worse.'

'I'm fine,' he says, reaching to put his sock back on, but he's frowning, and I know he's worried.

I don't know what to say. I'm not sure how much antiseptic would help anyway. He probably needs antibiotics, and there aren't any of those anywhere on the island. We need to get to the mainland for that. Liam pulls on his boot, huffing hard as he bends to tie it. He stands afterwards and stumbles towards the axe, sitting on the pew where I left it. I watch him as he swings it up over his head, wondering what the hell he's doing, but then he brings it slamming down with an almighty crash into the spot I had been sitting in.

'What are you doing?' I ask, cringing at the splintering noise and worrying that it might advertise our location to the man, which would entirely defy the entire point of us hiding here. Having said that, he must have discovered we've taken the gun by now and I'm sure he'll come looking at some point.

'Firewood,' Liam replies, as the axe head buries itself again into the side of the pew with a loud thwack. 'I'm going to build a bonfire on the cliffs. We need to signal the mainland. It's our only option.'

'We only have one more night to get through,' I tell him.

'And who knows what he might have planned,' Liam fires back. 'We have to get off this island and we have to get off now.'

Chapter Twenty-Seven

Liam makes short work of the pew, turning it into a pile of splintered fragments. He's pouring with sweat, stripped down to just a T-shirt and jeans, even though evening has fallen and it's growing cooler by the minute.

I jump with every blow as it crashes into the hard wood, covering my ears, terrified that the noise is loud enough to be heard on the other side of the island and imagining the man out there, searching for us, hearing us and coming running.

When he's finished, Liam starts stuffing some of the wood into his emptied-out bag. 'We'll carry the rest,' he says to me, pausing only to wipe the perspiration from his brow.

I look up at the stained-glass window. It's growing

darker by the minute. We gather the wood in our arms. Liam straps the gun over his shoulder with a strip of blanket that he's fashioned into a makeshift strap, staggers to his feet and together we exit the chapel. It's inky dusk outside now, the sky a deep mauve, and the wind is picking up and starting to howl, shaking the branches of the trees as we pass beneath them and making them creak. I look around in frightened anticipation, barely able to breathe. I feel eyes on me, somewhere out there in the dark. We're being stalked. I know it. But I can't see anything. I can just feel it, a prickling sensation crawling up my spine, sending goosebumps rippling down my arms and legs and stuffing up my mouth with a silent sob.

Liam is still limping; every single footstep makes him wince and hiss between clenched teeth with pain. He carries the bag of wood and my arms are loaded with another heavy pile and we make slow and unsteady progress, stopping every few feet for Liam to catch his breath. Every crack of a branch makes me spin around in alarm, imagining I'm seeing people standing between the trees.

We make our way down into a gully of the woods, and Liam leads us over the creek and up finally the last stretch towards the top of the cliff. Halfway up the steady incline I feel the first splatter of rain on my face. I cast a glance up at the sky and more raindrops land on my eyelashes and cheeks.

'Let's hurry,' Liam says, struggling to limp faster.

We make it to the top of the cliff as darkness really starts to fall. Panting, I throw down the wood and Liam kneels and takes his load out of the bag. I can barely make him out now in the fuzzy light, as he starts to build a tepee, carefully arranging the pieces of wood so they'll catch and burn brightly. Once he's finished, the bonfire he's made is about three feet high.

I glance out across the loch, shielding my eyes with my hands against the rain. In the far distance I can just make out a few glowing amber lights that must be Arduaine, the place that we took the boat over from. What are the chances someone will see the fire from all the way over there? And then what are the chances they will think it's anything other than a bonfire? Why would they assume it's a signal fire or an SOS?

The rain falls heavier, the wind whipping it into my face. I start to shiver and look at the stack of wood and the bonfire Liam has built. It's getting wet.

Liam is searching through his bag, frantically. 'Where are the firelighters?' he asks.

'I don't know. I thought you had them.'

He shakes his head. 'I put them in here,' he says, gesturing at the bag and then hunting through his pockets. 'At least I thought I did. Damn. Shit.' He swears loudly and then, unable to find them, he gives up and pulls a cigarette lighter out of his pocket. He clicks it and a tiny flame appears which he cups his hand around to protect from the wind. He tries to set it to the wood pile but the wood refuses to light. It's too wet.

Cursing some more, Liam pockets the lighter and rummages again through the bag. He pulls out the map of the island and I wonder for a moment what he's doing but then he sets the lighter to the corner of it and the map bursts into flame. Quickly, Liam shoves the flaming paper into the centre of the bonfire; he fans the flames desperately as I stand huddling close in order to feel the meagre heat.

Eventually the map catches on a piece of dryer tinder inside the stacked tepee and ignites. It's a feeble fire though, coughing out smoke and hissing in protest, the rain doing its best to fight it into submission. I glance once more out across the Loch toward Arduaine. I imagine one of the faint pinpricks of light is the pub – but no one will be out in this weather, so what are the chances they'll notice this tiny dot of fire in the distance on Shura?

I keep the thought to myself; Liam has not yet given up hope. He keeps fanning, trying to protect the flames by using his coat to shield it as best he can from the driving rain. It's a losing battle though and eventually the fire splutters out and dies.

Liam drops his arms to his sides and stares out across the water as if hoping he'll see the lights of a boat heading our way, a sign of rescue on the horizon. We're both drenched through now; my jeans are sodden and sticking to my skin and my feet are numb. The rain feels like needles being flung into my eyes. Thunder booms overhead, followed almost immediately by lightning striking the ground not twenty feet from where we're standing. I scream but it's cancelled out by another crack of thunder.

'Let's go,' Liam says, shouting to be heard over the storm.

The moon is invisible, offering not the faintest shred of light, and we make our way slowly down from the cliffs, slipping and sliding on now muddy paths, blinded by the rain, the thunder continuing to deafen us at regular intervals, shaking the earth. It feels as if the universe is a raging beast, opening its jaws and tearing into to the earth.

I am almost as frozen cold as I was when we fell in the loch. We trudge through the unrelenting rain until we reach the wood, Liam clutching on to me for balance. I almost stumble and fall several times and Liam swears under his breath, no longer able to hold in his frustration and pain. I try to gather my bearings and orient myself, despite the darkness and storm.

'So much for summer in Scotland,' I mumble to myself. Liam doesn't hear as my words are drowned out by yet another sonic boom of thunder rolling overhead and a flash of lightning momentarily lighting up our surroundings. I jerk on Liam's arm and pull him to a stop. He looks in the direction that I'm pointing in. I saw something moving in the wood, heading in our direction, but now I can't see anything at all. We've been plunged back into the shroud-like dark. I have the torch in my pocket, but I don't want to turn it on, in case it gives our position away.

A few seconds later another crackle of lightning illuminates the wood, and I spot him again, lit up brilliantly just for an instant. His face is ghostly white and he's wearing a black hood and standing not fifty feet from us. I'm not sure if he's seen us as we're shielded partly behind a huge fir tree. Liam's seen him too.

'He must have seen the fire,' Liam whispers to me through a clenched jaw.

Leaning his weight on his one good leg, he unstraps the shotgun and hefts it to his shoulder.

But we're swimming in darkness again, and the rain is torrential so it's hard to make anything out or to hear anything. We wait, battered by the elements and poised for an attack. Liam grips the gun tightly, rainwater cascading down his face in waterfalls.

The next moment a fork of lightning spears a tree not far ahead of us, and it's as though we're standing beneath floodlights.

I see him at once. He's standing still, staring right at us. Liam sees him at the exact same time. He swings the shotgun in his direction and pulls the trigger, but nothing happens; there's no blast, no recoil. I look at

Liam. He takes aim again, trying to focus through the rain, but the man has dissolved into the black. Liam fires anyway, into the void, but once again there's no bang, no crack of a bullet. The gun isn't working.

Liam snaps open the gun's twin barrels. He tips the shells out. 'Give me another shell,' he shouts.

I put my hands in my pockets but as I do, I catch a streak of movement coming our way.

'Liam!' I scream.

Liam turns to where I'm pointing, bringing the gun up and swinging it over his shoulder, ready to use it as a club. But nothing happens. The darkness is full. The ghostly echoes of the lightning are burned on my retina and I blink several times, but I feel as though I've been blinded. 'He was right there,' I say to Liam. 'Right in front of us. About fifteen feet away.'

I stand frozen, clinging to the oak tree beside me as though it's a rocky outcropping in a storm-tossed sea – the only thing keeping me from drowning. I don't dare move an inch, but I sense Liam stepping away from me and moving forwards. I try to reach for him, but my hand clutches at air.

'Liam?' I whisper, struggling to make my voice loud enough to be heard over the wind.

Liam doesn't answer. But then I hear a godawful, ear-splitting scream of agony as though someone is being eaten alive by wild beasts. I pull out the torch from my pocket, no longer caring about giving myself away, and with fumbling fingers I switch it on and swing it in a wide arc around the wood.

The beam lands on Liam. He's on the ground and, at first, I can't quite make out why – did he fall? But then I see that his leg is caught in a huge gin trap – the same one we saw in the castle. It's snapped around his right calf. He's clutching at it in complete shock and is howling in horror and pain. I'm too frozen to respond. All I can do is stare at the bloody metal teeth eating through his flesh and the blood pooling around him and his stricken face, but then I lift the torch and shine it straight ahead, to where the person was standing not seconds ago.

And there they are, still standing in the exact same place, watching me across the distance: a ghost.

PART TWO

Chapter Twenty-Eight

Eight Months Earlier

Mia

It's the kind of Christmas Eve you only ever see on Christmas cards. Snow fell this morning, covering the fields all around, inches deep, blanketing everything in such a profound silence it feels like we're cocooned in a world of our own.

Will and I went out for a walk this afternoon. The hedgerows were crusted with snow as thick as royal icing, and the only splashes of colour came from the red holly berries, which looked like drops of blood scattered on top.

Now, as evening falls, Will stokes the fire and I arrange presents under the tree and hang two stockings from the fireplace, singing along to 'Last Christmas' by Wham!, not caring that I'm out of tune. Will's laughing and singing along with me, and I have to stop for a brief moment to recognise how perfect the moment is.

Will's family are all down south and he was on call over the holidays, so we decided to stay put and I'm glad about it. It feels special – magical even. It's our second Christmas together but last Christmas we'd only been dating for a month and Will went to his mum's for Christmas. When he found out I had no family other than a half-sister in Australia, he invited me to come with him; but I didn't feel like I could.

Now I look around at the blazing fire Will has set and the coloured lights flashing on the tree and I find myself grinning uncontrollably from ear to ear.

I never thought I would ever feel this way: so loved and so happy. And yet, here we are. Will's perfect: good-looking, kind, thoughtful. He's patient, not just with his patients, but with me. I sometimes worry he's too perfect and that he must be hiding something.

'I told you I had my Boy Scout badge,' Will says, happily admiring the fire he's made from the logs he cut earlier in the winter.

I moved in with him a few months ago, when we decided to take the next step in our relationship. Up until then I'd been living in a room that I'd been renting from an old couple who had a big farm and no family. In exchange for room and board I'd help them with chores, and I became a de facto carer. It's how I met Will, who was their GP. The cottage belongs to Will – he bought it when he moved here a few years ago – but I've come to think of it as mine too, because he has made sure that I feel it's my home as much as his. There are photos of my parents on the side alongside ones of Will and me, and, though I didn't have much to bring with me, we chose the new sofa together and I made the curtains.

I finish hanging Will's stocking, singing 'It's Beginning to Look a Lot Like Christmas'.

I am still working for a few people in the valley, as a carer mainly, but also nannying for a GP at the same surgery as Will. At the same time, I'm applying to do a master's in psychology; Will's encouraging me to pursue a career as a therapist.

I look at him and smile and notice that he's still on his knees in front of the fire. And he's holding something in his hand.

'Mia,' he says as my heart starts to race. 'I love you. Will you marry me?'

My mouth falls open; I blink as he opens the little box and I see the engagement ring inside. I look back at Will, whose expression is halfway between hope and fear.

All I can do is nod.

He stands up. 'Is that a yes?' he asks, looking nervous.

'Yes,' I finally manage to shriek as Will sweeps me into his arms. 'Yes.'

We're both beaming so widely our teeth clash when we kiss. 'I love you,' he says again. 'And I'm always going to love you.'

I laugh contentedly; five minutes ago, I thought that I couldn't possibly be any happier than I was in that moment, but now I'm realising I was wrong. 'I love you too,' I say, my arms looping around his neck.

Will stops kissing me only long enough to push the engagement ring onto my finger. I stare at it in astonishment and shake my head. For some reason I never thought this life was permanent. I thought of it as temporary, even I after I moved in with him. But now it's like I've been gifted a future: a life shared here in Cumbria, in this village among the lakes. We'll be happy. We'll have children. We'll grow old together. Even as I think it, I'm aware of a tiny spark igniting in my mind – the idea that nothing this good, nothing this perfect, can last. I try to smother it out, but it's taken hold now and I can't shake it off.

Will pulls me to the sofa and lays me down on it, curling beside me, cradling me in his arms and kissing me, and soon my worries melt away. I sit up, laughing and tug off my top; Will joins me, laughing too, and we strip in seconds, frantically tearing at each other's clothes and falling into each other's arms.

We're so caught up in making love and in our happiness that, at first, we don't hear Jet's growls, but after a while they become so loud and insistent that we break off from kissing and turn our head to look. Our dog is standing with her paws up at the window, a low rumble emanating from her throat.

'Jet,' I say. 'What are you growling at?'

The curtains aren't drawn and all we can see is a black square of nothingness; we live deep in the countryside, surrounded by fields, and our nearest neighbour is half a mile away down a rutted lane.

Jet's growl becomes even louder.

'It's probably a fox or something,' Will says. 'Jet, be quiet.'

He gets up and crosses to the window and I shiver, aware of my nakedness now he's not there to warm me.

Will draws the curtains but now Jet is barking, relentlessly and aggressively, which is unusual. She's a good guard dog, but otherwise mild-mannered, even though she sounds frightening, which is exactly what I was hoping for in a dog. I grab the blanket draped over the back of the sofa and wrap it around myself, feeling a sudden sense of foreboding.

Will pulls on his jeans, commando style, and then his sweater.

'Where are you going?' I ask him, unable to disguise the tremor in my voice.

He walks to the kitchen and Jet bounds after him, racing past him, still growling and barking. She bats her paws against the back door, impatient to be let out.

I stand up, my legs feeling shaky. 'No,' I say to Will. 'Don't let her out.'

Will looks at me with a frown. 'It's just an animal or something. She can chase it away and then she'll stop barking.'

I open my mouth to protest but Will is already unlocking the door. Before it's even partway open Jet is shoving herself between Will's legs and darting out into the dark.

My heart is beating rapidly, and I feel faint. I'm breathing fast, almost hyperventilating. I try to tell myself to calm down. Will's right; it's no doubt a fox, or maybe even a sheep, escaped from the neighbouring farm. It's happened before. I'm being silly. It's that old fear that happiness must always be paid for rearing its head again, and I just need to quash it back down.

Will waits at the back door, shivering in the freezing cold, hopping from bare foot to bare foot. We can hear Jet outside in the distance barking, but all of a sudden there's a whimper and then silence. I hurry over to Will and grip his arm, peering past him into the blackness. My fingers grip the blanket around my shoulders as the frigid air pierces through to my bare skin.

'Jet?' Will shouts. 'Jet, come here!'

'Jet!' I call, adding my voice to Will's.

But she doesn't respond or come running. Will exhales loudly and moves to pull on his boots, which are lying, muddy, by the back door. 'What are you doing?' I ask. 'Where are you going?' I still can't shake the gut feeling that something is very, very wrong.

'Outside,' he says, as though it's obvious. 'See where she's gone. She's probably got her head stuck in a burrow.'

I frown. It's not likely; the snow is so deep.

'Or maybe she's fallen in a ditch,' he offers. 'Silly dog.'

'Jet!' I shout again, hoping against hope she'll finally come running inside, excitably shaking off snow, but she doesn't appear. Damn dog.

Will grabs his jacket from the hook and pushes past me. I snatch for his arm and he turns to look at me with a quizzical smile, but when he sees my anxiety, he pauses and kisses my cheek. 'Don't worry. I'll be back in a sec.'

And with that he's gone, leaving me standing in the kitchen, wrapped in a blanket, still feeling the pressure of his lips and the scratch of his stubble against my cheek. I put a hand to my face and hold it there. The anxiety keeps buzzing within me, like a fly hovering over decomposing meat; I can't bat it away and with every second that passes without Will returning it just grows louder and louder until it's an incessant hum in my head. My stomach is tied in knots and even though I'm shivering from the cold I can't move from the back door, peering through the glass to see if I can spot Will outside in the dark.

Why isn't the outside light on? I wonder, blithely. It's a motion sensor security light. It should have come on when Jet raced outside, and when Will stepped into the yard too. That's odd.

The anxiety I'm feeling cranks up another notch. My fingers dig into my arms. Where is he? Where's Jet? I glance at the oven clock; he's been gone for ages.

I move across the kitchen towards the counter where

the knife block sits, but just then the back door opens, and I let out a gasp of relief as Will walks in.

'Oh, thank god!' I say, a warm smile spreading across my face. 'I was getting worried. Did you find—?' I break off, my smile fading.

Will's expression is blank; his eyes are wide and filled with terror. He stumbles inside the cottage, tripping over the doorstep. I look up and see, over his shoulder, the shadow of a man, his hood pulled to hide his face.

He's holding a knife to Will's neck, forcing him inside.

I draw a breath, my knees going weak, and stagger backwards as the man forces Will towards me, gripping him by the shoulder and moving the knife to point into his back. He kicks the door shut with his heel and then he turns to look at me.

'Merry Christmas,' he says.

Oh, dear god, no. My mind scrambles, thoughts dissolving into blankness, as I stare at the man I now recognise as Ethan. How is he here? How did he find me? He has a knife in his hand. My eyes flick from that to Will's face to Ethan.

'Hello, Mia,' he says, smiling that familiar smile, one muscle twitch away from being a grimace. 'Did you miss me?'

My mind is white fog; a distant primal urge to flee or to fight stirs in my gut but my body has entered a state of paralysis. I am floating outside of myself. A sluice gate opens, and adrenaline floods my veins, but all it does is make my heart pound violently, while gluing my feet to the floor and sealing my lips shut.

I blink hard, wishing him away, but he's still here when I open my eyes. *How* did he find me here? And what does he want? I fixate on the knife in his hand, wondering what he plans on doing with it. Will's face is ashen. His eyes are saucers and he's staring at me with a warning, urging me to do something. But what? He knows who Ethan is. He knows all about him. I told him everything – about how I'd married a man who fooled me into thinking he was a prince when really he was a cruel bastard who took pleasure in inflicting pain. I told him how he beat me, humiliated me, starved me, controlled me; until one day, after planning in secret for months, I escaped him.

It took me a long time to open up to Will, because back then I didn't think I'd ever trust anyone again. But perhaps, even though Will has seen and kissed my scars, he didn't quite realise what Ethan is capable of. And now, I see from the terror on his face that he has finally understood. His expression is enough to bring me out of my frozen state.

'What are you doing here?' I say, surprising myself with the strength in my voice. There's no trace of the terror I'm feeling.

I lock eyes with Ethan, trying to get a grip on the reins before I gallop off into a full panic. I need to think clearly. I need to stay calm. Where's my phone? I think it's in the living room.

My glance skitters over the kitchen counters and lands on the knife block, which is just too far out of reach. I contemplate turning and sprinting for the front door. It would be a risk to leave Will, but it's me Ethan wants, so I expect that if I ran, he would come after me. But then I realise I'm completely naked, barring the blanket wrapped around me. I'm not wearing shoes either. And where would I run to in the snow? I weigh everything up, but it's too much of a gamble.

'Let him go,' I say calmly to Ethan, nodding towards Will.

Ethan smirks at me then shakes his head. His gaze drifts down my body and his expression darkens with fury. I grip the covering tighter around myself and think back to Jet barking at the window. I feel sick; Ethan was there outside in the dark, watching Will and me make love.

Will winces sharply and my eyes fly to the knife. Ethan's dug it further into Will's back.

'Please—' I start to stay, then stop myself. If I beg he'll only see it as an invitation to hurt him more. That's what he does. When he used to beat me, the more I begged him to stop the more it would egg him on. It was only when I fell still and compliant that he'd cease.

'Come into the living room,' I say, finishing my sentence. 'We should talk.'

Will looks at me, flabbergasted. His mouth falls open in shock, but I ignore him, focusing only on Ethan and willing myself not to show even a sliver of fear. He feeds on it. Even if I am so terrified that I can feel the pressure of a hysterical scream building in my chest, I need to push it down and stay calm. I need to focus on getting us out of this situation that I've got us into. Ethan narrows his eyes at me, and I know he's wondering why the sudden shift; he's thrown by it.

I smile back at him, amazed at how easy it is to slip back into the role I played for years: the obedient, submissive wife. My teeth threaten to start chattering and I grit them to make it stop, the whole time keeping the smile fixed in place. I remind myself that I am not that person from three years ago. I left that version of me behind, slipping out of it like an old skin, ripping it off when I fled for a new life, and a new identity as far from Ethan as I could get. *And now I am a new, stronger, braver version of that old me*, I tell myself. I fought so hard – gave up so much – to break free of him, and I am not letting Ethan take this from me. He doesn't get to destroy this life too.

What does he want? I wonder, as he continues to eye me with suspicion. Does he want me back? Or is he only here to punish me? The punishment will come either way, I know, but if there's a chance he still has feelings for me then perhaps there's a way I can get us out of this. Perhaps I can convince him I'm sorry, beg him to forgive me, tell him that I've missed him. He'll still punish me but perhaps he won't hurt Will.

I remember Ethan's punishments and as I do my

resolve wavers and I'm not so sure I have it in me to go along with this. For a split second I contemplate the knife he's holding, and I imagine myself leaping for it, grabbing it, twisting it out of his hand and plunging it into his neck. But I know I wouldn't have a chance of success; he's bigger than me, stronger too. And what if Will got hurt in the process? If it was me here alone, I'd fight. Or would I?

Ethan finally nods. 'OK. Let's talk. That's why I'm here after all,' he tells me. 'Partly, at least. I've been wanting to talk to you for a very long time. But you were very hard to find, Mia.' His lips purse in anger.

I don't say anything, but I wonder how he found me. Did I make a mistake? Should I have changed my first name as well as my last? I kept it because I wanted to keep something — just one thing — of my old self. I changed my last name, moved hundreds of miles, cut my hair, dyed it brown, threw away every remnant of my old life: my family, friends, job, credit cards, driver's license, birth certificate, social media, my national insurance number — anything that could be used to trace me. My parents died when I was a teenager so it wasn't as hard as it might have been to walk away. I have one half-sister who lives in Australia and who thinks I'm missing, likely dead by suicide, which is the way I set it up to look, leaving a note to that effect.

All my friends — those that were left, which wasn't many — assume the same. The police do too. That was the price for my freedom. Though I was never completely free from fear; I always wondered if he'd believe that I was dead, or if he'd come looking for me.

As the months passed and I stopped glancing over my shoulder every moment and started to feel more secure that he hadn't been able to trace my circuitous escape, the pressure lifted, but the dread never completely went away. It was always there, like a shadow chasing me. I used to think all the time about this moment, wondering what would happen if he did track me down. But I never let myself imagine it in detail because I knew that if he found me, it would only mean one thing: he would kill me.

'How did you find me?' I ask, unable to bear it any longer.

Ethan smiles slyly. He loves any chance to show off what he considers to be his superior intelligence. 'You applied for a master's in psychology.'

I frown. How the hell does he know that?

'You put your undergrad degree on the application form. They followed up with the alumni department at Bristol to verify your degree,' he continues, smirking at my bewildered expression. 'The administrator there is a very helpful woman.'

My heart stutters. Such a stupid, awful mistake. How could I have been such an idiot? I look at Will, tears bubbling up. I wanted something and so I let myself believe enough time had passed and that the risk was so low that it was worth it. I could kick myself.

'Come on, move!' Ethan says, nodding towards the living room. 'You want to talk, let's talk.'

I nod but pause before I turn around, looking briefly at Will. He seems frozen, eyes still set wide, not sure what the hell to make of what's happening – or of my compliance. I try to silently communicate to him to go along with it and I pray he won't try to tackle Ethan, who is much stronger than he looks. But Will is not that kind of man: he's gentle; not a fighter, a communicator.

'Look,' he says now, turning towards Ethan. 'Why don't you put the knife down—'

'Shhh,' Ethan warns him with a savage look in his eye.

Will falls silent, and Ethan pushes him forward. We walk into the living room, me leading the way. I glance around for my phone, my eyes scanning my clothes which are scattered on the floor in front of the fire.

'Get dressed, you slut,' Ethan says to me, the words coming out with a spray of spittle that lands on my cheek.

Without looking at either him or Will I gather my clothes and turn my back, slipping on my underwear with shaking hands and then discarding the blanket and quickly pulling on my clothes. The whole time I am looking for my phone but I can't see it and the landline is in the kitchen, too far to reach.

'You've put on weight,' Ethan comments.

My face burns with fury and shame, and I hate myself

even more for letting him get to me. I worked so hard to get his voice out of my head – to purge the constant critiques which played on a loop even once I left him. After I escaped Ethan, I wanted to gorge myself on all the food he used to forbid me from eating – cakes and chocolate – and have second helpings of everything. I was emaciated then. Now, I'm normal weight and healthy.

When I'm dressed, I turn around to face him, straightening my shoulders and back.

'Come here,' he orders.

My defiance immediately falters. I walk slowly in his direction, heart thumping. 'Get the duct tape from my bag,' he tells me. His face is cold and hard, and his eyes flicker dangerously. He's enjoying this. He likes having power over me. He always did.

He tosses his bag to the floor and I kneel and unzip it, a whimper rising up my throat when I discover a roll of thick plastic bin liners, as well as two rolls of duct tape.

'Hurry up!' he snaps.

I glance up and see he's resting the knife against Will's throat and blood is beading along the edge of it. My stomach folds over on itself; I need to do something now, before it's too late. But what?

Ethan pushes Will into the armchair and then he forces me to duct tape him to it, overseeing everything to make sure it's tight enough, before placing a strip over Will's mouth, gagging him. I glance at Will, my bottom lip trembling. 'I'm sorry,' I mouth to him. He stares back in disbelief.

I lunge for the fire poker, my fingers closing around it. I turn, swinging at Ethan, but he grabs it, wrestles it from me, and tosses it aside. *Shit.* Very calmly I watch him turn back and jab the knife into Will's side, not all the way, but several inches.

Will lets out a muffled bellow of pain. I throw myself on Ethan, gripping his arm and trying to pull him away, but he seizes me by the throat, holding me at arm's length. I see that this is fuel to his fire, so I stop struggling and fall still. I know if I fight back, he will become more violent. I'll unleash the monster within.

He smiles at me, recognising his power to control me. I look at Will. Blood is seeping through his sweater and he's bent over, panting. Oh my god. How hurt is he? He looks up at me, pale-faced, tears in his eyes.

'Please,' I beg Ethan. 'Please don't hurt him.'

I hate myself for begging, but what else can I do?

Ethan ignores me and turns to Will. 'You know she's married to me?'

Will, still hunched over and gasping, glares up at Ethan. He knows I was married to Ethan, and he knows, too, that we never divorced. When Will proposed to me earlier he knew that our marriage was, on paper, impossible. He knows my identity, Mia Smith, isn't real; that my real name is Mia Watkins. He's the only person who does know the truth.

He asked me once, after I'd told him all about Ethan, why I never went to the police and reported him. Why I never told anyone. I explained that I had never told anyone about Ethan and what he did to me because he was a policeman. Who do you complain to when your husband is one of the people you're supposed to turn to for help? One of the people sworn to protect you and keep you safe? There is no one. But, truthfully, a part of me was also too ashamed. I tried once to get help; I called a domestic violence hotline. But Ethan had a tracker on my phone and the beating he gave me almost killed me.

Even if I'd gone to the police and they had listened to me, even if they'd arrested Ethan, and he'd been charged and refused bail and found guilty and sentenced to jail – all big ifs – I knew one day he'd find me and get revenge. I'd spend the rest of my life waiting for the axe to fall. And if the police didn't listen to me, if they didn't arrest him, didn't charge him or if he didn't get found guilty in a court of law, I knew I was as good as dead. So, I did the only thing I could; I fled.

'You know what the punishment is for adultery?' Ethan asks now, looking between us.

A sob is trapped in my throat, but I refuse to let it out.

'If a man be found lying with a woman married to an husband,' Ethan intones, 'then they shall both of them die, both the man that lay with the woman, and the woman: so shalt thou put away evil from Israel.' Ethan looks between Will and me. 'Deuteronomy chapter 22, verse 22.'

I wince. He's channelling his mother. He would only ever quote the Bible when he was about to unleash violence; just like she used to do to him.

'Punish me, not him,' I beg. 'He didn't know about you.'

Liam studies me with a piercing look. Can he tell I'm lying?

'The Romans, the Greeks, the ancient Celts,' he goes on, 'they all punished adultery the same way. Death for both parties.'

I draw in a shuddering breath and my knees threaten to give way. Will grunts something angrily through his gag.

Ethan turns to me. 'You betrayed me,' he says.

'I'm sorry,' I say again, hating myself for saying it.

'There's something else in the bag,' he tells me. 'Get it. It's a present.'

I scramble to my knees. Sobs rack my body as I look though the backpack again, and the tears I've been holding back begin slipping down my cheeks. I pull out a gift wrapped in Santa Claus paper.

'Open it,' Ethan instructs me.

It's a box. And inside the box is a glass angel. I hold it with shaking hands.

'It's for you,' he whispers. 'I bought it for you the

Christmas you disappeared. I've kept it all this time hoping I'd eventually be able to give it to you.'

I give a quivering smile in response, wiping away the tears with the back of my arm. Ethan used to call me his angel. He had some messed-up logic; his mother – a religious fanatic – raised him to believe he was no good; she convinced him that he had the devil inside him. She would beat him, lock him up in the basement, starve him.

'You've saved me,' he'd tell me. 'You're my angel.'

'It's beautiful,' I assure him now. 'Thank you.' I weigh it in my palm.

'Why did you run away?' he asks, and there's a plaintive note in his voice that surprises me. I spy a chink of light in the darkness, a way out of the nightmare, and I grab it with both hands.

'I'm sorry,' I say again, reaching out a hand, and touch his cheek, fighting revulsion. He doesn't pull away. Emboldened, I let my fingers trace his face and I try to gaze at him with adoration. He loves adoration, craves it. He needs to be worshipped.

'Forgive me?' I plead.

He narrows his eyes.

I repress a shudder. Every cell in my body is screaming in panic.

'Maybe we can work things out,' I add with forced enthusiasm. 'You and me. We can be together again if you want. I'll go with you now.' I let my hand linger on his cheek and I stare at him with what I hope is tenderness, though inside I'm a quivering mess. 'I promise you I'll do whatever you want from now on. I'll be good. I'll obey. I'll be the perfect wife.'

Ethan's eyes widen just a little. Is he buying it? His hand comes up and I flinch, but all he does is stroke my hair, gently, like I'm made of gossamer. Then suddenly he pushes me backwards, down onto the sofa so I'm lying on my side. He lies down beside me, spooning me, one arm wrapped snugly around my waist.

I hear a growling from Will but one look in his direction from Ethan and he falls silent again. Ethan strokes my hair some more and then he nuzzles my neck. His arms lock around me. I am rigid as stone; it's like being held by a scorpion, and I fully expect the sting to come at any second. But instead of a knife to the chest, he kisses me, first on my temple, and then on my cheek and then the back of my neck, and I'm not sure what's worse; the knife blade or his lips against my skin.

I squeeze my eyes shut and try not to let out a cry. He breathes in deeply, sighing, then kisses me just below the ear. 'It's too late,' he murmurs.

I'm still holding the angel. It's heavy like a paperweight. Ethan reaches for the knife on the arm of the chair. As he turns, I smash the angel into the side of his head. He falls off the sofa, yelling, glass shattering over him.

I leap across him, stretching for the knife that has flown across the room. Just as I get hold of it his hand closes around my ankle and I'm dragged down, slamming my chin into the floor, glass embedding in my feet.

Next thing I know he's on top of me. He smashes my head into the corner of the table.

He heaves me to a sitting position. 'That was silly,' he says.

Dazed, I fight the descending darkness.

★

Barefoot, I sprint through the snow, a burning in my lungs, a heaving pain in my chest. Sobs rack me as I run. I left Will; I left him behind. The image of Ethan bringing the knife up and plunging it down brings a fresh wail up my throat. I hack up tears and snot as I move, stumbling and bleeding into the snow. I'm dizzy from hitting my head.

Blood screams in my ears. I sob Will's name. I need to get help. I need to save him. Maybe it's still possible. That's what's driving me on. That's what gave me the strength to stagger up and dive for the back door. It's what keeps me running now, ignoring the pain in my head and the stinging fire in my feet.

A louder roar suddenly fills my ears and for a moment I think it's someone coming to help, but then I glance over my shoulder and see two bright white lights heading towards me.

He's in a car. He's following me! Shit. I look left and

right trying to find an escape, but impenetrable hedges form barriers on both sides of the narrow lane. There's nowhere to run, nowhere to hide.

I press on, slipping in the snow, picking myself up. I look back over my shoulder as I run. He's gaining on me – the headlights are bearing down, dazzling me.

I dart left and hear the engine rev, getting louder and louder until it feels as if it's on top of me, and then pain explodes through my body. It's like being hit by lightning, and it forks down my limbs, splintering bone and burning flesh as I'm tossed into the air like a leaf. I hang suspended for what feels like eternity, before I land with a soft thud in the snow.

Brilliant white light fades to black.

★

A weight lands on my chest and I gasp for air, breathing in a mouthful of dirt. Pain sears through me. My body feels broken, each new breath sending shockwaves of agony down each limb, and my head throbs. I try to open my eyes but there's only a hazy darkness and one eye feels glued shut. Memories jostle sharply but I can't seem to grab hold of any of them. All I can hear are screams, but I don't know where they're coming from. It takes me a while to figure out they're my own.

Where am I? Sensations help me to remember: the

wet cold seeping into my bones is snow; that starchy scratchiness under my finger is a leaf; the smell in my nostrils is earth and leaves and the crisp frost of winter; that taste in my mouth is dirt and something else – blood.

The memory carves its way into my consciousness, slowly, painfully and meeting huge resistance. Will.

A sob rises up in my chest, the pressure of it building. When I let it out the pain ratchets to another level and blackness, comforting as a blanket, descends.

I don't know how long I'm unconscious for but when I wake the pain is still there, duller in some places and sharper in others. My hands, feet, and face are numb. My head pounds, and my chest feels as if a rock is pressing down on it; but it's my arm that hurts the most, burning as though it's on fire.

Will. The memory is sharper now. I see his face, the look of terror in his eyes, the awful frustration as he tried to wrestle free of the tape I'd been forced to wrap around his legs and feet.

I did this to him. Another sob rises up, accompanied by a scream. I don't black out this time. I remember the blood – so much of it. I remember his head, hanging down limply on his chest, the dullness in his eyes. I remember running because Will told me to, and I thought I could get help for him. I failed. There was the car, coming after me, chasing me down the lane. I remember looking back, seeing the headlights glowing, gaining on me, blinding me, before I was hit from behind, thrown into the air.

What if it's not too late? What if Will is still alive? What if I can save him?

I crack open my eyes and see a sliver of white sky above me. I try to move my hand and though it hurts – every muscle alive with its own excruciating sensation – I'm relieved that this arm at least doesn't feel broken. When I try to move my other one, however, I almost pass out. My shoulder must be dislocated, or maybe the bone is fractured. It takes me several minutes to breathe through it, to fight off the dizziness, before I can move again.

Finally, I manage to clear away the leaves, snow and dirt covering my face, enough that I can make out tree branches overhead, caked in snow, and a white frosted hedgerow. I must be in a ditch somewhere along the side of the lane. A branch lies on top of me. That's the weight on my chest. I push on it with my one good arm, closing my eyes and thinking of Will when my strength ebbs, pushing me towards a cliff of blackness. Powdery snow lands on my face, startling me awake.

I push more on the branch and it shifts and suddenly I'm able to breathe again. I gasp, drawing in breath after breath, each one clearing away more of the fog so that the soreness of my body is blotted by the ache of recalling everything that Ethan did to Will, how he hurt him, how he made me watch as 'punishment'. I almost give up, but the thought that Will might still be alive, might still be being tortured, drives me on. With renewed determination I force myself to sit up, and then to slowly drag myself one-handed, out of the snow-filled ditch.

I crawl onto the road, and then collapse, lying face down in the mud-splattered slush, tears rolling down my cheeks, until I catch my breath and haul myself onward. I'm shivering hard and when I finally manage to make it from my knees, to my feet, swaying and dizzy with the effort, I look down and see my feet are ragged and blue from cold. My jeans are ripped and bloody and when I look at my left arm, I see it's hanging uselessly by my side. My whole body is shaking – from cold or from shock I don't know.

I try to take a step and my legs buckle. I drop down onto one knee, a bolt of pain shooting through me like electricity. My eyes water, blackness pressing in at the edges of my vision. Up ahead I can see a blizzard of lights. I try to get my bearings. It's the cottage. I need to get there. Will. He's waiting for me.

Step by step, trying to push the pain into a far part of my consciousness where I can ignore it, I make my way up the lane. My brain struggles to process any more than the thought that I have to make it home. I have to reach Will in time. But as I get closer, another thought pushes its way to the forefront; what if Ethan is still there? He must have left me in the ditch, thinking I was dead. He covered me over with branches. But what if he's returned to the cottage? Should I turn around and head in the other direction, the three quarters of a mile to my nearest neighbour?

I halt, in the middle of the lane, taking in the frozen sky and a single blackbird flying across it. There's nothing but hedgerows and fields; it's as if all the colour in the world has been bleached out. But then my eyes land on a sprig of holly with its green leaves and red berries. It's Christmas, I remember. Christmas morning.

I keep going, knowing it's my only option, but I approach the house carefully, biting my lips to stop from howling out my grief, suppressing it all, using it to fuel my progress. I have one aim, and that's saving Will.

I crouch down low and sneak, panting, almost faint from the effort of dragging myself this far, to the window of the living room. I peer in, but I can't see anything through the crack in the curtain. I press on to the back door. It opens. I walk inside and cock my head for a moment to listen. The house hums with silence. But what if Ethan's upstairs? I pick up a carving knife from the block in the kitchen and then heave myself forward, stumbling into the living room.

I pause in the doorway, my arm and the knife falling limp to my side, a scream tearing out of my throat like a monster and then I fall forwards, tumbling to my knees and sobbing.

'No . . . No . . . No . . .'

★

Hours later I wake, my cheek pressed to the floorboards in front of the fire. It's dark out. My head still throbs; everything hurts, the pain radiating from not one single source but dozens. I remember why and try to slip back into the comforting depths of unconsciousness, but it doesn't work; my mind keeps pushing images to the surface, urging me to wake up and face things.

I open my eyes. The scent of bleach is strong in my nostrils. I stare around the room taking it in. The tree lights flash brightly. The presents sit beneath it, still unwrapped. There is no sign of a crime – that's what brought me to my knees before. Will isn't here. Neither is the chair he was in, nor the rug his blood had leaked onto. Ethan has wiped the place clean. He must have come back here and bleached everything. He's done a thorough job, from the eye-watering smell of things. Of course he has. He's an expert in covering up his crimes.

Did he carry Will's body out to his truck? I wonder. Did he wrap him in bin liners and dig a shallow grave somewhere in a wood, or pile him into another ditch, like he did me?

Earlier I thought about calling the police, I even picked up the phone, but then I put it down again. What good are the police to me? Will is dead. I know he is. I think he was dead when I ran. There was so much blood. If I called the police and told them what happened, then what? If they even catch Ethan and charge him it will go to trial. And even if they lock him away for twenty-five years for murder, all it will be is a temporary reprieve. Eventually he'll get out and then he'll come after me again and he'll finish the job. And if they don't catch him, but he finds out that they're looking for him, he'll know I'm still alive, and I'll be looking over my shoulder for the rest of my life.

A strangled sob erupts out of me. Will. I let this happen to him. 'I'm sorry,' I wail. It's then that I notice the engagement ring has gone from my hand. Where did it go? I look around in panic, but I know in my heart that Ethan will have taken it when I was lying in the ditch, unconscious. The bastard. White-hot hatred courses through my veins, filling up the spaces that were only yesterday filled with love.

I lie there on the ground for I don't know how long, until I can't physically cry any longer, and then I drift in and out for an endless time. I wonder if I can lie here forever, if maybe eventually I'll die too. I think that's I want, but then something slowly starts to stir inside me, awakening with the next day's sunrise.

I sit up. I am not ready to die, I decide. I am not ready to let Ethan win.

It takes an enormous effort to heave myself to my feet and to drag myself into the kitchen, ignoring the searing pain in my shoulder that threatens to make me faint and the awful sharp stabbing in my feet from where the glass is still embedded, but I do it because I know I must. I let the hate flow freely, and I use it as fuel.

I manage, one-handed, to make a cup of tea and collapse down into one of the chairs at the kitchen table. I force myself to eat some leftover mince pies because my body craves fuel, choking them down without tasting them, and when I'm done, I haul myself upstairs and into the shower. I don't let myself cry any more. I don't let myself think about Will. I don't let the voice in my head try to talk me out of what I'm about to do or throw logic bombs at my plan. I push aside thoughts of Jet and what might have happened to her because if I let myself think about that on top of everything else, I'll go mad. I'll break down. I won't be able to do what I've decided. I've already made up my mind and now it's just a case of making it happen, figuring out my immediate next steps. I can't think about anything else right now.

I don't need to make an entire plan, I tell myself. Not for the moment. I just need to focus on getting out of here, making myself disappear again, making the whole world think I've been kidnapped and most likely murdered, and making Ethan believe I'm still lying in a shallow grave, dead. I've had practice, at least.

Refusing to meet my own eye in the mirror in case it causes me to waver any more, I examine my face for cuts, dispassionately noticing the gruesomeness of my injuries. I wipe at the congealed blood the shower failed to wash from my nose and ear and examine the deep laceration to my palm, the fierce stinging helping to focus me.

I have a swollen cheek, a long slash down my cheekbone which I think probably needs stitches and which will leave a scar, and one of my eyes is puffy – all from the beating he gave me before he made me watch as he tortured Will. I bandage my hand, put a plaster on the cut on my cheek and dab antiseptic on the grazes on my arms and legs, before beginning to dig the glass out of my feet. It's a long process and I'm shuddering and gritting my teeth so hard I think I might have cracked my jaw. But finally, I get the last piece out and am able to stand.

It takes an age to get dressed and I almost pass out from the pain. I can't lift my arm and so I have to make do with doing up one of Will's shirts without threading my arm through the sleeve, and then putting on a cardigan the same way.

Next, I move around the room. I can't carry much, only a small bag, so I throw in some clothes and then I pause by the bedside table looking at the photograph of Will and me, emotion choking me. *Focus*, I warn. You've got this far. You can keep going. But I can't leave the photograph, so I pack it in my bag. I need something to remind me of what I'm doing this for. I find my jewellery box is missing. The bastard. He took my engagement ring, as well as a bracelet and a Celtic cross necklace that Will gave me. I wish I'd killed him now when I had the chance, back when we were married. I wish I'd stabbed him in his sleep. Or poisoned him. A life sentence in prison would be better than this. But it's too late for regrets.

An hour later I'm ready. I've gone through the house, every room except the living room, trying to figure out what to leave and what to take. In the end I can't take much because I can only take what I can carry, and I can't carry much as I'm too weak. At the back door, I pause briefly. This is my home; but it was my home with Will, and I can't stay here now, not without him. I wonder when someone will come by to look for us. Probably tomorrow when Will doesn't show up at work. I wonder what they'll think has happened here. Will they open a missing persons enquiry? Or will they know a crime was committed? Or maybe they'll think we've packed our bags and left for some mysterious reason.

People will tell the police my name – Mia Smith – but of course there will be no official record of me. No identity or birth certificate. They'll try to figure out who I really am and they'll fail, because in my old life I'm already dead. They will study the house and wonder what happened, and they will never solve it because Ethan has covered his tracks. I'm the only witness and I am not coming forward. I am going to take the law into my own hands. I'll show him justice.

When I step outside the door, I must cast aside the old me and become someone new. I must harden my resolve and stick to my guns. There won't be any turning back. But it's easier the second time. And it's easier now I have something to avenge. I will make Ethan pay. But before I make him pay, I will make him suffer. I swear this to Will and to myself. And then I leave the house.

I plot my route carefully, making sure that no one will see me. Luckily, it's Boxing Day – at least I think it is – and no one will be out in this weather. I can cut across the fields, circumnavigate the village and walk the five miles to Kirkby Stephen, where I'll catch a bus to Kendal and then take a train from there. I need to disappear without trace.

I'll head north, to Scotland, I think. Then I'll go to the hospital and get my arm treated. I'll need to give them a fake name and make up a story; nothing too suspicious in case they think I've been the victim of domestic violence and call the police. I'll tell them I fell off a ladder taking down Christmas decorations, that I hit the edge of a table when I fell, which caused the cut on my cheek.

I've fled my life and started another before; I can do it again.

Chapter Twenty-Nine

Day Seven

Laura

The ghost in the wood is a woman. And even at this distance, with her hood up and the lashing rain creating black and white static between us, I can make out her blonde hair. It's Mia.

She strides towards Liam, laid out on the ground, a high-pitched keening sound escaping from his lips as he tries in vain to pull apart the steel jaws clamped around his leg, and she crouches down beside him.

He looks at her and his mouth falls open. He stops screaming and falls silent. It's not as though he's seeing a ghost, but like he's staring at an avenging angel.

'Hi, Ethan,' she says to him. 'You should have made sure I was dead.'

Chapter Thirty

Mia

Ethan stares up at me like he cannot fathom that I'm real, his expression racing between disbelief, confusion and horror.

'Surprised to see me?' I ask.

His face twists into a grimace of pain. 'How . . .?' he pants, clutching his leg.

'How am I alive?' I help him finish. 'A miracle. The police and the papers reported me and Will missing, as you know. They never found either of us,' I tell him. 'But in my case, that's because there was no body to be found.'

I notice then that one of his hands is scratching in the muddy leaves. He's searching for the shotgun, which he dropped when the trap snapped shut. I reach over and snatch it from his fingertips just as he grasps it. 'You won't be needing that,' I tell him with a smile.

He bangs his head back into the ground in frustration, letting out a roar.

'Does it hurt?' I ask him, nodding at his leg. 'It looks painful.'

'Help!' he gasps, looking around. 'Laura!'

The rain is lashing down, pasting his hair to his skull. I can feel the droplets sliding down the back of my coat and along my spine, but I don't feel cold; I feel invigorated, alive with victory. I am free, finally, after all these months, years even, of fear. To see him here, at my feet, no longer the predator but the prey, is what I've been dreaming of. It's why I've done everything that I've done.

Still clutching his leg, he wheezes and tries to look around for Laura.

'You killed the person I loved,' I tell him. 'You made him suffer and you made me watch. And then you stole his identity, you piece of shit.'

'Laura!' he shouts again, his voice hoarse with effort.

I glance up and look at Laura, standing paralysed against a tree, shining the torch on us. She's a silhouette and I can't make out her expression.

'Laura! Where are you?' Ethan is desperate now.

She doesn't move.

PART THREE

Chapter Thirty-One

Eight Months Earlier

Laura

The door dings and I look up. A man barges in, carrying a large black Labrador cross in his arms. I rush around the reception desk to help him. The poor dog looks to be in a terrible state: it's panting, its head is lolling, and one of its hind legs is bloody and mangled.

'What happened?' I ask as I lead him straight through into a back examination room.

'I think it was a hit by a car. No collar. I found it lying in an alley.'

After the vet looks the dog over and confirms she'll need an operation to reset the leg, the man offers to pay for it. I take him out into the waiting room to prepare the paperwork and when I look up from the desk, I find him staring at me in such a way that immediately

I feel flutters in my stomach. He's incredibly good-looking and my cheeks start to burn under the intensity of his gaze.

'Hi,' he says before pausing a moment. 'I'm Liam. William really, but I go by Liam.'

I swallow nervously, always a little flustered by male attention, but even more so when it comes from someone so attractive. 'I'm Laura,' I tell him.

'Nice to meet you, Laura.' He smiles and my heart flips. He's tall, dark, handsome. He looks like he's stepped straight out of the pages of one of my romance novels.

I start to fill in the paperwork, my skin still warm beneath his gaze. 'Dog's name?' I ask, glancing up at him.

He shrugs. 'How about Isis?' he suggests.

★

'Where did you grow up?' I ask Liam on our first date.

His gaze, so direct up until now, wanders for a moment. He looks around at the other customers and then at the table. 'Kent,' he says. 'A small town. I got out as soon as I could. But my roots are Scottish.'

'I'd love to visit Scotland,' I say, slightly wistfully. I'm addicted to the *Outlander* books, but I don't tell him that's the reason. 'Do you still have family in Kent?' I ask instead.

He shakes his head. 'No. My father disappeared when I was young,' he says. 'And my mother died eight years ago.'

'I'm sorry,' I tell him.

He shrugs. 'It's OK. We weren't very close. She was a difficult woman.'

I cock my head. It's an unusual way to describe a parent. He gives a tight smile.

'She must have been proud of you for being a detective.'

He shakes his head. 'Not really, no. Nothing would have made her proud. She was very religious. I could never do anything right. Black sheep and all that.'

'I'm sorry again,' I say, moved by his honesty.

He smiles at me, and it's such a lovely open smile that the butterflies in my stomach multiply. I feel almost giddy with excitement.

'What about you?' he asks. 'Any family? Ex-boyfriends I should know about?'

I pause, thinking about Paul, who I haven't heard from since Christmas Day. I've sent him several texts, but I think he's ghosting me. I shake my head. 'No,' I say. 'No boyfriend. Just my mum.'

'Good,' he answers with the smile that I'm growing to love.

★

'Oh, he's ever so lovely,' my mum giggles as we watch Liam mending the fence in the back yard. 'It's nice to have a man around here who's good with his hands.'

I bite my lip to suppress a smile.

'I'm amazed he's not married already,' my mum says.

'He was,' I tell her.

My mum looks at me, her expression eager. 'What happened?'

'I don't know much, only that she cheated on him. He won't even tell me her name. He says she broke his heart. He's still not quite over it, I don't think.' I bite my lip. The truth is, I sometimes catch Liam scowling and when I ask him what the matter is, he puts on a smile and tells me nothing is the matter. But one time he did admit that he sometimes thinks about his ex and that the pain of her betrayal still wounds him.

My mum must see the expression of doubt on my face as she pats my hand. 'Don't you worry. He loves you; I can tell.'

'Do you think?' I ask her. 'He hasn't said it.' But we've only been dating six weeks so it's not surprising. It's a bit early for declarations of love.

'The way he looks at you,' my mum says, sighing once more. 'It's so romantic. And look at those roses he bought you. It'll be a ring next, just you watch.'

I slap her hand away, laughing. 'Mum!' I giggle. 'We've only been going a few months. It's a bit soon for wedding bells.' But I can't stop grinning, touching the necklace and thinking of the dozen red roses back home in my kitchen that he bought me for Valentine's Day. He even bought my mum a single red rose too, much to her delight.

'Where are you going tonight?' my mum asks.

'We're staying in,' I tell her. 'I'm cooking.'

My mum's eyebrows raise. 'You're cooking?' she asks. 'Is that a good idea?'

'Don't be mean,' I laugh. 'Liam wanted a home-cooked meal. I've planned it all out.'

My mum still looks doubtful; she knows my cooking skills are sub-par.

Just then Liam walks in the back door. 'All done,' he says, setting the hammer down. 'Nice and secure now.'

'You are a love,' my mum tells him. 'Let me make you a cup of tea.'

'Thanks,' he answers. 'That'd be great.' He looks at me. 'Then we should get back.'

I nod, even though we only just got here twenty minutes ago, and I know my mum was looking forward to spending time with us.

'It's fine, pet,' she measures me, understandingly. 'Liam's a busy man.'

'What about that bit of carpet at the top of the stairs that you needed fixing?' I say.

'That can wait,' my mum says. 'Not to worry.'

I look at Liam with a pleading expression.

'I've got to install those security cameras,' he replies with an apologetic shrug.

'What cameras?' my mum asks.

'Oh,' says Liam, washing his hands at the sink. 'I'm putting up some cameras at Laura's place. You can never be too safe.'

I hand him a towel to dry his hands. He takes it, smiling at me. 'Got to take care of my girl,' he adds, putting his arm around me and kissing my cheek.

Later, when we're home, Liam gets to work on installing the cameras and then connecting them up to an app on his phone. 'This way,' he tells me. 'I'll be the first to know if anyone tries to break in.'

I lean on his arm. 'Thanks so much.'

He kisses my temple. 'You're welcome. What time's dinner?'

'Eight?' I say.

He frowns. 'Can we have it earlier?'

'Oh,' I say, 'um, sure. I'll just have to figure out the timings again but that's fine.' I hurry off to get started. The chicken needs time to marinade.

When I finally put the dinner in the oven, praying it turns out OK, Liam walks in, freshly showered. 'Here,' he says. 'I got you something else.'

I turn around and find him holding a gift-wrapped box. I take it, feeling overwhelmed. 'What is it?' I say. No one has ever given me so many gifts before. I feel bad as I only bought him a book of poetry by Robert Burns, which I'm worried he didn't really like.

'Open it,' he says.

I do and I find a beautiful black silk dress. 'It's gorgeous,' I exclaim.

'Try it on,' he tells me.

I nod and hurry towards the stairs, only to find him following me up them and into the bedroom. He obviously wants to watch.

My mouth opens and my throat goes dry. Little palpitations shake my heart. I'm very self-conscious about my body and, so far, Liam and I haven't been intimate, besides kissing. I'd been wondering if tonight was the night that we might go further, but I'm nervous. What if he doesn't like what he sees?

'Go on,' he encourages.

Anxious, I take a deep breath and pull off my jumper and then my T-shirt. Standing in my bra and jeans I glance at him. He's staring at me with naked desire and I feel the heat rise up my chest.

'Beautiful,' he says. 'Now the jeans.'

I undo them and step out of them, feeling awkward and on display. No one has ever asked me to take off my clothes in front of them.

'Now put the dress on,' he says.

I do as he asks. It clings to my hips and boobs. 'Will you do me up?' I ask, turning my back to him so he can pull up the zip.

He does, kissing my shoulder blade. I inhale sharply.

'It's a little tight,' he tells me, forcing the zip.

My cheeks flame.

'If you lose a few pounds, it will fit like a dream,' he tells me.

I nod, feeling ashamed. Does he find me unattractive? Am I overweight? I thought I was fairly normal. My chin wobbles and I tell myself not to cry.

He turns me around to face him and lifts my chin. 'I love you,' he says, kissing me.

My heart stills. My chin stops wobbling. Love? He's said the L word.

'I love you too,' I breathe.

He pulls back, tucking a loose strand of my hair behind my ear. 'My angel,' he says.

I laugh. I like being called that. 'Oh god!' I exclaim. 'The dinner!' I race for the door. I've forgotten all about the chicken.

By the time I pull it from the oven I can see it's overcooked. The sauce has all dried up and the skin is scorched. Damn. Liam comes to stand by my shoulder. 'That looks like a dog's dinner,' he says glumly.

'I'm sorry,' I say, almost bursting into tears.

He doesn't speak for a while and I can tell I've disappointed him. I turn to face him. 'I really am sorry. I wanted it to be perfect.'

He finally smiles, though it looks forced, and strokes my cheek. 'It doesn't matter. We can get takeaway.'

'Really?' I ask, still downhearted.

He nods. We order an Indian takeaway and eat it by candlelight. Liam's phone dings as I serve up. I glance at him, wondering if it's work, as he's often on call. 'It's the app,' he says. 'It lets me know if there's motion at the back door.'

I frown. 'What's at the back door?'

'The cat,' he answers.

'Tiger?' I ask, rushing to the back door. 'How did he get outside?' He's only three months old. He can't be let out yet and I'm strict about making sure he stays in.

I open the door and find my little orange cat, meowing pitifully in the cold. I scoop him up and bring him inside. 'How did he get out there?' I ask.

Liam shrugs, spooning curry into his mouth. 'Must have escaped somehow.'

I frown. 'My poor love,' I say, cuddling the cat against my body for warmth. 'He's freezing. I'm so glad he didn't run off.'

Tiger slinks around my chair, rubbing against my ankles. Liam looks at him with a scowl. I don't think he likes cats as much as dogs. And Tiger must sense it, as he's taken to spitting and arching his back whenever Liam comes too close.

After dinner, Liam takes me by the hand and, without a word, leads me upstairs. My breath catches. We're going to make love. I'm so nervous; I don't want to upset him.

'Do you want a shower?' he asks when we reach the bedroom.

I don't because I had one a few hours ago, but I nod anyway and take one, as he's obviously hinting that I should. When I come out in my dressing gown, I find Liam sitting on the edge of my bed. 'There you go,' he says with a smile. 'Lovely and clean. Come here.' He holds out his hand.

I step forward and he undoes the belt on my dressing gown so that it falls open. I swallow, flames rippling up my body as he runs his fingers across my stomach and hips and then kisses me just below my belly button. He lets out a groan. 'Are you mine?' he asks in a murmur.

I stroke his hair, holding his head against my stomach. 'Yes,' I say.

'You've saved me,' he murmurs. 'You know that?'

I hold his head against my stomach, feeling his grip on me tighten as he burrows his face against my belly and breathes in deep. 'I thought women would only betray me, but you're different. I'm so glad I found you.'

'I'm glad too,' I say, feeling my heart fill up with love.

He lays me down on the bed and then he takes off his clothes. He lies beside me and pushes my legs apart and I let out a gasp. It's all going a bit fast. I've never had a good sexual experience, and I was hoping with Liam things would be different. I want to tell him to wait, but the words are frozen on my tongue. It hurts when he pushes inside me, but I can tell he likes it. He's happy, and that's what counts.

'Is that good?' he asks.

I nod, tears prickling my eyes.

'Tell me,' he urges. 'Tell me how good it feels.'

I have no idea what I'm meant to say – I can't speak – but he's insistent. 'It's great,' I mumble, mortified.

Finally, it's over.

He rolls off and then he looks at me, shaking his head in wonder and grinning. I feel so relieved. He seems to have liked it. 'I love you,' he says.

'I love you too,' I answer, feeling a glow inside.

He gets up to use the bathroom and I lie there, feeling as though I'm being swallowed up by the mattress. I don't know what to think. Perhaps it's normal and I've just watched too many movies and read too many unrealistic romance novels. Maybe my body isn't made the right way. A little niggle in my mind wonders if I should tell him that I'd like to take it slower next time, but then the thought of actually coming out with the words makes me want to curl into a ball and die. I'd never be able to admit that to him. I wouldn't want to hurt his feelings; he's so sensitive to criticism, thanks to his mother.

When he comes back to bed, I smile at him and he stretches out beside me, pulling me against his chest. I close my eyes. At least this feels good. I feel safe and protected – and I'm loved! For the first time in my life.

'I was thinking,' Liam says. 'How about we move in together?'

I look up at him, astonished. My first thought is that it's a bit quick – we've only been dating a couple of months – but then I think about how much I love him.

'Yes,' I say, my heart bursting with happiness.

★

'Where were you?' Liam asks the moment I open the door.

'The bus was late,' I murmur, putting down my keys.

He scowls at me. 'No, it wasn't.'

'It was Sonia's birthday at work. They had a cake.'

He lifts his eyebrows.

'I didn't have any,' I assure him. 'I just stayed to sing happy birthday, then I came straight home.'

He narrows his eyes like he doesn't believe me. I know he has trust issues because of his ex, so I smile reassuringly and walk towards him, but my heart is thumping hard and I feel as if my voice is strangled. 'I wanted to get back to see you, but I didn't want to be rude.'

He softens a little. 'I don't like it when you're late. I worry.'

'I know. I'm sorry. Did you have a bad day at work?' I ask.

He nods gruffly.

'Do you want a massage?' I ask him.

Liam nods again, more enthusiastically this time.

I'm exhausted after a long day at work, but I shrug it off and lead him to the sofa. Massages often lead to sex and though I'm getting more used to being vocal in bed, which is what Liam likes, I'm still no better at actually telling him what I like. I feel like it's too late now and I don't want to make him feel inadequate. He likes praise and flattery and I'm happy to give him that. I want him to feel important to me, because he is, and honestly, it probably is good sex and the problem is likely with me.

When Liam came into work the first time, I saw the envy on my colleagues' faces. They couldn't believe how gorgeous he was. They think I'm lucky. Having seen my mum and dad fighting all the time, I know that no relationship is perfect. Everyone has to make compromises and if the only one I have to make is to offer kindness and to flatter him, then I can do that.

As I knead his knotted shoulders, I can feel him start to relax. I wonder if now might be the time to discuss the bills and how we'll pay rent. He hasn't offered yet to contribute, but I think it's just because he's so busy. He says he has a lot of cases to deal with, so I decide I'll wait and ask him in the morning.

But I don't ask him in the morning because he has to leave early, called in by his boss to work a domestic violence assault. 'The husband beat his wife half to death because she didn't have dinner on the table when he got home from work,' he tells me, downing his coffee in one swallow and grabbing his keys.

I breathe in deep, shuddering, and then kiss him goodbye. All day I can't stop thinking about the poor woman, and I hurry home after work, anxious to make sure our dinner is served up at six, just after Liam gets home. I laugh at myself as I pour pasta into the boiling water. It's not like Liam is violent, and he'd never hit me. He just gets hungry after a long day at work and likes to eat at the same time each evening.

He likes to taste the food and then score me, too, very occasionally offering up a handshake. I've bragged to my mum that I've now had two handshakes; something I'm very proud of. I'm becoming an even better cook than she is. She has asked when she might get to taste some of my cooking and judge for herself, but it's hard to find the time, what with work and Liam.

After I put the salmon in the oven, I notice that Tiger's saucers of milk and food are still full. *That's odd*, I think to myself. Usually when I get home from work, they're both empty. I realise I haven't seen him since I got home.

'Have you seen Tiger?' I ask Liam.

He shakes his head. 'No. When's dinner?'

'Soon,' I tell him. 'Tiger!'

I search the entire house for the cat; I look under

the beds and in the cupboard under the stairs and even in the kitchen cabinets, but there's no sign of him.

I open the back door and let out a scream. 'Oh my god!'

'What is it?' Liam says, rushing into the kitchen. He gasps when he sees what I'm looking at.

Tiger is lying outside on the doormat. His little ginger body is twisted, his neck broken. I drop to my knees, sobbing. 'What did this to him?' I ask in bewilderment, cradling his tiny body in my lap.

Liam kneels down beside me to examine the cat. 'I don't know,' he says, equally bewildered. 'It looks like an animal maybe. A fox?'

I glance around, tears running down my face. I've never seen a fox in the back garden. 'Poor Tiger,' I wail. 'How did he get out?' I shake my head.

Liam nods at the window. 'The window's open,' he says. 'He must have got up there and climbed out.'

I look up at the window over the sink. That's weird. I never open it; the latch sticks. 'I didn't open it,' I say.

Liam shrugs. I open my mouth to ask if he did, but then I shut it again. I don't want to accuse him. Maybe I'm mistaken and I did open it, and then forgot. And now poor Tiger is dead. I stroke his fur, bent over him and snivelling.

'Do you think there might be something on the app – from the camera – that would show us what killed him?'

Liam shakes his head. 'I doubt it. I'd have to go back through hours of footage as well. Come on,' he says, pulling me to my feet. He takes the cat from my hands and walks into the kitchen, pulling a plastic bag out of the drawer.

'What are you doing?' I ask him, shocked.

'Disposing of him.'

'You can't just throw him away,' I yelp, reaching for the cat.

Liam looks taken aback and seems about to ask why not, but he stops. 'Do you want to bury him?' he asks.

I nod, still crying.

'OK,' he says. 'I'll dig a hole in the back garden.'

'Thank you,' I mumble.

'Why don't you make a coffee for me while I do it?' he says.

I bite my lip and nod, tears still welling.

'Stop crying,' he tells me, looking annoyed. 'It's just a cat.'

'It's not just a cat,' I say, with a quiver in my voice. 'How can you say that? I loved him.'

Liam's eyes turn steely, but then he nods and forces a smile. He puts his spare arm around me. 'Of course. He wasn't just a cat. But we've got Isis.'

I know that's true, and I love Isis; in truth she's become more my dog than Liam's, as I'm the one who walks her and pets her and feeds her.

We bury the cat in the back garden, and Liam even

says a prayer aloud over the grave. I take his arm and we walk back inside.

Smoke wafts in the kitchen and the smoke alarm starts to blare. I forgot the salmon in the oven. Oh my god. I rush to take it out, bursting into tears again. When I place the blackened mess on the counter, Liam takes one look and then glares at me. 'Now what am I meant to eat?'

'Sorry,' I say. 'I'll make something else.' I'm flustered, unsure why he's so angry at me. It's hardly my fault I forgot; I was upset about Tiger. As I move around the kitchen, trying to rustle up a replacement meal, Liam yells at me. I can feel myself flinching under his words, thrown back to being a child listening to my father bellowing at my mother.

'You're useless,' he spits. 'I've been working hard all day.'

'So have I,' I mumble under my breath.

'What did you say?' he asks furiously, rounding on me.

I shake my head. 'Nothing. How about a pizza?' I pull one out of the freezer.

'My god,' he says, shaking his head. 'You care more about that damn cat than you do about me.'

'That's not true,' I argue, trying to placate him. 'I'm just tired and upset. I was trying to think of something that would be quick and easy, but I can make you whatever you like. How about spaghetti bolognese?' I ask, knowing it's one of his favourites.

'Fine,' he replies, begrudgingly.

Later, in bed, he holds me and kisses me and tells me he's just stressed, and he didn't mean to shout at me. I tell him I understand. I've come to learn that Liam is triggered whenever he feels love being withheld. I reassure him that I love him more than anyone in the world and I won't ever leave him or betray him, soothing him like an anxious child.

He doesn't believe me at first and when, exhausted by the long day and wanting to sleep, I ask him what I need to do to make him believe me, he tells me that he needs me to be more demonstrative. I thought that I was, but I agree to make more of an effort.

'You're always spending time with your mum, rather than me,' he complains.

'She's sick,' I tell him. 'You know she needs me. And I've hardly spent any time with her,' I say. 'I haven't seen her in almost two weeks.'

'I need you,' he argues.

I stroke his hair. 'I know,' I tell him. 'And I'm here for you. But my mum does need my help. I need to take her to her appointments. She can't go alone. And she's still getting over her last bout of chemo.'

Liam says nothing but I can hear his teeth clenching against each other. It's hard for him to understand the bond I have with my mum and he gets impatient whenever we have to go over there, and then he'll often make an excuse as to why we have to leave almost immediately. It's strange, because my mum loves him and she's kind to him. I haven't told her about the arguments we have, because I don't want her to worry. She's so excited by the thought I've found love and the prospect that we might get married, and I don't want to let her down or disappoint her. And I don't want to disappoint Liam either.

'I love you so much,' Liam whispers, clutching me tight. 'I don't ever want to lose you.'

'You won't,' I assure him, melting a little at the little boy lost in him and how much he obviously needs me.

Before we drift off to sleep, I think again about raising the issue of the rent and the bills, but it doesn't feel like the right time. I brought it up with him a few weeks ago, but before he could answer a text came in from work and he had to leave. He was gone for more than twenty-four hours – working a double shift – and when he came back, he brought me flowers and took me straight to bed.

*

The next day at work, I'm deep in thought, trying to puzzle out all the issues that Liam and I seem to be facing. I'm exhausted from so little sleep. Often I have to soothe his anxieties long into the night, and it's starting to have an impact on my health. I have dark circles under my eyes. Earlier Sonia joked that I must be having a lot of sex to be looking so tired, and I smiled wanly at her but wasn't able to reply.

I want to ask her advice on how to talk to Liam and whether it's normal for men to be so possessive and want to know where you are all the time. I don't have much of a frame of reference, given my past relationships, but I'm too embarrassed. Besides, Sonia's been cool with me of late; she's stopped inviting me to the pub. I suppose I told her no too many times.

So preoccupied am I with thinking about Tiger and the argument Liam and I had, that I make a near-fatal error at work. I give a dog who's in for a standard teeth-cleaning procedure too much of the drug I'm asked to administer. The dog very nearly dies, and I run in panic from the room, after Doug shouts at me. I hyperventilate in the kitchen, tears pouring down my face. I've never made a mistake like that before. I'm always so careful. I think of what could have happened – of having to explain to the owner their pet died on the operating table – and I'm grateful Doug was able to step in and save her.

When he comes to find me ten minutes later, he puts his hand on my shoulder. 'I'm sorry I yelled,' he says. I flinch, reminded of Liam saying the exact same thing.

'What's going on with you, Laura?' Doug asks. 'You seem distracted.'

I swallow away the lump in my throat and shake my

head. 'I'm fine. I'm just a little tired,' I say, unable to meet his eye.

'Really?' he asks. 'You seem very stressed these days.'

I nod, my stomach folding into knots.

'Is it your mother?' he asks, sympathetically.

I shake my head. 'She's doing OK, actually. The doctors say she looks like she's going to beat it.'

'That's great,' Doug says. 'I'm glad. If you need to take some time off, though, for whatever reason, let me know. We all value you here; you're a great colleague and good at your job, but we can't have mistakes like that one again.'

I nod again, grateful that I'm not being fired.

'I am going to have to write this up,' Doug says, grimacing apologetically. 'For the other partners. It's part of the surgery's policy whenever there's a critical error.'

My stomach knots itself even tighter and I bite my lip extra hard to stop from crying. 'I understand,' I tell him, looking at the floor.

He doesn't say it in as many words, but he means I'm on probation. If I make another mistake, they'll definitely fire me. The thought of that is overwhelming. What would I do without my job?

'Why don't you take the rest of the day off and go home and get some sleep?' Doug suggests.

I thank him and grab my things and leave. The shame is a black hole inside my chest. My face burns. I don't want to go home. All I want is my mum, so I head to her place. I need to confide in someone and I know she's the only person who can make me feel better.

'What's happened?' she asks, as soon as she sees me.

'I just messed up at work. They could have fired me,' I sob, as I fall into her arms.

'Ahh, there, pet,' she says, stroking my hair and pulling me inside. 'I'm sure it's just a mistake and it'll all be OK.'

I follow her into the kitchen. She puts the kettle on, but I tell her to her sit down and I make the tea, feeling the weight of weeks of stress fall from my shoulders just by being with her in the home I know so well, just us two, even though guilt is eating me up at how long I've been away. It feels safe here. It feels more like home than my own place, and that makes me sad.

'I wish I still lived here,' I blurt.

'Why?' my mum asks. 'Aren't things good with Liam? I thought you were happy he moved in?'

'I am,' I reassure her. I pause. I want to admit to her that things aren't going well, but it feels like failure, and she looks so tired that I don't want to trouble her. I smile. 'Things are great. I just miss you, that's all. I'm sorry I haven't been to see you.'

I pour the hot water into the mugs.

'It's OK, I know you're busy,' she says with forced happiness, but I can tell she's disappointed.

'Liam's had so much on; and there was all the unpacking.' That's actually a lie. Liam only brought one bag of clothes, and no personal items or furniture either. He left it all with his ex – he says he couldn't stand seeing anything that they'd once shared.

My mum nods, understandingly. 'Shall we watch some *Bake Off*?' she asks as I hand her a cup of tea.

I say yes, even though I'm watching the new series with Liam and he'll be upset if he knows I've watched it without him. But he won't find out. It was a tradition with my mum anyway, even before I met him.

We sit down on the sofa and my mum takes my hand and squeezes it. I squeeze it back and rest my head on her shoulder. 'Why did you stay with Dad?' I ask her, as she rummages for the remote.

She looks at me askance, frowning. 'Why do you ask that?'

I shrug, drinking my tea. 'I just wondered.'

She sighs. 'I shouldn't have. I was an idiot. I thought he loved me and if I just loved him enough, in the right way, that he'd be fixed. But it wasn't about me. He just wasn't capable of loving anyone. He didn't know how. He was an angry man, your father.'

I swallow hard.

'I should have left,' she says with a sad sigh. 'I shouldn't have let him treat me or you the way he did.' She smiles at me, her eyes welling up. 'I'm sorry. It's my biggest regret.'

My chin wobbles.

'What's the matter, love?' she asks, anxious.

I think of opening up and telling her, but the thought of disappointing her is too much. 'Nothing,' I say. 'I just feel sad. Probably that time of the month. It's nothing.'

She turns on the TV and flips to the *Great British Bake Off*.

★

I make it home at the same time I would normally return from work and find Liam already back. 'Oh,' I say, surprised, as a feeling of dread sweeps over me. 'You're home early.'

As I put the keys down on the plate by the front door, I sense the atmosphere. I'm attuned to it, like a barometer. My stomach flips and then tightens; my spine stiffens.

'I wasn't feeling well,' he says. 'Came home early.'

'Oh no,' I say lightly, injecting extra concern into my voice. 'What's the matter? What can I get you?'

'Where were you?' he barks.

I shake my head and let out a little laugh. 'I was at work.'

'No, you weren't.'

Shit.

'I went by to pick you up and you weren't there,' he snaps. 'They said you left early. Where did you go?'

I swallow, my gut writhing with anxiety. 'I went to my mum's to check up on her.'

He looks at me. 'Liar.'

I take a step back, shocked at the venom in his voice. 'I'm not lying,' I stammer. 'Call her if you don't believe me.'

He comes at me so fast I don't even have time to let out a scream of fright. His hand is around my neck, making me gasp.

'You lying bitch. Who were you with?' he growls savagely in my face.

'My mum,' I sob.

The punch to my stomach comes so suddenly that I fold double, seeing stars, pain exploding throughout my body.

He pulls me by my hair so I'm standing tall, winded and unable to breathe.

'Go and make me a cup of tea.'

I drag myself into the kitchen and start making tea, bent over and shaking like an old lady.

Later, in bed, he rolls over and holds me. I stifle a moan, and he shushes me and strokes my hair.

'I'm sorry, my angel,' he says. 'You just made me so angry,' he whispers in my hear.

I nod meekly against his shoulder. 'I'm sorry,' I whisper.

He lifts my chin with his finger and looks me in the eye, his expression so full of love and adoration.

'Marry me,' he says.

I'm stunned speechless. I look down and see he's

holding a huge diamond ring in his hand. I look back at his face. He's smiling, his eyes filled with hope.

'Yes,' I tell him.

*

We organise the wedding in less than three weeks. I have fully convinced myself that the punch was a one-off event and I vow to do better and not trigger him again.

I am swept up in the excitement, though I keep it from my colleagues; I even take off my engagement ring when I go to work, aware that they'll think I'm rushing into things. Liam wants it to be a private affair and I agree. It's more romantic this way – like an elopement – which he suggested, but I refused. I couldn't do it to my mum; she'd be broken-hearted if she didn't get to see her only daughter walk down the aisle.

I've never seen her so happy before. She's glowing with the news of the big day; you'd think she was the one getting married. She helps me choose a dress, something I barely ever imagined doing. It's fairytale-like: simple and white and elegant, with a high neck and a lace veil, almost 1940s in style. I know Liam will like it as it's modest and timeless.

We get married at a registry office. Liam slides the ring onto my finger and tells me that he will love, honour and cherish me until death do us part. I do the same, adding in the traditional 'obey' because he asked me to, telling me that he was a traditional guy. After the ceremony, which is shorter than I'd expected it to be, I get changed into another dress – more casual – and we have lunch at a local gastropub. Liam gives a toast and we drink champagne and eat scallops wrapped in prosciutto. Liam keeps leaning across the table to kiss me and my mum keeps taking photographs, having put on the hat of official wedding photographer after we decided not to waste money on one.

My mum weeps when we head off hand in hand after the meal. We need to get home to get ready for our early morning flight to Greece the next day. She kisses me on the cheek and tells me she loves me and is proud of me and that she can't believe I'm a married woman. Neither can I. I keep looking down at the gold ring on my finger, marvelling at it.

'See you when you get back,' she tells us, giving Liam a big hug. 'Have a wonderful honeymoon.'

It's the last time I ever saw her.

On the way to the airport the next day I get a call. My mum has fallen down the stairs and broken her neck. She's dead.

I cannot believe it. To have come through cancer, to be almost in the clear, and for this to happen. It's too much to take on board, and for days I'm in denial and then just angry. Eventually the anger fades to sadness.

'It's OK,' Liam says, hugging me on the day of

the funeral. 'I'm here. I'll take care of you. Don't worry.'

If only he'd fixed the carpet, I think to myself. She wouldn't have tripped. She'd still be alive. The thought percolates in my mind and I keep thinking about how if Liam hadn't been in such a hurry to install those security cameras, he could have fixed the carpet like he promised, and my mum would still be here.

I turn into a walking zombie. I cannot eat, sleep or do anything. Liam lets me stay in bed for two weeks 'moping', as he calls it, but then he starts getting impatient. 'Cheer up,' he tells me. 'You're so goddamn miserable all the time.'

'Sorry,' I mumble, blowing my nose.

'If anyone should be upset,' he goes on, 'it's me – I had to cancel the honeymoon. I lost a load of money.'

'Why didn't you fix the carpet?' I blurt, unable to keep it in any longer.

He turns and looks at me, blinking a few times. 'What did you say?' he asks.

'If you'd fixed the carpet, she'd still be alive,' I say, my lip quivering.

It's like being at the epicentre of a bomb blast. Punches land on my body, and then kicks after he lets go of my throat and I sink gasping to the floor. Finally, starlight bursting at the edges of my vision, it all fades to black.

★

Liam left me on the floor and went out for the rest of the night, returning at dawn. He found me on the sofa, where I'd managed to drag myself in the middle of the night when I regained consciousness. He asked me why I wasn't in bed, and then what was for breakfast.

I walked into the kitchen without a word, wondering who I'd become in the space of a night. I felt like I was sleepwalking, like I was watching myself, unable to fully believe the situation I was in. The voice in my head was urging me to do something – to get the hell out of there – but I knew I wouldn't. I had no control over my own decisions any more.

'I'll stay home too today,' Liam told me. 'I'll take care of you.' He came up behind me and my body went into a state of panic, freezing, heart pounding, a trickle of sweat rolling down my spine as he put his hands on my shoulders.

I managed another nod, a sob building in my chest that I knew I had to hold on to and not let escape. If I tried to leave, what would he do? It would only make him angry if he thought I was abandoning him. And we're married; I can't just leave him.

Liam calls in to work for me and tells them I have flu. My head throbs like it's clamped in a vice. Every breath causes a spear of pain to shoot through my chest and I wonder if I've broken a rib or two. Black and blue bruises blot my skin like ink stains. When I look in the mirror, I am shocked at the stranger staring back.

If I told someone I'd been in a head-on collision with a lorry they'd believe me.

My bruises are slow to heal, especially the ones on my face, so Liam keeps calling into the surgery to tell them I'm still sick. I stay in bed each day until I have to drag myself up to make dinner. When I sit down with him to eat one night, he pulls away my plate before I can take a bite. 'I don't think you need that,' he tells me. 'Maybe it's time you tried that diet you've been on about.'

I'm barely eating anyway. I haven't been able to get much past my lips since my mum died. But when I do manage to force something down, he controls how much I eat and of what. I'm light-headed, and the shadows under my eyes are more pronounced than the fading bruises on my face and body.

In my dizzy state it's hard to fight it. The thought of escaping him is too much: I can't seem to imagine how to do it; I don't have the energy or the clarity of mind to make a plan. And I don't have anywhere to go to now, luckily for Liam. I have no friends and no family to turn to.

Luckily for Liam. The thought rings in my head, circulating like the sound from a Tibetan bowl being rung. It echoes around my skull. *Did he kill her?* At first, I dismiss the idea, but then it's as if it's been planted in the weak compost of my mind and taken root. I look at him out the corner of my eye as he watches football on the TV. I study his hands as he picks up the remote and when he cuts through his steak. *Did he push her down the stairs? Did he kill my mum?*

He was jealous of her; of the time I spent with her. And I have no shadow of a doubt that he is capable of killing. Sitting beside him on the sofa, pretending like we're a normal couple, a shudder runs up my spine. He puts his arm around my shoulders, pulling me against his body, and I feel myself tense; I order myself to relax so he doesn't suspect anything and get angry. But the thought won't shake from my mind. I woke up in the middle of the night on our wedding night and Liam wasn't in the bed. I fell back to sleep, and he was there, beside me again, when I woke up in the morning. But what if . . .

'What is it?' Liam asks, frowning at me with an annoyed expression.

I'm staring at him in shock, sick to my stomach, the terrible awareness sinking in that I'm right. I know I am. He went to my mum's house in the middle of the night and he killed her. He pushed her down the stairs. He made it look like an accident. He knew about the carpet that was sticking up on the landing, because he had promised to nail it down. But he never got around to it. Of course he didn't! He was setting it all up to get her out of the way. He wanted her dead. He didn't want to share me. And if my mum was dead, I'd have nowhere to go. *Oh my god*. My brain struggles to process the thought. What if I'm wrong? I might be. But equally, as I stare at Liam, I know that it is within the realm of possibility. *Well* within it. And the fact that I can even think that about the man I'm married to is terrifying.

'What?' Liam asks angrily, shoving me away. 'Why are you looking at me like that?'

I can't stop staring at him. It's as if I'm seeing a demon in human form right in front of my eyes. But quickly I force my face to return to blankness and offer him a smile. 'I just love you, that's all,' I say.

★

I have guessed that Liam has been lying to me about his career. I should have figured it out sooner, but now it's obvious he has no job to go to. I don't know if he ever had one, or if he was even a detective at all. Did he lie to me? I imagine he plucked the profession out of the ether, knowing that him being a detective would lull me into a false sense of security. I wonder, too, if he pretended to work for the police in order to later scare me into submission. How can you report a policeman for domestic violence?

I know he killed my mother. And I know he killed Tiger too. How can I have ignored for so long something that was staring me in the face?

I have been such a fool that if I wasn't so numb, I would die from shame. And I think, because of that, I am able to hold it back; to confine it in some far recess of my mind which I can ignore. I cannot face it. Not yet and maybe not ever. I try to tell myself that he's fooled everyone, not just me. He's a consummate actor – he charms everyone he meets, hiding the real Liam from the world. The real Liam is a monster, but he keeps that monster concealed. I do my best not to antagonise the monster. I don't want to wake him.

At first, I maintain a completely blank expression, but then, after he tells me I'm a miserable bitch, I learn how to fake a smile. Very quickly I come to realise that If I smile, speak only when spoken to, and never argue with him, criticise him or ask questions, I am safe.

After two weeks, the bruises are mostly gone, and those that remain can be covered by clothes or make-up. Liam praises me for looking so lovely and slender and takes a renewed interest in my body. I lie there, stiff as a corpse, my bruised body aching anew. I close my eyes and pray for it to be over each night. Each time his lips brush one of my bruises I gasp, but he thinks it's in pleasure. I worry about getting pregnant, as he's stopped using protection, but I don't bring it up as I don't want to risk an argument.

My mind wanders during sex, though I'm blasted back into reality when I hear him shouting at me to show some goddamn enthusiasm and stop being such a frigid bitch. I learn too to fake enthusiasm: I start hearing myself as though from a million miles away. It pleases him and he starts to treat me more kindly. *Perhaps everything is OK,*

I tell myself. Perhaps I can do this. It isn't so hard. I've found a way to manage. I just have to pretend. Pretend to the world and even myself. And always, always smile.

The only time I can't pretend is at night when the dreams come. In all of them, I'm trapped in some dark dungeon-like place and I'm being chased. I'm terrified, but no matter how hard I try to find a way out, I can't escape. I wake up screaming and Liam is getting more and more frustrated, telling me I'm ruining his sleep and demanding to know what I'm dreaming about.

To stop myself from annoying him any further, I force myself to stay awake. It isn't hard. I drink a lot of tea, and my palpitating heart and taut nerves help too. Liam doesn't even go out to walk Isis; instead he lets her out into the back garden to do her business. He orders groceries online using my credit card, and sometimes he orders a takeaway for one. He still controls my phone and I daren't ask about returning to work. I daren't ask anything at all. I wonder if we'll continue like this forever, living imprisoned in this house, never leaving, but I know not to ask.

The only time I let a tear slip out, Liam notices at once.

'Why are you crying?' he snaps.

I bite my lips shut and blink away the remaining tears.

'Do you miss your mum?' he sneers.

I don't answer.

'She was just your mother. I'm your partner. I'm your soulmate. I'm all you need.'

I nod.

Work calls to ask when I'm going to be back. It's been two weeks. Liam can't make any more excuses, and my bruises are mostly faded, so he makes me call them back and tell them that I'm quitting.

★

Liam returns to 'work'. I don't know where he goes. I don't care. He knows that I won't leave, so he doesn't need to stay. The security cameras will tell him if I leave the house, and I assume he has installed a tracker on my phone, so I don't use it or make calls. He takes my laptop with him so I can't do anything online.

I lie in bed with Isis every day, staring at the ceiling, then I make myself get up at four o'clock in the afternoon to take a bath, get dressed and cook dinner, making sure it's piping hot and on the table at six on the dot. Three courses, every day, as Liam requests. He checks the fridge and cupboards every day to make sure I'm not sneaking food when he's out of the house. The one time that he believes, wrongly, that I've eaten something in his absence, he removes all the food from the cupboards and padlocks the fridge, leaving out only what I need to make dinner.

I wonder how the bills are being paid and keep expecting red notices to fall through the letterbox, until one day I notice that Liam is flush with cash. He has sold my mother's belongings. I wonder if he's banking on selling my mum's house and then using the money. I almost hope that he takes it and runs, but the more acquiescent I get, the happier he gets, and I know that I'm digging my own grave either way.

One day Liam comes home early. He finds me in the bath. I'm crying without even realising it. He kicks open the door and looks at me in fury. 'Why are you crying?' he demands. 'I am sick to death of your crying and moping and your sad face. You were supposed to be better than all the others.'

I stifle my tears.

'Do I not do everything to make you happy? Do I not worship and adore you?' he asks.

I nod.

He lunges forward, takes my head in his hands and thrusts me under the water. I struggle but he holds me under. He's going to kill me. I realise it with a shock. I swallow a lungful of water, my chest exploding with pain. I can see him grimacing as he forces me under. I kick and thrash but I'm no match for him.

I start to lose consciousness and he suddenly lets go and hauls me upright. Coughing and spluttering, I hang over the edge of the bath, gasping for breath. I know not to let out another sob in case he thrusts me under again.

Liam gets up and walks out of the room. I sink back into the bath.

PART FOUR

Chapter Thirty-Two

Mia

'Laura!' Ethan yells again, looking past me to where Laura is standing with her back pressed to the tree. She doesn't move.

'She's not going to help you,' I say to him.

He glowers at me, his lips white, stretched taut against the pain of the trap snapped around his leg.

'Do you know why?' I ask him.

I see the understanding start to seep in even before I tell him.

'That's right. Because she's been helping me.' I gesture at the island. 'We did this all together. Lured you here. I thought about all the ways I wanted you to suffer. I wanted to give you a taste of your own medicine. How did you like it?'

Laura appears at my side. She's found the courage to

come near the injured animal now that she knows he's disabled in a trap. She hovers at my shoulder and Ethan looks between us, shaking his head in confusion, trying to piece it together. If only he knew what it had taken to plan all this; what lengths we've gone to, not just to escape from him and make sure he never makes another woman his prey, but to punish him the way he deserves to be punished.

'Laura,' he says to her, pleading. 'Help me!'

She doesn't say anything.

'Do something! My leg . . .' he sobs.

I stand up and look at Laura. She gives me a tremulous smile. I smile back at her and then we hug each other, clutching each other hard, leaning into each other. 'We did it,' I whisper in her ear.

I feel her nod against my shoulder. Her body, rigid from months of tension and frighteningly skeletal, collapses like a building's foundations giving way after an earthquake, and she staggers against me. But then she takes a deep breath, straightens and pulls back, finding another sub-foundation of strength within her. She looks me in the eye and even through the still pouring rain I can make out the glimmer of determination in her expression; the courage that I knew was in her all along, and which at first she doubted. Ethan couldn't stamp it out, no matter how hard he tried.

'What are you doing?' Ethan yells at her. 'Laura, please?'

Laura squeezes my hand and then she kneels down beside him. I worry for a moment that her softness and fragility will make her cave, that the sight of the blood on his hands and the gory mess of his leg will make her change her mind and want to help him. And I'm afraid, because that isn't the plan. The plan is to watch him bleed to death.

'Go to hell, you bastard,' Laura says, and I realise she's a lot stronger than she looks.

Quick as a viper Ethan grabs her wrist and she lets out a yelp of fright, struggling to pull free. He won't let go; he drags her towards him so her face is pressed to his. 'You bitch,' he hisses. 'I'll kill you.'

'Like you did my mother?' she shouts back at him, still struggling to free herself.

I smash the stock of the gun into his shoulder and he lets go with a scream of fury. Laura scrambles back through the mud away from him, and I help her to her feet.

'She was in the way,' Ethan cries. 'It's your fault. All that time you were spending with her.'

Laura lets out a sob. 'You did kill her?' she asks, almost plaintively, as if until that moment she hadn't been sure. Now, faced with the confirmation, her agony is writ clear across her face. But then the grief twists into something new; into anger. 'She was my mum! She'd been ill!' Laura shouts. 'She needed me!'

'*I* needed you,' Ethan says, still clutching his leg, the pain eating his face.

He looks between us, seeming to realise that neither of us are going to help him and that there's every chance we might leave him here like this.

'You won't get away with this,' he says, fear flooding his face.

Laura wipes her hand across her face, drying her tears. 'Yes, we will,' she replies with a smile.

Chapter Thirty-Three

Laura

Two Months Earlier

I'm standing at the sink, peeling carrots, when I feel the strange sensation that I'm being watched. I've been feeling it a lot recently, and I've even started to wonder if it's my mother's ghost, watching over me. But when I look up, I see a woman, dressed all in black, despite the warm summer sun, standing still as a statue by the far fence.

We back onto an alley. She must have jumped over. I don't scream when I see her though – that instinct has been beaten out of me – but my heart rate doubles, and I grip the knife I'm holding tighter.

The woman beckons to me. I stand there, frozen. But she beckons again. Finally, I move to the back door, as though in a trance. If it was a man outside I would call the police, but the fact she's a woman reassures me. Isis is at my heel and when I open the door, instead of barking as she normally does at the sight of a stranger, she races across the garden towards the woman, her tail wagging furiously. She jumps up in delight, licking her face, and the woman pets her, smiling ear to ear, tears falling.

It's only then I remember the security camera that Liam installed. I glance up at it. It's pointed at the back door, not at the garden. If he's watching via the app on his phone, which goes off any time someone approaches the door, he will see me going outside. But he won't see where I go in the garden.

I walk towards the woman. She smiles at me. 'Hi,' she says. Though her words are warm, there's a hardness to her.

I shake my head, terror gripping me that Liam might return at any moment and find her there. I'll get into trouble. 'What are you doing here?' I ask in a whisper. 'Who are you?'

'I'm Mia,' she says.

'Mia who?' I ask, confused.

'I know what's happening to you.'

I stare at her in shock. 'Who are you?' I ask.

'I'm the one before you,' she says.

I frown. What does she mean? It dawns on me then that she must be Liam's ex. The woman who cheated on him. 'His ex-wife?' I ask her.

She nods, her lips pursing in distaste. 'Yes. I guess we're still married though, technically, so not quite ex.'

I almost collapse to the ground. He's still married. I glance down at the engagement ring on my hand and my own wedding band. That must mean Liam and I aren't married. Laughter bubbles up my throat, mixed in with relief.

I notice that her gaze has followed mine and she's looking at my rings. She gasps, a hand flying to her throat. 'That ring . . .' she says, staring at it with tears in her eyes, 'that was mine.'

I frown. 'I don't understand,' I mumble, still in shock.

She looks up at my face. 'Are you OK?' she asks.

'What do you mean?' I ask, instantly on the defensive. What if this is a trick? What if Liam's put her to this to test me?

'Is he hurting you?' she asks, looking me directly in the eye.

I freeze, my legs trembling.

'I know what Ethan's like,' she goes on.

'Ethan?' I ask, even more confused.

She nods. 'Yes, that's his real name. He's not Liam.'

'What?' I say, my brain turning inside out. I don't understand. What does she mean, he's called Ethan?

She shakes her head angrily and snorts. 'William Carrington. I can't believe he's calling himself that.'

'He doesn't,' I tell her. 'He goes by Liam.'

'He's not Liam or William,' she spits angrily. 'That was someone else. Someone I knew. Someone I loved. He stole their identity. After he killed them.'

My mouth falls open. 'What do you mean?' I stammer.

She studies me but doesn't explain. 'Is he hurting you?' she asks again, this time squeezing my hand for emphasis.

I start to say no, but then I change my mind. Something about her strength inspires me. I nod. 'Yes.'

And when I finally admit the truth to this stranger, I feel an unloosening in my body as though the knots keeping me together are coming undone. *He's done this to someone else*, I think. *He's killed someone else.* I reel from the confirmation that I was right.

'It's OK,' Mia tells me. 'I'm going to help you.'

I blink at her. 'You can't,' I whisper, glancing back at the house. 'You need to go. He could be back any minute.'

She nods. 'I'll come back tomorrow after he's gone out. I have a plan. But I need your help.'

I shake my head, terrified. 'I don't know. If he finds out . . .'

She grips my arm tight and looks into my eyes. She's blonde, blue-eyed, beautiful despite the scar running down her cheek and the dark circles under her eyes. 'Do you want to get away from him?'

I nod, tears welling up. 'But I can't.'

'I know you're scared,' she says. 'I know what he's capable of.' Pain is etched on her features. 'But you're going to get away from him. And then we're going to make him pay for what he's done. Do you understand?'

The fierceness in her voice stirs a dormant part of me that I thought had vanished for good. I nod and she turns to leave, walking towards the fence at the back of the garden. I want to ask her a thousand things — how did she find us? What does she know about Liam and the things he's done to me? How long has she been watching? What's her plan? But the question I ask is: 'Do you promise?'

She stops and looks over her shoulder. 'That I'll get you out of this?'

I shake my head. 'That we'll make him pay.'

Chapter Thirty-Four

Laura

'Laura,' Liam begs, his voice sounding weaker, the blood leaking out of him onto the muddy ground, washed away by the rain.

I look down on him, feeling no sympathy and no regret. I don't even feel bad to see him in pain. If it was a fox caught in the trap, I would feel something, I would cry, but with Liam I am only relieved. His eyes search my face. He can't believe I've betrayed him.

But I have. I've lied to him. I've lied to everyone. Like Liam, I became an actor, better than him even, because I knew what the consequences were if I failed. Every smile, every touch, every gesture of kindness or tenderness has been pretend.

I have feigned being in love with him, faked being the perfect, adoring wife, for every second that we've been here. And there is some triumph in that. In knowing that I have tricked him just like he tricked me. Every time he touched me, I would shudder, and he took it for pleasure, when really it was revulsion. Every time he held my hand, I had to fight not to yank it out of his grip. Every time he kissed me, I had to kiss him back as though I meant it. I have learned to contain my terror and my grief and my hatred; to mask them behind a smile.

I have had to hide my innermost thoughts from everyone, even from myself. I have kept them locked away in a far recess of my mind, so they would never reveal themselves, accidentally slipping out and tracing a path across my face that he might notice. I have forced the real me into hiding.

I lied to my mother, to my friends and to the world, at first because I was ashamed and then later because it was the only way to survive. And finally, because it was the only way to escape. I have gritted my teeth and smiled until my face ached, because I knew it would be worth it to one day be free of him.

It was easy in the end, a simple matter to convince Liam that I'd love a holiday, that I think it might help me to heal; and what place more romantic than Scotland? He agreed eagerly, thinking it was a sign that I was moving out of my depression and finally starting to be happy again. And in fact, I *was* starting to become happier. Now I had a purpose and I could see a faint chink of light on the horizon, my spirits did lift. Hope was a tiny flicker at first, it didn't dare to flame bright, and I feared that any moment it might be snuffed out. Now though, as I look down on him, caught in the trap, bleeding out, the hope burns as brightly as the lightning still scoring the island.

I couldn't have done it alone, of course. It's Mia who made it happen, who devised the plan and carried most of it out. She'd been plotting for six months before she even met me. After she made her way to Scotland she went to a hospital and had her broken arm fixed, then she found a grotty place to rent with cash and no questions asked.

Afterwards, she used her remaining money to hire a private detective to find Liam. Her plan was to lure him somewhere private where she could kill him. She even bought a gun for the purpose. But then, after the private detective found him, following Mia's lead that he might have turned up at a vet's with a wounded dog on or around Boxing Day, and she learned that he was already involved with another woman – *me* – she knew she'd need to change her plans. That was when she first approached me, appearing in the garden that day and scaring the life out of me before offering me a way out of my nightmare.

The only part of the strategy that we couldn't work out was where to carry out the revenge. It was solved when I first read my mum's will. There was a life insurance policy and I was the beneficiary. I was to receive three hundred thousand pounds. I knew it was my mum's way of looking out for me when she was gone, and I also knew that there was no better use for the money.

I told Mia about it and managed to keep it a secret from Liam. I gave Mia my ID documents and she opened a bank account for me online and called the insurance company pretending to be me. Once they paid the three hundred thousand pounds from the policy into the account, Mia used half to buy the isle of Shura, which was going cheap, though neither of us knew the reason why.

The idea was to trap Liam in a place where he couldn't escape, so he'd know what it was like to be hunted by an invisible prey; what it was like to be stalked, to be victimised, to be starved, to be controlled; to, above all, feel fear. We wanted him to know just a sliver of what we have endured at his hands.

I thought it might be too difficult to pull off, too twisted a revenge, when really all I wanted was for my nightmare to be over.

'It's never over,' Mia argued. 'If we don't do this, he'll kill you eventually.'

Her words seeped in. I knew they were true. The bruises on my body seemed to throb with the knowledge too.

'And he'll get away with it,' she went on. 'And then he'll find another woman and do the same to her.'

I closed my eyes and took a deep breath. Killing someone – becoming a murderer – was that something I could do? Was it the right thing? Was it right to make him suffer the way he had made us suffer?

I thought of my mother and I knew the answer was yes.

'He's a policeman,' I said, weakly. 'How can we manage to trick him?'

Mia snorted. 'No he isn't. I found out from the private investigator I hired. He's not a policeman or a detective. He never was. He lied to us both. It was to make us afraid, so we'd be less likely to report him. He's never had a job. He's been living off money his mum left him.'

I had suspected it, but hearing the truth was altogether different. My whole life was a lie; nothing felt real any more, except for one thing: the terror coursing through my body; a feeling that never faded or ebbed but just kept building like a floodwater, always rising.

'I'm ready,' I said, turning back to Mia and looking her in the eye. 'Tell me what I need to do.'

Our plan took a while to work out. Every day Mia would sneak into the back garden over the fence and I'd go out with Isis – or rather Jet – and we'd hide behind the shed and discuss the plan. Mia gave me a throwaway phone, too, which I hid on silent in a plastic bag, taped to the underside of the bed.

She visited the island and worked everything out and when she came back, she explained how she would hide on the island in a cave at the base of the cliffs. Mia wanted not just revenge, but, as she put it, to *fuck with him*. 'I want him to feel the fear that I felt; that *you* feel,' she told me, with a steely glimmer in her eye. 'I want him to know what it's like to have someone control your life and then destroy it. I want to make him play the game and lose.'

She told me all about Will, and what Liam did to him, and I told her my theory that Liam had murdered my mother and my cat. Mia's hunger for revenge fuelled my own. Every day that we plotted I grew stronger, imagining my freedom. Things improved when Mia, pretending to be me, registered at a new GP surgery and managed to get me a prescription for anti-depressants and the pill, which she slipped me and I kept hidden in a box of tampons.

We arranged to communicate once we were on the island via cryptic notes left beneath a pile of stones on the beach resembling a cairn, something I built on the first day there and which I told Liam was a memorial for my mum. Whenever one of us had a message we would replace a stone from the top of the pile to signal the other person. Mia also left a note in the guest book — a deliberate coded message for Liam — which he didn't get, but which made me smile.

'*Stay was cut short unfortunately, but it was wonderful*

until then. Tried looking for the burial site but couldn't find it. I look forward to visiting in the future. A warning to guests; stay away from the cliffs. A fall could be fatal.'

She was referring to her life with Will being cut short, and referring to her own burial site, the ditch Liam left her in. She warned us away from the cliffs because at the bottom of them was the cave where she was camping out, hiding, waiting to put our plan into action.

The satellite phone in the cottage was my idea, to make sure Liam didn't get suspicious from the very beginning, but we made sure that we took the charger out of the box. I have to say I enjoyed watching Liam's frustration when he realised we had no means of escape and no one to call for help. It was beyond satisfying to see him going through just some of the terror he made me feel every day.

I used the cairn to warn Mia that there was a fourth, unexpected stranger on the island. I hadn't been able to believe it at first – the chances of it seemed so impossible – and it wasn't until Liam and I found the squatter's campsite in the castle that I put it together and realised we weren't alone.

I wanted to pull the plug immediately on our plans and left another note for Mia in the cairn, but she wouldn't have it. We'd come this far, and she thought it worth risking it. She believed whoever was holed up in the castle would leave us alone, not wanting to get caught. And they did leave us alone. The problem was that Liam thought that they were the person who had stood at the window watching us; that they were responsible for the etching of the word 'DEVIL' on the window and the electricity being cut and the food being stolen and the woodpile being wrecked, when in fact it was Mia who had done it all. When I lay in bed listening to her scratching the word 'DEVIL' into the window downstairs, I was terrified that Liam would wake up and catch her. I couldn't sleep for fear he was on to us.

I tried everything I could to keep Liam away from the castle, to stop him from confronting the stranger, but of course he wouldn't listen.

When he discovered the boathouse, I had no time to warn Mia, and so the only thing I could do was to throw myself out of the boat. I knew if we left the island then that was it – all our plans would have been for nothing. So, even though Liam has left me terrified of water, as soon as he took his eyes off me to look over his shoulder, I launched myself over the edge of the boat and into the freezing waters of the loch. If I drowned, I told myself at least I would die on my own terms and it would be my choice.

I was the one, too, who left the glass angel on the ground by Liam as he slept. Mia wanted him to see it; she believed it would be the final puzzle piece that would jolt his memory and make him realise who

344

was stalking him and why. But when I woke up, I remembered the story Mia told me of how she'd fled through the snow with her feet bleeding, glass splinters embedded in them, and so I placed it where I knew Liam would step on it.

I wanted to make him suffer; to let him have one more taste of his own medicine.

While he went hungry, I was eating trail mix that I'd hidden in my pockets. When he asked me to grab the shotgun shells at the castle, I did, but I also picked up the empty ones from the pile of rubbish and while he slept, I was the one who replaced the shells he'd loaded in the gun with blanks.

And all the while, I remembered my mother and I remembered the beatings he'd given me and I thought about what he'd done to my cat and to Will and to Mia, and who knows, maybe even to other women before her.

He thought I was weak and that I would never fight back. He got that wrong.

'I need help,' Liam begs weakly, flopping backwards in a river of mud.

The rain has almost completely eased; the thunder and lightning are rolling off and out to sea.

'There's no help coming,' I say to him. Then I crouch down beside him again, no longer afraid that he has the strength to hurt me.

Mia joins me. Liam looks between us in disbelief,

clearly still shocked that he's fallen victim to our plot, struggling to understand how Mia is alive and how we managed to fool him.

His face crumples and he lets out an almighty bellow of rage. It's the cry of a lone wolf caught in a trap. He knows his time is running out, and that no one is coming to help.

The Stalker

Pain engulfs me. My leg feels as if it is on fire, like it's being roasted over an open flame. The metal teeth of the trap have torn through flesh and are sucking on the bone.

I throw my head back and howl in agony as much as in rage. When I open my eyes, Mia is still kneeling beside me. My angel. I still don't understand how she's here. I buried her in a snowy ditch. She was dead.

There was a big search for her and Will. I followed it online. But they never found the bodies. I study her. Is she real? She doesn't look like herself. There's an expression on her face that I don't recognise. It comes to me just then what it is: defiance. She isn't afraid of me and she wants me to know it.

I let out another howl of frustration, my hands squeezing my leg, hoping to stem the bleeding and mute the pain. The jaws won't give though. The metal teeth keep gnawing.

With tears in my eyes I glance at Laura, my other angel. Why is she not doing anything to help?

'Help me,' I say to her again, as the flames lick higher. I can feel my heart straining as blood leaks out of me. My hands are hot and sticky with it.

Laura looks at me not with the same defiance as Mia, but with something I recognise all the same. It's the look my mother used to give me: disgust. Like there is something wrong with me; like she hates me, like she sees the devil in me.

I blink in surprise. Has Laura been pretending all this time to love me? How has she hidden it so well? I thought I knew her. I thought she was different.

I lift a hand to touch her cheek but she pulls away and my hand flops to the ground. 'You were my angel,' I say to her. 'You were meant to save me.'

'Guess you're going to Hell then,' she says.

Chapter Thirty-Five

Laura

We stand up and watch Liam as he slowly bleeds out. Still, I feel nothing except relief. I understand finally what the Celts were thinking when it came to meting out justice to those who'd committed crimes against the tribe.

When Liam finally takes his last breath, it feels as if a great dark weight has been lifted off of me. I feel unshackled. The fear that's crippled me these last months dissolves like my breath in the cold night air. It's there one moment, gone the next. I could take flight.

I turn to Mia, who stands beside me like a statue, head bent, not taking her gaze off Liam's face. She grinds her teeth and breathes hard as she looks down on Liam's body and her shoulders start to shake violently. I put my arm around her. 'Are you OK?' I say.

She clings to me. 'No.'

I hold her tightly. 'It's OK,' I whisper. 'We did it.'

'He isn't coming back,' she says. She pulls back to look at me and I see that she doesn't mean Liam.

'Will?' I ask.

She nods, tears falling down her cheeks. I soothe her. She swallows hard and wipes her arm across her face.

'Here,' I say to her.

She looks down. I'm holding out her engagement ring. She takes it, her face stricken, before she fights off the sadness and smiles at me through her tears. She slips the ring onto her finger. 'Thank you,' she says. I unclasp the Celtic cross and give that back to her too. Her bottom lip wobbles, but only for a moment, and then her expression hardens.

'You should go,' I say.

'I know,' she answers. 'But what about you?' She glances down at the body.

'I'll be fine,' I tell her, and I mean it.

Mia and I hug one last time before she walks off through the woods towards the cliffs, where she'll find her boat and pack her things and leave, like the ghost she is.

In a few weeks' time we'll meet again. She's given me back my life and I'll give her back her dog.

Chapter Thirty-Six

I watch Mia walk away, heading for the cliffs, and then disappear from view into the first tinge of dawn light.

When I turn back around, I see a man standing a few feet away. I let out a gasp of fright. I recognise him instantly. It's the man from the pub who was watching me strangely and who told me about the island being haunted. He's the man who's been squatting in the castle, whose boat and gun we stole. How long has he been standing there? What did he see? Did he watch Mia and me together talking over the body?

'What happened?' he asks gruffly, nodding at Liam's body.

My heart rattles like a freight train. I knew there was a risk if Mia and I kept on with our plan once we knew that he was on the island too, but it was a risk we had to take. We couldn't back out. I did my best to keep Liam away from the castle, not wanting him to blame the wrong person, and I hoped that the man would steer clear of us too.

'There was an accident,' I stammer to the man. 'He stood in an animal trap.'

He narrows his eyes at me. 'That's odd, that,' he says. 'Because I know this island back to front and there wasnae any trap here yesterday.'

Oh god. I can feel the tremor starting in my ankles, riding up to my knees. He glances at his shotgun, which I'm holding in my hand.

'That's mine,' he says. 'You stole it. And my boat.' He reaches for it and snatches it out of my hand.

'I'm sorry,' I say, stumbling backwards. 'And about the boat too. It capsized. I'll pay you whatever it takes to replace it.' I risk a look in his eyes. He's scrutinising me with a hard stare, and I flush to the roots of my hair. He looks at Liam's body. He knows I'm lying. He knows this was no accident.

He turns back to look at me. 'No matter,' he says.

My heart skips a beat. I blink at him not daring to breathe. But he says nothing more. He's waiting for me to talk.

'You're a McKay, aren't you?' I blurt.

He frowns at me, taken aback, but I can see that I'm right.

'It's your mother and brother, Elliot, who are buried

352

on the island, isn't it?' I ask, jerking my head in the direction of the churchyard.

'How do you know that?' he asks, gruffly, frowning at me.

'I saw the flowers on the grave earlier.'

I noticed them when we returned to the chapel after we stole the gun. A bouquet of thistles and autumn leaves filling the vase that had been toppled over just the day before. That's when I figured out who the fourth person on the island was. Liam was too focused on his foot to notice them, thank god. I saw the flowers and thought about the No Trespassers sign and suddenly it all made sense. The gravestone said 'beloved brother'. It wasn't Andrew McKay on the island. It was his son. His *other* son. It was the only thing that made sense.

'I'm sorry for what happened to them.' My nerves are electrified. I feel as if I'm walking on a tightrope over shark-infested waters.

He nods to himself. 'Aye. Well, I'm sorry for what happened to him,' he says, nodding at Liam but keeping his eyes fixed on me. I know that he's searching my face for some reaction to his death. I should look anguished, upset, grieving, in shock. And I'm not displaying any of those emotions. I'm giving myself away with my total lack of feeling.

'You've got blood on your sleeve,' the man comments, nodding at my arm.

I look down and notice the dark stain on the white

cuff of my sweater. There's a circle of dark bruises too, a bracelet of them running around my wrist, Liam's parting gift to me. I tug the sleeve down, hoping he hasn't noticed, but when I look up at him, it's clear he has.

'My father was a sick bastard too,' he says.

The breath catches in my chest. I lock eyes with him. A long moment passes.

'I saw the way he was with you in the pub,' he finally says. 'From the moment you walked in I could see you were afraid, though you were hiding it well.'

I am stunned at his words. I thought I was a consummate actress. That I was hiding my fear from the world.

'I spent my life around a bully,' he goes on. 'Watched my mother put up with it for years. Always wished she'd leave him, but she never did.'

My lungs refuse to fill. I feel as if I'm being held underwater, but then suddenly I'm bursting to the surface and drawing in air. I take in a ragged breath.

'You had bruises,' he says, gesturing to my neck.

I remember I was wearing a scarf in the pub. I'd started taking it off but noticed he was looking at me funny and kept it on, reminded that the scarf was hiding the bruises on my neck that Liam had put there a few nights before. My hand flies to my neck and an echo of a shudder runs through me as I remember Liam kissing the five bruises in the shape of his fingers. They're still there.

'I wish I'd had the courage to stand up to my father before it was too late and he did what he did,' the man says to me now.

I don't react. I'm so used to keeping a blank face – or trying to, at least. But then I remind myself that I don't have to fake anything any more. 'I'm sorry,' I say, letting emotion transform my face. It feels as if a dam breaks. All the tension I've been holding on to starts to crumble and I let out a choked sound.

'You OK?' he asks, taking a step closer.

'I will be now,' I answer, giving a shaky smile.

'You going to leave him here?' he asks, nodding disdainfully at Liam.

I think about how Liam told me that dead criminals in ancient times would be left out in the elements for the animals to eat them. It seems fitting.

'I'll tell the police when I get back to the mainland,' I say. 'The boatman's coming in a few hours.'

The man nods. He doesn't offer to undo the trap around Liam's leg or move him somewhere sheltered.

'What about you?' I ask. 'How will you get off the island?'

He takes out a small notebook and pencil and scribbles something down. When he's done, he rips it off and hands it to me. 'When you get back to the mainland, call this number. It's my friend Joe. Tell him where I am – my name's Jamie – and ask him to come and get me.'

I take the piece of paper and put it in my pocket. I still can't believe that this stranger is going to cover for me when he knows what I've done.

'Thanks,' he says to me.

I nod.

'You could stay here if you wanted to,' I blurt.

He shakes his head, an unhappy look on his face. 'It's not my land any more. I don't own it. My father was in debt. When he died everything had to be sold.' He exhales loudly. 'But I still come out here, to tend the graves. It'll always feel like home.'

'I know the new owner,' I admit. 'She'll be OK with you staying.'

He narrows his eyes at me, and then a small smile creeps onto his lips.

'She might even need a caretaker for the cottage,' I add.

He considers it for a while, the smile still playing on his lips. 'Tell the new owner I might be interested in that.'

'I will,' I say with a smile.

We say our goodbyes, exchanging emails, and I return to the chapel and rescue the bird, Hathor, from its box. She's unhappy with me for having left her alone so long. I carry her outside and sit down, exhausted, among the gravestones. The sky is flushed pink and the sun is chasing the shadows away. I carefully unfold the bandages around the bird's wing.

'How's that?' I ask, setting her down on the ground.

She caws loudly at me but then hops away, flapping out her wing, ruffling the feathers. I decide it's probably too early for her to fly and I move to pick her up again and rebandage her, but before I can, she flaps her wings and takes off into the air, rising higher and higher into the morning sky.

I stand up and watch her fly towards the sun.

Acknowledgements

This is my twentieth-something book and I would like to thank Amanda, my agent, who has shepherded every single one of them. I am indebted to you for your support.

I am grateful too to Mady, my film agent, who has also supported me for almost a decade now. We finally did it! My first adaptation is finally greenlit. Hopefully it won't be the last.

When I think about my journey as an author the thing that strikes me most is that I had no creative writing background or knowledge before I started, not unless you count being an avid reader and watcher of movies and TV. And yet, what I did have was the confidence to try, cultivated in large part by my parents, and an attitude of fuck it, cultivated in large part by my husband and the advice of my brother-in-law: 'what's the worst that could happen?'. That advice has served me well (it also serves me as a storyteller when I'm trying to figure out what plot direction to go in).

I am lucky and blessed to have the support of my husband, John, and our daughter, Alula, as well as the encouragement and cheerleading of some amazing friends, most especially: Vic (always my first reader), Alby, Nichola, Rachel, Lauren and Clarissa.

Thanks also to Tessa, and my sister-in-law Sarah, for their medical knowledge and help with the details.

My least favourite parts of writing a book are the copy-edit and the proofing, so enormous thanks are due to Felicity Radford and Tony Russell for taking the hard work out of it and making it easy.

Finally, last but not least, I would like to thank the amazing team at Avon for their hard work and dedication. Molly, my editor, has an eagle eye and I so appreciated her skill. Also thanks to Helen Huthwaite, Ellie Pilcher, El Slater, Becci Mansell, Catriona Beamish, Sammy Luton, Hannah Avery and Elisha Lundin.

Two friends go on holiday.
Only one comes back.

A twisty holiday read for fans of *The Holiday*
and *Date Night*.